'Collins' brand of macho, streetwise and often vicious prose . . . here achieves a new tautness that helps maintain a frenetic pace and a genuine suspense. Collins has bridled the voice of the malcontent and produced something that is rare enough in contemporary Irish fiction: a well written and socially conscientious novel' *Times Literary Supplement*

'Collins is a novelist with superbly controlled inventive vitriol' *Glasgow Herald*

'[Collins] makes apparently simple materials work powerfully . . . his aim is exact and his effect eerie' *Observer*

'Michael Collins is a considerable stylist . . . his prose has a thoughtful, sinewy quality, a kind of subliminal toughness of mind' *Daily Telegraph*

'The best I've read this year. Prose throbbing to the rhythm of Auden's "Night Mail" script, but with serrated razor-wire as cutting edge. Unputdownable' *Time Out*

'Collins is operating at a level that's beyond the reach of most of his practising colleagues' *Toronto Globe & Mail*

Reading Collins . . . is like being mugged in a savage land' *The Times*

'Readers should be grateful to Collins. He is a stylist, blessed with the gift of having something worth saying well' *Scotsman*

'Colourful, surreal and vividly characterised . . . already prompting comparisons to Joyce and Beckett' *The List*

Michael Collins was born in Limerick in 1964. His fiction has received international critical acclaim and his work has been translated into numerous languages. His first book was a *New York Times* Notable Book of the Year in 1993, his short story 'The End of the World' was awarded the Pushcart Prize for Best American Short Story and the *Toronto Globe & Mail* selected his most recent collection of stories as 'one of the must-read books of the year'. *The Keepers of Truth* won The Kerry Ingredients Book of the Year Award for Best Irish Novel and was also shortlisted for the Booker Prize.

By Michael Collins

The Meat Eaters (stories)
The Life and Times of a Tea Boy
The Feminists Go Swimming (stories)
Emerald Underground
The Keepers of Truth

The Feminists Go Swimming

MICHAEL COLLINS

PHŒNIX

A PHOENIX PAPERBACK

First published in Great Britain by Phoenix House in 1996
This paperback edition published in 1997 by Phoenix,
a division of Orion Books Ltd,
Orion House, 5 Upper St Martin's Lane,
London WC2H 9EA

Reissued 2001

A CIP catalogue record for this book
is available from the British Library.

ISBN: 1 85799 978 9

Printed and bound in Great Britain by
The Guernsey Press Co. Ltd,
Guernsey, Channel Islands

DEDICATED TO MY WIFE AND PARENTS

Acknowledgements to

Maggie McKernan
Professor William O'Rourke
Professor Nancy Cirillo
Department of English at UIC
Rich & Teri Frantz
Richard Napora
Spike & Wicklow

Contents

The Feminists Go Swimming

This is based partly on a true story where women protested at a gentlemen's bathing area beside the James Joyce Tower in the early seventies.

The men couldn't say exactly when they had first noticed the parked cars near the entrance to the Gentlemen's Bathing Place called the Forty Foot. There had been bad weather, cold rain and wind for a long spell. The men came after early Mass, down along the coast road and then descending the rocky passageway to the bathing area and the cold sea. Most of them were older men, retired from civil service jobs. The daily swim gave a certain order to their lives. They took pride in being able to swim in inclement weather, in feeling that they belonged to a harder breed of men. On these wet days, they came on bicycles or walked with duffel bags slung over their shoulders, heads bent to the ground. They did not speak, only grunted and shook their heads, counting off who had come and who had not.

Clustering beside the stone walls that shielded them from the wind, they undressed, folding their shirts and trousers, tucking damp socks into their shoes, breathing deeply. Sometimes it was hard for the older ones among them to get their clothes off. They teetered in the wind, struggling silently, never accepting help, balancing amongst the jagged rocks.

When they were ready, some went off behind another wall, checked the wind and pissed. Others did calisthenics of some kind, rotating their naked hips and torsos, hiding from the brunt of the wind and rain, slapping their withered skin, making it turn red and sting, feeling the invigoration of blood running through the veins. On rainy days they would already be soaked and shivering, covered with goose pimples. They watched each other to see who was looking the worse for wear, always posing and talking about the great weather, even when it was lashing rain. It was part of the game. Then one of them would trot off toward the grey waves, hunched over like a prehistoric creature, moving carefully over the stones and disappearing into the churning sea. The others followed, rubbing their arms and blowing out hard, and then they too vanished, the heads bobbing up seconds later between the swells and waves, sleek and bald like seals. They swam in winter for only a minute or so, and then came out.

Afterwards, when they were standing around naked and wet, they felt the blood flowing to their extremities, a tingling sensation of warmth. Someone had always heard a good joke lately. They discussed politics and sports, depending on the occasion and the weather, stepping from foot to foot, slapping their hands together, the water beading on their bodies.

They brought their own tea and bread and ate and drank among the shielding rocks, the sea crashing behind them, and they felt secure and glad that another day's swim was over. None of them had been alive when the tradition of swimming naked first started, but it had become a great institution, making the place somehow atavistic. They were a fraternity of men, naked creatures inhabiting a place of men that had been handed down through generations. They didn't know if it was the nakedness or the swimming or the tea, or if it was all of it that brought them close together, or because nothing ever changed down at the hidden Bathing Place For Men Only.

It was on a clear day in March, still freezing but bright, when only the hardened swimmers were coming to the Forty Foot, that Morrissey, the auctioneer, said, 'There's some women sitting up in a car by the road. When they saw me coming, one of them got out and took a picture of me, and then jumped back into the car.' Morrissey spoke with his usual frankness, sitting down on the stone bench and untying his laces with his big fingers. He had great handlebar whiskers, an eccentricity that he used to complement a polished English accent when he bargained over expensive houses and property listings.

'And what did you say?' Norris, half-undressed, said, scratching the thin grey hair on his chest. He was the oldest of the men who still came for the daily swim.

'What the hell could I say? I thought it was reporters from the papers at first, but they didn't ask me for my name or anything. Just snapped the shot and then popped back into the car. The bloody cheek of them. We've become a spectacle these past few years, if you ask me.' He set his shoes beside his white feet and wiggled his toes, little worms of dirt between the cracks.

'Another magazine doing a special on us, I'll bet,' Norris said. He felt slighted that the people in the car had not seen him coming down. After all, he was the oldest of the daily swimmers. He liked to see himself quoted in papers. He said things like, 'I remember swimming on the morning that this or that happened.' Swimming was his sole claim to fame. Norris bent over and touched his toes. Two deflated breasts hung from his chest, the small nipples like brown scabs. He straightened up as he heard a bicycle bell sounding. 'That must be Giblin,' Norris said. 'A clear sky brings them out, doesn't it? We haven't seen him in weeks.' They moved closer to the long narrow stair that led back up to the road.

'Morning.' Giblin saluted somebody up on the road. Neither Morrissey nor Norris nor any of the others heard the response, but they heard Giblin roar, 'You whore!' He came into sight again, furious and moving fast, his bicycle lurching as it descended the steep steps into the Forty Foot.

'They called me a male chauvinist pig,' Giblin shouted in an incredulous manner, almost spitting. The bicycle jumped out of his hands and rolled straight down the steps towards the water.

Morrissey ran out and stopped it from toppling into the sea. 'Is it them up in the car?' he said, holding the bicycle steady. His breath fogged in the cold air.

'You saw them?' Giblin took his bicycle back and put it beside the wall. 'What did they say to you?'

Two younger men in Adidas track suits, who had been

standing some way from the older men, came over and listened, grinning at one another.

'This one comes out of a car and takes a photograph of me, and when I smile, she gives me a look that would sour milk. They're not your girlfriends up there, are they?' Morrissey said, eyeing the two younger men.

'We don't know any girls,' the taller of the two men grinned. He had a chiselled body, his shoulders broad and tapering to his waist. 'But maybe one of them fancies you, Morrissey.'

Morrissey looked at the two and felt slightly inhibited. He tried to suck in the weight around his belly. They had only begun swimming around Christmas. He was surprised to see they were still coming. He gave them a cautious nod and straightened his moustache. Until they arrived, he had been one of the younger men there, even though he was in his forties.

Giblin checked the bicycle. The wheel seemed a little out of shape. 'Christ.'

The two young men stood looking at Morrissey. He looked at them. 'What are you looking at? Go on off, there's nothing going on.' Morrissey turned his thick buttocks on them and went to whisper something to Giblin.

The two young men walked off toward a cluster of rocks which jutted out into the waves. They always dived in from that spot.

'Maybe they just wanted to speak to someone,' Norris said. Standing naked, now a small skeletal figure, the outline of his spine arched visibly, showing each vertebrae. 'I think I'll . . .' Norris wished for a moment that he'd read the morning paper. Maybe something significant had occurred.

'Stop awhile,' Morrissey said, turning again to Norris. 'Leave them alone.' Morrissey had his shirt untucked from his trousers and his tie loosened at his neck.

Giblin checked his bicycle.

'I'm telling you, there's been too much talk about this place. We're liable to get all sorts coming down here to grind their axe,' Morrissey went on.

4

'What do you mean?' Norris said.

'Forget it.' Morrissey turned and went towards the wall.

A hoary frost remained, despite the cold sun climbing into the sky. Another two men came down, a priest fresh from his eight o'clock Mass and a retired policeman. The priest and the policeman were inseparable. 'The law of the land and the law of God together.' The policeman walked very close to the priest, his head tilted, speaking seriously, the way he always did. His breath steamed and it was as if smoke were coming from the priest's ear.

Norris was about to ask them if they had seen the women when Morrissey and Giblin gave him a cold look. Morrissey twitched his long moustache. He could see that the two young men were amused by the idea of women putting Morrissey and Giblin under surveillance. He gave them a dismissive glance. The taller man had on red swimming togs.

'How are you, men,' the aging policeman said, as though he had come upon a group of criminals up to no good. He had his hands behind his back, as was his custom when he walked the town.

'Grand,' Morrissey smiled. 'Great day.'

'It's not a bad day at all,' the priest answered, loosening his collar and taking off his coat. 'We had a good turnout at Mass. Thank God it's getting brighter in the mornings.'

'Not that it'll hold up with the breeze. There's a forecast of rain for later morning,' Giblin said. He looked in a disgusted manner at his bicycle and then up at the road. His mind was distracted with the women.

'Are you all right, Giblin?' the priest said, looking at the bicycle. 'Do you have a flat?'

'Spokes are a bit bent, Father.' Giblin rubbed his jaw. 'Just spokes, Father.'

The priest smiled and turned to the two young men standing off to the side. 'Good morning. It's good to see you down again.'

The taller young man saluted the priest with a dip of his

head. 'Fine morning, Father.'

The priest had his towel under his armpit like a Swiss roll. 'Well, we'd better start then. It's cold enough down here.' The salty air had a peculiar cold sharpness which filled the lungs in early March. It was a dangerous month for swimming.

The day was extremely crisp and blustery, so they had to go around to the east wall to undress out of view of the steps. Usually someone watched to make sure that no dogs strayed down.

'Are you still looking at selling that church up the way, Father?' Morrissey said as he undid his tie. It was the first word he had spoken to the priest.

'And good morning to you, Morrissey,' the priest said, annoyed.

'Right,' Morrissey said. 'Nice morning to freeze your arse.' He smiled at Giblin, who averted his eyes.

'I had a call the other night, Father. I'd see you right in this. There's parties willing to pay cash up front for the church.' He raised his thick eyebrows, and his moustache moved like a creature on his upper lip.

'God forbid it should come to that,' the priest answered, looking up to the sky. 'What does it say for a people when they begin closing their churches?'

'True enough. How right you are.' The policeman made a sour face and repeated what the priest had said.

Morrissey scratched his chest, letting his belly feel the cold air. 'Ah,' he sighed. 'This is the life.' When he was finished with his antics, he turned and looked at the priest. 'I'd get you a good price on that church, Father.' He touched his moustache as if to affirm his seriousness. 'I'd see the church right, Father.'

'Who would buy it?' The priest stopped, a rotund figure in stockinged feet.

Morrissey's shirt billowed in the wind.

'It wouldn't be those Mormons, would it?' the priest said, pointing a finger at Morrissey. 'Is that what you're on with again?'

Morrissey rolled his eyes. 'Isn't this an age of ecumenicalism? Father, there's not a soul out by that church. There's no point having this dog-in-the-manger attitude. You'd do well to get what you can. It's all the same God.'

The policeman sensed a row developing. He stood beside the priest, his big naked body creased in rolls of fat as he tipped his stomach forward. 'If you weren't such an eejit, Morrissey, you might be dangerous.'

Morrissey took his shirt off and turned around, affronting the policeman with his hairy buttocks. 'You know best then,' he smiled, winking at Giblin.

The two younger men had hard muscular bodies, the flesh still tight around the neck, armpits, and legs. Their stomachs were flat, hair coarse and black. They began doing push-ups on the flat stones.

'They're in great shape,' the priest said, staring at the pair. He wanted to avoid a row with Morrissey. 'I remember when I was young like that.'

The old man, Norris, was already undressed and still curious about the women up in the car. He was sure they were from a magazine. He went off with a towel in hand to have a look up the steps to see if they were taking pictures. He reached the bottom of the steps, put the towel around his waist and climbed up towards the road. A car engine was running. He could see the exhaust smoking behind the wall. He went up further, trying to broaden his shoulders and tighten his face for a good photograph. He was ready to quote famous events he remembered, and how they discussed them down at the Forty Foot. He'd been photographed numerous times through the years at the Christmas morning swim.

Two women stood off to the side of the wall, peering through the cracks. One of them held a camera, and shouted 'Pig!' popping her head up over the wall. 'Pig!' she shouted again.

Norris flinched and the corner of the towel fell out of his fingers. He fell backwards, trying to grab the towel, and hit his head on the steps. The two women ran down a few steps. 'Pig!' The one with the camera took shots of Norris, who looked dazed, trying to squirm away. 'Get that shot!' the other woman shouted. Norris's small bony buttocks were exposed to the camera as his legs curled up. The woman crouched down, turned the lens in the camera, focusing on the small testicles packed between the legs.

Two other women got out of the car and ran to the edge of the steps.

'We have one!' the women down below shouted.

Norris grabbed at his towel and recovered enough to turn and stumble back down the steps. When he got to the bottom, he turned a corner and sat down on a stone which had been carved into a chair.

The women stood halfway down the steps, but they didn't dare come down into the Bathing Place. 'Look,' one of the women said. They looked at droplets of blood on the steps. 'He's cut.'

Norris's knees and the left side of his thigh were grazed. His elbow had a gash on it. He shook badly. He touched his head, feeling a lump, but there was no blood. 'Jesus Christ,' he muttered. His small knees hit together.

The priest came out from behind the wall and saw the state of Norris.

'What in the name of Jesus happened?' he cried, rushing over. He squatted on his fat, hairless legs, the knee caps severely red from years of kneeling.

'I fell. It's nothing. I fell on a bit of seaweed over there.' Norris pointed towards the water but there was no seaweed, only stone and the sea crashing off behind it. 'It's nothing,' he said again. 'Really, Father, I'm all right.'

'Are you sure you're all right? You'd better dip that in the water to clean those cuts.' The priest stood up. His buttocks were very round and big. They had stretch marks on them. He looked bewildered. 'You weren't even over by the sea. Where did you fall?'

The policeman came out from behind the wall with his hands hanging at his side before Norris had time to answer. 'What's all this?' he said.

'Give me a hand here,' the priest said. The two of them stood over Norris.

8

Blood had begun to dry on Norris's legs and elbow. His torso was very thin and his hip bones showed as he sat with his hands over his crotch, ashamed, hiding his small gooseberry testicles. 'I'm grand,' Norris said softly.

'Let's get you cleaned up,' the priest said. 'You've been down here too long Norris. It's not good to be down here for this long with nothing on you.'

Norris had taken out his dentures earlier, so his face was sunken and he looked all that much older as he sat there looking up. His adam's apple moved in his throat as though he were trying to suppress tears.

'It happens to the best of us sometimes,' the priest said, softening his tone, looking pityingly at Norris. The priest knew that when Norris went it wouldn't be the same at the swim. He slapped the pads of his big hands together suddenly, winking. 'Let's get you sorted out then.'

'I just slipped,' Norris said meekly. He tried to turn his head to see what the women were doing, to see if they'd left. He was afraid to tell the priest.

Morrissey and Giblin came out together from behind the rocks and saw Norris. They were in no humour for swimming. Morrissey had it in for the policeman.

'What the . . .' Morrissey shouted. He raised his eyes to the road and then looked at Norris. 'It wasn't . . . Jesus Christ.'

Norris swallowed feebly, and nodded his head. He lowered his eyes.

'It wasn't what?' the priest asked. 'What are you talking about?'

'He fell down,' the policeman said frankly, raising his hand to point, and then not knowing where to point.

Morrissey and Giblin were shocked. They felt the sudden vulnerability of their nakedness. The women were obviously mad and that camera might be anywhere. They couldn't believe they would do something like that to Norris. He was like everybody's grandfather. Morrissey moved nervously towards the long narrow stair ascending through the rocks to the road. His rotund body tensed, ready to attack. He wasn't going to be made a fool of by women.

'Give us a hand with Norris,' the priest said.

The two younger men stood on a rock, preparing to dive into the sea, oblivious to what had happened. They looked back and waved at Morrissey. Morrissey waved back despite himself. He knew they would tell the priest and the policeman about the women. Morrissey was hoping the two young men would just jump in and start swimming.

The two young men whistled over. 'Are you ready, Morrissey?' the one in the red togs shouted.

'Go on!' Morrissey shouted savagely. 'Go on, for the love of Christ!'

'What's wrong with you?' the priest said.

Morrissey shuddered.

Norris waited in the stone chair silently. He was freezing cold.

'Well, let's get him down to the water and clean him up then,' the policeman said. He and the priest assisted Norris to his feet. They felt strange touching another naked man, and they tried to make contact only with his outstretched arms. 'There you go now.' Norris was a light burden. They took him down to a concrete area where boats were launched and set him down at the edge of the water. He held the rusting iron bars and dipped his thin legs into the choppy sea. His face winced as the salt water stung the wounds.

The two younger men were already swimming off towards an island of rocks.

Morrissey and Giblin stayed back and looked at one another. They turned and looked up towards the stairs again. Giblin spoke first. 'What the hell are we afraid of, anyway? Let's go up there and kick the shite out of them ones. I'll get my bicycle pump and we'll sort them whores out. You know what they are, don't you?' Giblin said. He had a hard face that went well with clothes, but when he was stripped bare, the rolls of fat at his middle pulled at his shoulders and spine and made him look almost hunched. When he tensed, his body rippled.

'Bra burners,' Giblin said. 'That's what they are.'

Morrissey squinted. 'Feminists. That's what they call them now. They want the same thing as the bra burners, though, but the difference is they hate men. I'm telling you they're a right bunch of trollops,' Morrissey went on. 'I see them all the time at auctions. Pretentious bitches with an education and a grievance against mankind. And stingy fuckers, mind you.'

'Lesbians,' Giblin said. He stepped nervously from foot to foot. He had a very small penis, a nib of redness covered with coils of ginger hair. He turned his back on the steps.

Morrissey rubbed his face. He felt stubble. He only shaved after his swim. 'Let it go for a bit. They're probably gone now. What we need is to discuss this someplace else, get ourselves organized and prepare for this sort of thing.' If he had been dressed, Morrissey would have put his hands in his pockets at this stage, or touched his cap. Instead, he smoothed his moustache. He felt uncomfortable and irritable and wanted to just put his clothes back on and leave. 'Let's sort Norris out first,' he said finally. 'They're gone.'

Giblin cast one last look.

Norris was only grazed, nothing serious. He was smiling and talking with the priest and the policeman. 'Well, all the same, you come up by the house with us afterwards and have a cup of tea and a bit to eat,' the priest insisted. His round face was flushed with the cold. When he smiled he had very good teeth, one of the advantages of having the best dentists through the church. 'I always have to have brown bread and tea after I come down here,' the priest went on. 'You have to put back what you expend. That's a law of nature.'

Across the bay, the blue sky began to darken. The wind changed to a northerly direction. The men became conscious of the cold. 'Let's get this over with, shall we, gents,' the policeman said, turning to Morrissey and Giblin. They resigned themselves to a cold, reluctant swim and plodded toward the sea.

The priest rubbed grease onto his arms and legs and

kneaded his buttocks. 'God, it's cold.'

'We should forget it,' Giblin said.

'And break our record? Not on your life,' the priest protested.

The two young men were swimming through the dark water, out towards a small island of rocks, something that none of the others had done in years.

'It's good to have young blood like this here,' the priest said, his hands on his hips.

Morrissey crouched down and took a swab of grease and rubbed it into his arms.

'I remember years ago, when we'd race out there and back,' the priest smiled. 'You remember that?'

The policeman grinned. 'It's been a long time.' His big red face broke in a smile.

'I think that we should acknowledge those young men more than we do. We're all friends here.' The priest eyed Morrissey, his eyebrows arched on his forehead. 'You're too hard on them, Morrissey, We should be glad to have them.'

Morrissey spat into the sea. Tiny hairs stood on his arms and legs, the grease glistening on his skin. 'Let's see if they're here next year. We don't want every Johnny-come-lately here with us. And look at that one fellow off in his red togs, what's that all about? You're supposed to wear nothing down here.'

'Well, Morrissey, why don't you tell him to drop his togs?' The priest winked at the policeman, who only caught the hint of humour and opened his mouth in an enigmatic manner.

Giblin broke into a smile.' That's a good one, Father.'

Morrissey gritted his teeth.

Norris still sat with his legs in the water looking abjectly out at the sea. He was perished and alone, a man who had been attacked in his own domain.

The sea heaved, a wave crested, foamed over the lip of concrete running between the men's feet. The five men shuddered. They had been standing around too long. The swim needed to be one continuous movement on days like this, an uncalculated journey from their house to the sea and back again. Their routine had been disturbed.

'It's too cold.' Morrissey turned back.

'I'd like to see you swim out to where they've gone,' the priest said smugly. 'You're too resentful of others, do you know that?''

Morrissey rolled his eyes and turned. 'Johnny-come-latelies coming down here. They're down here to laugh at us. Do you know that? Well, I won't be made a fool! Do you hear me?' His words swirled in the cold blustery air. The tide swelled and belched another wave onto the smooth slipway. 'You live in a dream world, Father. You think you can ignore everything.'

'Are we here to swim or get our death?' the policeman interrupted, looking stoically out at the gnarled rocks seething with foam.

Norris stood up and shivered.

The priest dismissed everything with a smile. 'That's it, Norris.' He put his hand on the balding head like he was baptizing a child.

Norris crouched at the edge of the water and dabbed his elbow, cupping water with the other hand over his elbows. 'They're only scratches.' He stood up. 'I think I'll get dressed.'

'Grand,' the policeman said. 'I don't like the look of this sky. There's rain out there on the bay.'

'Why don't you go on up with him, Morrissey, and don't catch a cold yourself,' the priest said, and jumped into a breaking wave without waiting for Morrissey's response.

Morrissey grunted, ran on his flat feet and dived, submerging himself in the freezing water, whipping his legs in and out, holding his breath, going out into the sea, feeling the power of his body buoyed by the salty water. He surfaced into a crawl, not daring to stop and look around, moving his arms in steady strokes, trying to establish a rhythm.

The other three trod water and then caught sight of Morrissey's head appearing and disappearing amid the waves. 'Now you've got him going,' Giblin said, laughing, keeping his chin above the water. 'He's mad as hell.'

The policeman went on his back and blew a thin spout of water.

'He's not a bad sort,' the priest said, as he splashed salt water on his forehead in a sign of the cross and sank beneath the waves.

They stayed a few minutes in the water until the shock of sudden exhilaration gave way to the beginnings of hypothermia. They swam over to the rusting iron bars by the slipway and climbed out.

Norris had a towel around his waist and a dingy undershirt on. He pointed to the speck of Morrissey's head. He was halfway to the island, bobbing up and down in the swell of the ocean.

Out on the island of rocks, the two younger men stood watching Morrissey fight the waves. A dismal drizzle began. 'Come on,' they shouted, but they did not dare go into the sea and interfere with Morrissey.

The four men on the slick, worn concrete looked out to sea. 'Jesus, he's a desperate man,' Giblin said. 'You got him all worked up, Father.'

The women had come down the steps and taken the men's clothes. They all wore shiny black raincoats and bathing caps, giving them a strange, androgynous look. They spread out across the slipway, behind the men.

The priest massaged his rubbery skin, reddened from the cold. He leaned over and touched his toes, shuddering, 'God, it's brisk enough.'

The leader of the women grinned. 'Now,' she whispered and the others let the raincoats fall off their shoulders. They were completely naked, each revealing a single letter on their stomachs: L, I, B, E and R. Flanking the end of the line a monstrous woman's grotesque breasts hung, half obscuring the double letters on her stomach: TY. She, too, wore a hideous bathing cap that stretched her face into a grimace.

The leader shouted, 'We've come to swim!'

The four men turned and saw the women. 'They're back!'

Norris shouted.

The wavering word LIBERTY moved on the women's bellies.

'Mother of Jesus!' the priest shouted, and instinctively jumped into the sea again. The policeman and Norris followed him.

Giblin covered his small penis and scrambled away to a buttress of rocks. 'Jasus Christ!'

Norris emerged from under the water and clung to the railing, a small curled-up creature, like something that had been extricated from its shell.

'We've come to swim,' the leader of the women shouted. The four younger women looked at one another, shivering. The heavy woman on the end moved on her elephantine legs, the marks from her bra and pants reddening in the cold air.

A cauldron of heads bobbed in the great depths of the water. The policeman fought to keep above water. His massive arm came out of the water. He repeated the only thing which came to his head, 'This is private property!'

Giblin stayed behind the rocks.

'We are entitled to swim here,' the leader of the women shouted.

A wave curled and broke on the outer rim of rocks, sending a scud of foam over the policeman's head. His head emerged again. 'You . . . You have to be a member to come here.' He said it with the felicity of a man who believed in laws.

'You have to be a man!' the fat women scoffed.

The woman with the letter R sized up Giblin with a camera and snapped a shot. The bulb flashed, Giblin scurried away. She took more shots of the men in the sea.

'Have some Christian decency!' the priest shouted from the water. 'It is too cold for this sort of bravado.' The sea heaved and he disappeared.

The rain fell in ice cold droplets. The women hesitated. The cold had already begun to numb them. They weren't used to it. The leader went over to the fat woman and they whispered together. The younger bony women remained, looking at the men.

The leader turned and stepped back from the slipway.

'We'll take their clothes on them,' the fat woman said, nodding her head.

'We're not going in?' the girl with the letter B said.

'We're taking their clothes!' the fat woman said defiantly. The leader nodded her head and repeated. 'We're going to take their clothes this time.' The rain had made their bodies mottled and red, slightly incapacitating them.

'We're coming out,' the policeman shouted, and swam toward the rusting iron bars beside the steps. Norris struggled out, then the priest and finally the policeman. He was the only one who didn't cover himself. The other two leaned over cupping their hands over their genitals. 'You are trespassing.' The policeman pointed to the worn sign on the stone wall. His left ankle was festooned with dark seaweed as he moved toward the women.

'Watch him,' the fat woman said, instinctively looking to see that the narrow stairway was clear for an escape.

The women moved back cautiously.

Out on the sea, the rain fell in a slanting mist. The faint noise of the men out on the rock drifted inland.

'Morrissey!' the priest roared. There was no sign of him. The two young men on the rocky island looked towards the land. 'Holy Mother of God,' the priest shouted. 'He must have gone down.'

The two young men out on the island dived into the sea.

Giblin came out glumly from behind his rock, walking sideways like an embarrassed crab.

'Where is he?' Norris whispered, hunched over.

The sea surged and subsided. The priest saw a struggle out near the island. 'Over there.' He crossed himself. 'I think they have him!'

The women looked sceptical. The fat one turned to watch for men coming down the long steps. She didn't want to get trapped.

The policeman's voice gained authority. 'There's a man drowning out there.' He pointed at the sea and plodded up towards the women and then stopped. He looked like some hideous Frankenstein's monster with his big arms extended.

'Stand back!' The fat woman had a stone in her hand.

'Forget them,' the priest shouted.

The policeman stopped and glared at the women. 'There's a man drowning.' He turned from the women. 'Out near the island!'

The women saw nothing. 'They're lying!'

The leader leaned down and got out a piece of paper from her raincoat. She stood up and began reading. 'We are here today to protest against the exclusion of women . . .' The rain was falling too heavily for her to read with any sort of ceremony. Her teeth chattered. She looked to the other women.

The four men looked pathetically out to sea. 'We should go in,' Giblin said hesitantly. But they were too cold to go into the water again. Their limbs were blue. The salt air and the rain had stiffened their muscles.

Even the women hesitated, moving close to one another, squeezing the word LIBERTY tight together.

The priest had his back to them, shouting at the rolling waves, his body jiggling as he moved.

Norris turned around. His wounds were fresh and swollen. 'You stupid women! There's a man drowning out there . . .' He pointed frantically. 'If you don't believe us, count how many pairs of trousers you have there.'

The women counted seven pairs.

'What did I ever do to you?' Norris cried and put his hands to his face when he saw that the women understood that the men were not lying. 'What did we ever do to you?'

The women set the clothes down on the rocks. They put on raincoats and disappeared up the narrow steps.

There was no sign of the three men. The sea crashed against the rocks, a vicious dark green. They heard the screech of tyres up on the road. The women were gone.

The priest was on his knees, his hands together, blessing the dead out in the sea.

When the men gathered their clothes, they could not put them on because their fingers were so numb. They tried to pick things up between their wrists or pinch things, like inept lobsters. They had to help one another drape shirts over their backs and step into their underwear, pulling the pants up over the genitals. They could go nowhere until that was done. The priest managed to get a towel around his waist. They left their shoes and socks behind, walking in their bare feet.

'What will we say?' Giblin said, sniffling. Spit drooled from his numb lower lip.

The priest fumbled with a towel, visibly shaking. He stopped and looked at Giblin. His lips could hardly form the words. 'You . . . You saw them on the way in, didn't you?'

Giblin looked down at the grey stone.

Norris, his dentures in his hand, did not look at the priest either. 'We thought they were with the . . .' Norris stopped talking.

The policeman stood dumbly, unsure of what to do. He waited for the priest to say something.

They moved out from behind the wall, the sea heaving its heavy mass against the land. They consciously didn't look at it.

The priest's legs burned as he tried to mount the long steep steps.

'What will we say?' Giblin said.

'We . . .' The priest fumbled with his towel. It fell on the ground. He bent over and tried to pick it up.

Giblin looked away.

'We will say what happened,' the priest said when he got the towel around his soft middle. 'The men drowned swimming to the island.' He continued up the steps penitently.

'But, the women?' Giblin said.

The priest's face had turned an icy blue. His jaw stiffened. 'The men deserve a decent, quiet burial without scandal.' He coughed and held the phlegm and swallowed it again. 'Without scandal,' he said again.

Giblin kept staring at the priest. 'But if the women say anything?'

'They won't,' the policeman said flatly, putting his hand on Giblin's shoulder. 'They won't.'

Giblin wriggled out from under the policeman's grip, still looking unsure. 'But the women . . .' Giblin looked dumbly at the priest.

The priest stared at him. 'Because two things happen simultaneously, does that mean they are related?' It was the kind of line he might have used in a sermon. 'Are we agreed?' the priest said firmly to Giblin.

Giblin nodded. 'Agreed.'

Norris looked up at the priest. 'Agreed, Father.'

The sun came out again and streamed down the narrow stair. They all had to squint their eyes and look away. They moved silently past the flaking black sign with the white words, 'Forty Foot. Gentlemen Only.'

Up on the road the policeman waved a car down. It began to pull over slowly.

The priest looked at the policeman and then at the other two. 'The men drowned swimming to the island.'

The End of the World

The end of the world was a school day. There was even homework due. It seemed strange. It was hard to think of homework due on the day the world was set to end. The priests stood before the classes and paged through the maths books and the Irish books and picked out problems, the odd ones from one to fifteen. A long passage of Irish was assigned.

The day before the end of the world was like any other school day for Patsy. He was walloped twice, once in Geography and then again in History. He was pure thick, a dosser of the highest order. The priests said no boy alive could have that little aptitude for a written language.

There was going to be no let up on educational pursuits on that day. The routine was well established. Catholicism guarded against idlers.

Patsy travelled the cold corridors between classes, obligingly good-humoured. He gripped the ribs of the heaters with his calloused hands, squeezing the hot iron. Patsy's ability to take abuse gave him a formal status among the other fellows. He let the strap lick its way up his palms and wrists. It didn't hurt him the way it hurt the others. In English class he was caught with the word 'Armageddon' written in his notebook where he should have had his homework listed. Tierney demanded, 'Where did you get that word?'

Patsy shrugged his shoulders. He held his hands out for punishment, but Tierney punched him in the face. Patsy fell out of his desk. His nose bled. 'Where did you get that word?' Tierney roared again. He was a head taller than Patsy and had huge sloping shoulders and a strong rugby player's neck. 'Where did you get that word?'

Patsy finally admitted he'd seen it in an American comic about Superman saving the planet. His nose was still bleeding. The bell rang for the next class. Tierney kept Patsy back and then the two of them went down to the toilet and filled up a basin of water.

'Hold your head back, you fool.'

Tierney smelt of chalk dust, tobacco and cheap aftershave, an odd middle-aged mixture. Patsy tilted his head back and inhaled. He thought how nice it would be when the end of the world came.

Tierney breathed hard through his nose. 'Stop moving.'

Patsy held steady. He presumed there would be no school in heaven, and that all things would be revealed to him. He maintained his solemn ignorance, especially in the presence of a man who could beat him to death. If the world had gone on a little longer, Patsy felt he would have got back at Tierney. But now was a time for forgiveness. Patsy knew the beating was frustration on Tierney's part. The school had lost early on in the Munster school rugby championships. Tierney was the coach.

'There you are now,' Tierney said.

Patsy knew Tierney was in his element in this sort of sideline Order of Malta antic, stuffing cotton up a bleeding nose or moving smelling salts under some poor eejit's nose who'd taken a hard hit out on the rugby field.

'Head off now, Patsy.' Tierney shook Patsy's hand and said, 'May we meet in heaven, please God.'

Patsy took the hand in a genial manner, winked and said, 'Maybe they'll have an ol' rugby championship in heaven, Mr Tierney, please God they will, Sir.'

Nobody was really sure how the world was going to end. The Pope was supposed to open an envelope that held the secret of Fatima.

The Religion teacher was a pious and ancient priest, Father Mackey, a shrunken piece of leather in a black robe who told stories about the Famine and what it did to Ireland. He came around every week and spoke about the missions in other countries and always tied things up by relating a story about the Famine. On the day before the end of the world, the classes were brought together in the study hall for what everyone thought would be a sermon by Father Mackey.

It began without a prefatory remark. The boys were still chatting when Father Mackey climbed up on the podium, teetering with old age, his rosary beads dripping from his fingers: 'Now, boys, how will the world end?' He asked it three more times in the same modulated but croaking voice. He'd been a heavy smoker of rolled cigarettes in his day; his neck was cut up from numerous operations. The boys had to lean forward in their desks, trying to catch what he was saying. The question finally reached everyone. The place was dead silent. Nobody had actually mentioned the end of the world all day. It was unspeakable. It was good to talk about it finally. There were questions that needed to be asked.

'How will the world end?' Father Mackey said again.

'Maybe an angel will come down,' the school swot said resolutely, standing up.

Father Mackey had a stooped spine, and when he smiled it became a perfect arch. 'Could somebody draw what it will be like?' Father Mackey gasped for breath.

Father Mackey looked out over the assembly. The grey vacuity of the back of the room contrasted with the intensity of the boys before him. A window rumbled, letting in a cold rainy breeze.

'Draw me a picture, boys,' Father Mackey said. 'How will the world end?' he repeated over and over again. 'Draw me a picture.'

The boys worked away in their copybooks. Father Mackey checked the drawings, walking up and down the aisles kneading the rosary beads through his fingers, the holy abacus of his millions of Holy Marys and Our Fathers. The beads were famous. The cross of Jesus dangling from them which Father Mackey had touched to pagan black babies in Africa had made the devil leap out of them screaming. Everybody knew what a cannibal was in Father Mackey's class.

'Go up to the board, Donovan, and draw what you have,'

Father Mackey said, holding Donovan's limp hand, his finger provisionally on a bead, halfway through a decade.

Donovan drew a picture of an ark pulling in down at the city docks. People were getting on in twos.

'What . . . What's that?' Father Mackey asked, pointing to a small creature that looked like a dog.

'It's a dog, Father. It's me and my dog getting onto the ark down at the docks.' Donovan touched the knot of his school tie, suddenly self-conscious. Maybe dogs weren't going to heaven. He assumed a schoolboy position of defence, cowering sideways, holding his hand over his ear.

Father Mackey put his skeletal fingers together in prayer. 'Sweet Jesus, humour at this hour . . .' His eyes looked to heaven.

Somebody else had a flying ark driven by Noah through the sky. The boy was asked to draw the picture.

The priests at the doors were shaking their heads in an ambivalent way. This was no time for cod acting. Everybody was scared.

The English boy Wilson stood up and said, 'My mother says the Germans killed all the Jews in the world. That is why we are going to die.' Wilson's father had died in the trenches in France. His mother was Irish.

'Was Jesus a Jew?' Father Mackey asked Wilson.

Wilson said nothing.

'Are we part of the Church of Ireland or the Church of Rome?'

The class mumbled back and forth among themselves. This was a trick question which Father Mackey always asked them, but they never could remember which was the right answer.

Wilson ran to the door crying. The priests let him go.

Father Mackey's spine was still arched. 'Let him alone, God love him. He will be with his father soon.'

'When Wilson sees his Dad, will he . . . Well, you know, Father, Wilson's Dad was blown up. Will all the souls of people look like new?'

'Everybody will be about thirty,' Lawlor shouted. 'That's

what my mother says. The age of Jesus – thirty three – isn't that right, Father Mackey?'

'That seems reasonable,' Father Mackey coughed. His head turned a boiled pink colour; his lips trembled. He had lost control of the boys.

'You mean we'll be thirty as well?' Kingston shouted.

'No, our mothers and fathers and all the grannies and the old fellows, they'll all be thirty. We'll be the way we are, right, Father?'

'That seems reasonable,' Father Mackey's small head turned to the priests at the door. He needed help.

'Will we have wings?' a fellow asked from the last row.

Patsy said, 'When the Pope opens the secret of Fatima, will the world begin to end at that moment?' He had seen something like it in his comics where codes had a message in caps saying: THIS WILL SELF-DESTRUCT IN 5 SECONDS.

Father Mackey sat down on a chair and spread his legs, leaning over, drawing breath. 'You boys should be praying, not scheming.'

'What happens if he doesn't open it, Father?' Patsy pressed on.

The two boys beside Patsy moved out of the desk and shoved in beside some other fellows. Then there was a moment of silence. Father Mackey said to Patsy, 'Are we part of the Church of Ireland or the Church of Rome?'

Patsy said, 'The Church of Ireland,' and twitched his injured nose.

'Come up and reproduce your drawing, Patsy.'

Patsy went up and drew a picture of Jesus coming down on the great orb of the sun which was in his copybook. He had seen something like this in the same *Marvel* comic from America that had the Armageddon. But, in the comic, Superman came down to save the world. Patsy ad-libbed from the original drawing in his copybook and added a big 'J' on the chest of Jesus in a diamond and a great mushroom cloud rising above the smiling face.

Father Mackey took Patsy by the arm. 'What's this?'

'It's Jesus. Don't you see the J? It's how He saved the world from nuclear war. Armageddon, Father.' Patsy gave the class a pat, apish stare.

Everyone thought Father Mackey was going to break in half. His body creaked and cracked audibly as he went at Patsy. He was flogged before the class, his hands held out before him. Each wrist in turn took the long tongue of the leather. The nosebleed opened again with the pressure of his face holding back expression. Patsy managed a smile at the end. The boys wouldn't look at him. They turned to the fogged windows. This was the eve of the end of the world. Everybody resented Patsy's antics. It was supposed to be a time of prayer and family.

Father Mackey raised his small leathery hands and roared, 'The end of the world has nothing to do with Supermen or nuclear war!' He referred to something from the Book of Revelations.

Patsy was beginning to understand something. He swallowed the sweet trickle of blood, but he knew he was winning. He remembered something back at his house about how the world was saying the Church and the Pope had done nothing, even though they knew the Jews were being burned alive. He figured Superman would have been on to that.

The school ended an hour early for everyone to get a start on their homework. The senior boys went to the back of the class and began their tasks. Even Patsy worked hard, labouring over a long division problem. Over half the class had completed their homework before they left the study hall. However, Patsy was one of the unfortunate who would go towards eternity with the nagging spectre of long division remaining as one of those earthly conundrums. He braced himself for the patent sideburn pull from a priest who saw him struggling with the dual anxiety of ignorance and diminishing time. 'You're pure thick,' the priest said, but didn't touch him. Then the bell rang and the boys were let out.

All the boys walked silently down the long drive to the school gates, sometimes stopping, looking back at the great structure of the school in the field, flanked by grazing cows. The priests lived off in one section of the school. The evening was getting dark, a trail of lights crawling from the town off in the distance. The priests had solitary lights on in their small rooms, each one distinct and cold. Patsy stopped and began laughing. The other fellows around him moved away. He pointed at the priests' quarters. 'Jasus, look at that. Just think of them eejits spending their last night praying alone.' He had stopped laughing by the time he had said it.

'What happened to your nose?' Patsy's mother said when he came into the kitchen.

'I bumped into a door.'

'God Almighty . . . Do you ever stop?'

Patsy gawked at her. He liked the sweaty look of his mother with pots steaming around her. She smelt of cabbage.

'Well, change your shirt and get ready for Mass.' His mother had bought a big roast and cooked the family's favourite dish for the eve of the end of the world. She'd even bought a block of ice-cream.

Patsy felt in great form. He went out of the kitchen and looked in on the small living room. Everything was like Christmas, the best tablecloth spread out on the table, the good cutlery and china. A big fire going.

Patsy's father came home in solemn humour. He nodded at Patsy and noted the damaged nose. 'Acting the maggot until the end, no doubt. Do you have any fear of hell?' he said passing into the kitchen. 'Are you ready, Mother?' Patsy's father took off his shirt and filled the sink. He rubbed a cloth between the rolls of his white belly, washing his face, ears and neck, then shaving.

Patsy waited with his sisters in the living room. He heard his mother. 'I've your shirt ironed.'

'Grand job,' his father said. Then there was a long silence.

The lashing rain streamed down the living-room window. If the world was going to end, this seemed the weather for it. Patsy looked in the mirror and touched the soft scab forming on his nose. It had turned a dark brownish black.

'You told a lie, Patsy,' one of the sisters said. 'You'll go to hell for that, you will.'

Patsy spat on his palm, parted his hair, and plastered it with saliva. 'I wonder if Rita O'Brien will be up above?' he said, and winked at his sisters.

'Do I have to warn you again?' Patsy's father said, coming into the room.

Patsy stepped away from the mirror.

'Now cut the messing out, Patsy. Did you wash?'

Patsy nodded. The girls eyed him and made a face.

'Let's get going then. Look lively. Mother? Are you ready, girls?'

The girls smiled. Patsy gawked after his father.

'You told another lie, Patsy,' the two girls whispered.

The street was black with people. The town accepted the raining, cold vulnerability, the penitent slogging their way to Mass, all the houses oozing the black dribble of the faithful. For all the crowd, the street was silent, only the scrape of shoes, or the occasional cough. Patsy's mother had had her hair styled, protecting it now with a transparent rain cap.

All the churches were packed. Patsy stood with his parents, bewildered, cold, and hungry. A tremulous singing began in strained discord and died. Teeth chattered. From the ceiling, the faded murals looked down silently. Twenty minutes passed and nothing started. Patsy thought of the food warming at home. He looked at his father's severe face. 'Pray,' his father said. 'This is your last chance of salvation.'

A priest came out and announced there would be confession first. A rumble of thunder rolled through the vault of the church. The dark mahogany doors of the confessionals opened. Patsy was astonished to see that there had been priests in them since they had come in. The confessions were administered rapidly.

In those few minutes, the earthly mysteries of sin were revealed, the dark mouths pouring out guilt; drunkards who beat their wives, boys who had harboured impure thoughts, and the mystery of the young girl who had been murdered three years earlier revealed by a man with his lips pressed up to the mesh.

Patsy sat freezing in his seat. The Mass was long and arduous; Patsy listened to none of it. He looked around for Rita O'Brien.

The priest said nothing about how it would end. 'All is in God's hands,' he said, breathing through the speaker, sending a storm of breath through the congregation. 'Pray to our Blessed Mother in heaven, the intercessor of all our petitions, the patron of our Parish.' The priest left the altar in a billow of white cloth followed by a gang of altar boys swinging incense. The perfumed blue smoke lingered on the altar.

Patsy felt a grim satisfaction. To his mind it had the look of a bad trick. He had known this would happen. But sure, hadn't the others? The congregation looked at one another.

Patsy went with his father to the side altar. The priests peered silently through the bars of the confessionals, their eyes unblinking, watching people light candles. The world seemed ready for its end to Patsy.

The small side altars crowded with people. The brass boxes were so full of money that people had to leave the pennies on the floor of the chancel. Patsy took a small candle off a pale blue saucer and gave it to his mother.

More candles were brought up from the storage room. The congregation scrambled to get them for petitions, passing around lit candles to light the others. A constellation of light trailed up and down the aisles when the small altars filled.

Patsy lit his own candle and placed it beside the squat red candles of his sisters and his parents. His father's eyes moved over his family. He had always wanted to die without a sin on his soul. It was the death he had prayed for. 'Forgive me,' he whispered to all of them. 'I wasn't the father I should have been . . .' He stopped.

Patsy swallowed. Even he prayed for the end of the world at that moment.

*

At home the meal was eaten in silence, the lingering smell of incense in their clothes. The Mass had drained them. Patsy didn't even start a row when he got a small helping of ice-cream.

Patsy and his father pulled the couch over to the fire. The girls curled up on it. His father and mother drank the last of the tea. Then Patsy's father got up and went out to the hall. He came back in his coat, with his hat in his hands. He sat down next to his wife and closed his eyes.

Patsy went out to the bunker and filled up the bucket with coal, something his father would have objected to if the world had not been going to end. Patsy set two blocks and a bed of slack on the fire. His parents had committed their souls to another life. He looked at the fat of his mother's arms, his father's weak mouth, vacant and dark. His father had a formal dignity, his hat set on his head; a practical man, ready to lead his family on a journey.

Behind Patsy the dishes remained, the remnants of their last meal on earth, the shrivelled roast guarded by a ring of potatoes. Patsy looked out of the window into the darkness. The street stood in dark rain, the beginning of a great flood? How was it going to end? A seagull took sanctuary on the windowsill, its eyes shining. Fiddle music drifted on the rain from some house. He hoped death would come in sleep. His lips touched his mother's head, then he placed a hand on his father's shoulder. He tucked the blanket around his sisters. Stretching out before the fire, he knew he would not dream as his eyes closed for one last time. He whispered his last words on earth. 'I am sorry for what I done, Jesus.'

It was the radio next door that woke Patsy. He turned over, his shoulder blades stiff from sleeping on the floor. He sat up slowly, looking around. His parents had taken their shoes off during the night. The room was still darkish. Patsy turned his head to his sisters.

The sounds of the day filtered into the room, the hiss of tyres on the wet road outside, the clank of the milk bottles being left on the porches.

It would have been good if the world had ended during the night. In the kitchen, he put the kettle on the boil. When he came back in, they were all awake. Nobody knew what to say. The big meal from the previous night still hung in the air.

His father worked the embers of the fire and got a small red coal and blew on it, fanning it with bits of paper. It took quickly.

Patsy took the milk from the porch. The street was empty.

'Well,' his father said. 'Let's move the couch back then.' It all seemed like a cruel joke. Were they going to die during the day, separated from one another? Patsy's mother went over to the table and cut slices of meat off the roast, wrapping them up in the evening paper. She kept curling her long grey hair behind her ear like a schoolgirl. Patsy stood in front of the mirror, touching his nose, watching his mother's reflection. He went up to the bathroom and washed his face with cold water then came down again.

The girls stayed in the room with their mother. Patsy opened the front door. A dirty day for the end of the world, the clouds low over the city. God must have hated his own image to let the world run down to this horrible rain. He had destroyed Sodom and Gomorrah by fire.

Patsy pulled the collar of his coat up around his neck. 'Come on,' said his father, as the front door closed. Patsy could hear the girls crying behind it. Patsy stopped. His father shook his head. 'Leave them be.'

The two of them walked silently, Patsy's father pushing his bicycle. Patsy yawned deliberately to pretend he was thinking about nothing. 'Da?' he said, looking straight ahead.

'What?'

'Isn't it true St Patrick said Ireland would never be drowned in the end?'

Patsy's father slackened the pace. His eyes had a glassy look.

'I'll tell you, Dad, I wouldn't fancy a drowning . . . Like would it be a sin to try and keep swimming, or like should you . . .?' At that moment Patsy saw Rita O'Brien at her doorway. She stood desolate, her mother in her dressing gown holding her hand. Patsy thought that was a good one all right. The state of Mrs O'Brien, going to meet St Peter in her dressing gown. Jasus, didn't that beat all. Patsy raised his voice. 'May we meet on the other side of eternity, ladies.'

'In the name of God, will you give it over,' Patsy's father said with a sudden halting stiffness. The bicycle front wheel jack-knifed and rolled into a wall. The O'Briens' front door closed.

At the end of the street his father stopped and balanced the bicycle against the wall. 'I'm off then,' Patsy said.

Patsy's father tried to say something, reached for Patsy's hands and held them. But Patsy turned aside and stiffened. 'It's nothing, Dad, please.' Patsy's hands were blistered, the callouses bluish-white from the cold.

'Bastards,' his father whispered, touching the knuckles of his son's hands. 'No, I should have done something.' He showed his own hands, the leathery skin sealing hidden secrets. They had shared the same fate, years of abuse, the backs of sticks. Patsy had inherited the ignorance of his father.

Patsy made a hard face, trying to pull his hands back. 'Forget it.'

His father let him go. 'I knew and I did nothing. That can't be forgiven even by Him up there!' His voice quaked. His father closed his eyes. 'I let it happen under my nose.' He shook his fists. 'Those dirty bastards!' he roared. 'Those dirty bastards up there at that school!'

Patsy saw the O'Briens' door open slightly.

At lunchtime nobody wanted to go outside. Sandwiches were left on the windowsill, uneaten, half drunk bottles of milk in doorways. The fear hung solidly as the day wore on. The sky cleared in patches. Patsy loitered around the toilets, smoking a cigarette with some other fellows. He felt sick thinking of how he had caused such trouble in school and drawn the beatings on himself, and now his own father was going to go to hell because he felt guilty at not standing up for him . . . Patsy knew he should have said something. He shouldn't have left his father standing there like that.

Patsy went out into the yard. The air smelt of fire. It came from down in the town. The priests came out and crossed themselves. 'It has begun.' The sun turned a dark orange off over the town, then the first drift of light smoke descended on the school. Embers floated in the air, pulsing a deep red, carried on the wind. The boys shielded their heads with their coats and peered off, seeing that even the church steeples were on fire. In a few minutes, the smoke filled the horizon. The town was obscured. The hot smoke burned Patsy's eyes.

'We will go to the chapel to wait for Him,' Father Mackey cried, shivering and wheezing with the drifting smoke.

Patsy went back into the toilet. It was true. The world was ending. He slumped down on the ground, curling up. His people were dead. The smoke seeped in through the doors and windows. Patsy tasted it. His face touched the cold porcelain urinal. He had robbed his father of a good confession. His father was dead now. Who else had sinned since last night, was his father to endure purgatory alone? Patsy called out to his father as though he were haunting the earth already. There was no response. 'I deserved it!' Patsy screamed. 'Da, I deserved it! You couldn't have done nothing for me!'

Glass smashed in the background, as boys screamed and ran toward the chapel.

Patsy shivered and curled further into the cold urinal, shaking in loneliness, afraid of what he had to do. He swallowed and opened his mouth. 'You fuckin' bastard, God!' his voice trembled, feeling the sin enter his soul. 'Yes, you up there! You ol' fuckin' bastard, God!' He waved his fists at the damp ceiling, weeping with moisture. He would be with his father.

A priest ran into the toilet and glared at Patsy on the ground. The priest blessed himself, crossing the air with his long finger. 'God have mercy on us!' The priest took Patsy by the arm. 'What are you saying?' He dragged Patsy with him.

'Even the churches are on fire,' Patsy laughed.

*

32

In the chapel the boys were on their knees. Father Mackey held the host from the chalice in his old hands. 'He will enter it now in his own flesh and blood.'

The priest pushed Patsy up to the altar. He whispered something to Father Mackey. Two priests held Patsy steady.

Father Mackey quivered and shouted, 'Repent in the name of Jesus!'

Patsy struggled. Two other priests held his arms apart. Father Mackey croaked, 'In the name of the Father, and Son and Holy Ghost I absolve you.' He sprinkled holy water on Patsy, holding the tip of the chalice cross to Patsy's head. Patsy let out a roar, tore his arm free and slapped the chalice with the back of his hand. The small cross cut his hand. Father Mackey collapsed and the chalice toppled on the cold marble. 'Fuck the lot of you! Let youse all burn in hell!'

The congregation of boys went insane at the horror of Jesus coming down the road hearing this roaring blasphemy. Hands dragged at Patsy, tripping him by the ankles, pulling him down into the mire of bodies, the twisted faces of desperation, boys without mothers and fathers, screaming boys waiting for Jesus to come and save them, and here was a boy who didn't care and wanted them all to die and live in hell . . . They fell on him, grabbing Patsy's face and holding him, hands clasped over his mouth to keep him quiet, to stop the devil in him. Patsy lay deep beneath the pile of bodies, crushed and twisted.

Amidst the flames and smoke in the town, the wailing started. 'Where are our sons?' a woman cried. The girls from the convent had come home dazed and confused when they saw the smoke. The men had abandoned the factories. Farmers came in from the fields. But where were the boys?

The boys' school stood off by itself outside the city on the Cork road, a great grey building at the end of a long drive. The place was deserted. There was vomit and blood on the floors, copybooks flung around the place. The classrooms were empty, chalky numbers and sentences still on the blackboards, school-bags beside the desks, everything overturned. They saw

33

the ark pulling in down at the docks in the study hall. Someone mentioned the last plague that had visited the House of David, the slaughter of the firstborn sons. A wailing went through the cold empty school.

'We must pray!' a priest said with ponderous religiosity, raising his hands.

Mothers called out the names of their sons as they moved toward the chapel.

The boys and priests hid behind the altar. The place was in darkness except for a few candles domed in red glass.

The people stopped outside the locked door of the chapel. 'Go on,' someone whispered.

'It's locked,' a man answered.

'Locked?' The word murmured among them.

'I hear something,' one of the men whispered, his face up against the door. The crowd swelled and heaved forward.

'Break it down,' the priest said.

Four big men pushed the outer door, forcing the pews piled against it to crash against the marble floor. First one person and then everybody began shouting the names of the boys.

'We believe in One God, the Father Almighty . . .' the priests inside shouted, seeing the shapes of creatures like demons with arms extended, piling through the door. The boys sobbed the words, then stopped as they clamoured over one another, desperately trying to escape the lost souls from hell coming towards them in the dark.

In the study hall, the boys' names were read off a list by Father Mackey, who kept his eyes solemnly to the floor. People were shaking, holding their sons. The absurdity of the day was beyond them. But they did not dare curse or complain. It was still the day that the world was to end. The sky had turned pitch black from the rain and smoke. There was no electricity. The town had come to a standstill.

Two names were called out over and over again: Patsy, and Gerald Taylor. Everybody else had been accounted for. The boys' fathers went down with three other men to the chapel. A candle lit the way.

Under the benches they found a body. The head was unrecognizable, it had been trampled so badly. The men turned away and blessed themselves. They looked through the rest of the shambles and found Taylor sitting in a confessional.

'Are you an angel?' Taylor wept as his father took him in his arms.

Patsy's father sat down beside the broken body and blew out the candle he had carried.

The men stood to the side. They waited for a long time, listening to soft crying.

'Come on,' Malloy whispered tentatively, putting his hand on Patsy's father. A match flared. The light of a candle moved over the body, passing its yellow aura over the bloody face down to the huge hands clapsed together. The candle trembled. The small scarlet imprint of a cross was embedded on one of the hands. Patsy's father collapsed.

The day passed into night and into the next day. The secret of Fatima was never revealed. It was said that the Pope fainted when he read it. He kept the secret to himself.

Patsy's funeral was held three days later, at a makeshift church down at the parish community hall. His was the only death associated with the end of the world. They did a lovely job with him. The hands were never separated. A bishop came to verify the mark of the cross on the left hand. It was pronounced a miracle. The red imprint on the hand looked as though it had been touched up. It was a perfect cross. People pressed pieces of clothing against it to get holy relics. They came from all over the place.

A cast was taken of the hands. The priest gave a sermon disputing the rumour that it was the thousands of candles in the churches that had set them on fire. He said, 'It was a sign, a miracle. We have been given another chance. We must rebuild the temples of the Lord. We must clasp our hands like Patsy, with the faith of one who was taken to heaven, who gave us the very symbol of faith.' The priest looked at the dark mahogany coffin, then spread his arms apart. The congregation bowed their heads.

The priest looked up, tears in his roving eyes, his hands clapsed together like Patsy's. His mouth opened, 'From now on there will be two collections at Mass, until we have a sign that our work is done.'

The Horses

There was mutual recognition from the start – I'm nearly sure of that. We got to talking as though in mid-thought, and so was friendship established.

Now that I think about it, he did look up and ask about the two-thirty race at Leopardstown.

He had stopped lecturing at the university some time in the past. That much he offered from the start, presenting himself as a candid approximation of shambled intellectualism, with his down-turned hat and oversized coat, dressed entirely in shades of grey and black. He hinted at some philosophical disagreement he'd had with his department which I could never make head or tail of.

He exists in my memory now in the shadows of Mulligan's Public House, almost invisible in his black coat and hat with his stout before him. His silence was deathlike when he had nothing to say. He'd sigh now and then, his hands deep in his pockets. He might even have been taken for sleeping at times, if you didn't know better. You had to come close to him to see his angular back, his hunched shoulders, and what amounted every few minutes to a surreptitious turtle movement of his neck and head. It was only after putting yourself in this precarious and compromising position, almost leaning over into him, that you saw the slits of eyes and a face that came to a smouldering tip of cigarette, and you understood he was not sleeping at all, but thinking.

I was fascinated by the sheer economy of his expression in those quiet moments that came after his midday meal. He was a thinking man all right, tucked away with his own thoughts. There was company in his solitude though. Sometimes he told me something over our lunch, a point of philosophy that had been troubling him. I could only offer up the occasional nod, 'You don't say,' or 'Is that so?'

The pub emptied after lunch, leaving us to the hollow coldness, the ring of silence in our ears, the condensation on the walls, the abandoned plates of mash and fatty bits of meat, the half-drunk pints which I drank from when low on money. He seemed to sleep through it all, almost hibernating. I sat near him throughout the afternoons, holding a paper to the light coming from the street.

I had no job. He had no job. It was as though we didn't really exist. I'd read off the horses for the afternoon races to him, more or less speaking aloud to myself. I'd think he was sleeping, but from time to time his right hand would materialize from his pocket and arrive at his pint which he drew to his chin and tipped to his open mouth. A moment later, with the index finger of his right hand, he cleared off the wetness on his upper lip. I could see him staring at me. He was awake, listening to me.

What was estimable about him from the start was his unwillingness to accept blame for anything, and his dispassion for those who found him interesting, people who encroached on him in the afternoons. He only wanted to hear me read to him.

He spoke sometimes about his philosophies, interrupting me. I never minded. He'd take my arm when there was a point he wanted me to get. He blew smoke into my face in agitation when he saw I had it all wrong, by his accounts. One day he asked me if I knew of Ortega. I said, 'When's he running?' His nails sank into my arm. He swallowed and released me. I ordered another drink before he spoke again. He told me he felt – how does it go now? Yes – 'half immersed in nature, half transcending it'. He said: 'We are given the abstract possibility of existing, but not the reality.'

'Or the money,' I offered up, and touched his glass with my own. 'Or the money,' I repeated to myself, laughing the way I do sometimes.

He never laughed when discussing his philosophies. I came to learn to listen and say nothing when he was with his philosophies.

I think if it wasn't that I knew my horses, he would have given me up from the start. You see, I've always had a fair amount of luck on the horses – not that I bet or anything. I keep a mental note when a horse I have an eye on shows. I play on the sidelines. As he might have put it: I liked the abstract possibility of playing, but not the reality.

I assumed he shared the same interest. But then I remember finding a docket on the floor of the pub one afternoon not long after I'd begun reading off the horses. I assumed he'd dropped it when he got up to go to the toilet. He'd won £30 on a horse I'd picked. I set the docket on the table. When he came back, he saw it there, though he didn't pick it up. He said nothing about it to me, gave me not even a nod of thanks. I said nothing to him, of course. There was no point starting a row.

I picked horses then with a certain suspicion throughout our time together. I was never sure about him. You see, there were horses picked which didn't win, place, or show. I was right more than I was wrong – I'll say that much – but he said nothing either way. I'll tell you straight, I'd prefer to give a nod in the right direction to another than gamble with my own money. In the long run the odds are against you.

I have always considered myself a good friend to my fellow man. I am not in the main suspicious. To tell the truth, I never actually saw him place a bet in all the time I was with him. In fact, I couldn't even be sure he was betting on my picks. When I thought back to the £30 docket, for the life of me, I didn't know how he could've been able to back the horse, since we'd been at the pub together, and he'd not gone near a betting shop, and the race had been run before we parted company. The docket remained a mystery. Maybe it had fallen there by chance from another man before us, which seemed a reasonable enough explanation – not that I really gave the incident much consideration.

This was our routine. You see, I'd read the papers after the midday meal, as I have stated already, and he'd be there with me. Now, he'd always excuse himself and head to the toilet around a quarter past two, and spend a good ten minutes on average in there. Of course, during our acquaintance, I never actually timed him or felt obliged to see that he was in there. I just knew it was a habit of his, a sign of a regular constitution. Now, I will have to say that he was, at the time of going to the toilet, informed of my opinions on what horse looked good. I only say that as a point of fact, to set the record straight. You see, the races ran at two-thirty and quarter past three. Well anyway, he'd return, and we'd stay at the pub until four twenty-five, when I'd take leave of him, as my bus came before his did.

Anyway, the year of our friendship progressed in a plodding certainty. There probably isn't a word that describes the non-committal and yet exacting punctuality of our meetings. I met him in town at exactly half-ten in the morning, rain or shine. Again, nothing we ever agreed upon. We just met. All I'll say is you could set your watch by him.

But now that I think about it, in the light of everything, it must have been the other way around. He was always there before me. It was I who arrived at ten-thirty on the stroke, Monday, Wednesday, and Friday. You could set your watch by me. You see, I had my breakfast at nine o'clock at my digs from the woman in charge and then began my walk at a quarter to ten, heading into town, stopping to buy the paper before meeting him. Although I have never owned a reliable watch, in a Catholic country you don't need one – if you follow my point. The church bell sounded as we shook hands every day. I remember it distinctly now. I admit it comes as a sort of shock in a way. There had been some governing principle to my movements all along.

I couldn't say with all honesty that we were the best of friends. For instance, I never asked him what he did at night, nor was I ever asked to join him out where he lived for a drink. I, for my part, never extended an invitation to my own place. I didn't even know if he was married. He didn't wear a wedding band. I only knew that he had once been associated with the university, information he'd offered up at the very beginning. He offered nothing else about himself. And yet, when I think about it, in all our times together we were never short for a word when it was needed.

We always went around St Stephen's Green, if the weather permitted, or went in by Hanna's Book Shop. He paged through books on philosophy with titles like *Beyond Good and Evil, Systems of Logic, The Social Contract.* He asked me one day if I knew about tabula rasa and I said: 'When's he running?' He nearly spat in my face.

A scheme somehow started, from the beginning of our meetings in town, where I bought at the pub on Monday, he on Wednesday, and myself on Friday, and so forth over the weeks. I say it against myself that I have been bad at even marginal puzzles, and somehow it fell that what I'd thought was a fair alternating of expenses was working to my disadvantage. There could have been no duplicity on his part — I'm sure of that. You see, I always start things on a Monday. It's the way I was brought up. I never knew quite how to bring the matter up without insulting him. I was sure that if the scheme had begun on a Monday with him buying, he'd have taken the burden of the slight oversight and said nothing. I begin things on a Wednesday now.

Although there was no exit from the pub at the rear of the bar, there was a window above the toilet bowl which exited to street level. This was kept partially open for obvious reasons, and might have allowed a man of his size to fit through and exit to the alley. The betting shop was only around the corner, and he could have gone about his business in a matter of minutes and come back in through the window, and none would have been the wiser. To my credit, I never followed him into the toilet, although on one occasion I chanced to go in after he'd been gone for a while, went about my business, and took note of the closed stall door and the tips of a pair of shoes. There were no words exchanged, so again, I'm without unequivocal proof that he was in the stall. But as I have said, at the time, my only motivation for going in there was to relieve myself. You see it's only in the recounting of events that things become suspect. The possibilities of a situation become limitless.

I waited for a rainy day. When he came back from the toilet, he was as dry as a bone. I dropped a pen and looked at his shoes. Dry. I hated myself for it. I wanted to say 'Sorry' for some stupid reason, to take his hand and say, 'I've had this ridiculous notion . . .' I said nothing though and left at four twenty-five since – as I've said – my bus came before his.

One day he says to me, after he'd paid for our Wednesday lunch, when I thought he was thinking to himself, 'What day do you go up to the track?'

I looked up from the paper. His hat was tipped down over his forehead. It was like addressing a shadow. 'Never,' I said.

He shifted in his space and took his drink, swirled it and drained the contents. He held the glass up in the air, and the barman said, 'Same again, gents?'

'If you never go up to the track, how do you get your information?' he said.

It was one of the first times I was sure he was listening to me earnestly. 'I follow the results in the paper.'

'It's a matter of statistics?' he said suspiciously, almost jockeying himself forward. I could see his eyes looking at me from under the rim of his hat.

'Not exactly.' I hesitated. 'You see, there are articles written about the races, who did what and when. You get a sense of the field, what happened in the races . . .'

'Go on,' he said.

'Well, different reporters write about the races. They might make mention of an also-ran, some comment that strikes you.'

He balanced on his buttocks and hesitated as our drinks were set before us. 'It's a matter of interpretation. Is that what you're saying? That's a good one.' The table trembled. 'Go on. You've never been to the track . . . It's a matter of literary interpretation, is it?' he insisted, then stopped. A handkerchief masked his mouth as he coughed.

I moved my head back from him.

He cleared his throat. 'Go on.'

'It's a matter of style, of manner, I suppose.' I felt the sweat run down my back. 'You see, I will only read certain columnists on certain days. Dermot Leary never has a good thing to say about anything on a Monday. But catch him on a Thursday. Do you follow me?' I would have said more, but he put a finger to his lip.

'You're talking about something you've never seen . . . Jesus Christ.' He whispered it more to himself than to me.

I would never have put it that way myself, but that was the height of it.

He leaned back into the bench. His face was invisible.

I said no more, and he asked nothing else. I went back to the paper, and he to his thinking. I began reading off the horses as usual a few minutes later. I glanced at him in the mirror across from us, afraid to look at him directly.

He was in the toilet at a quarter past two as usual.

I met him one morning and got a whiff of aftershave which I'd never smelt on him before. I said nothing, and we went on our walk. On another occasion, I noticed his nails were clean. Again, I said nothing. I have no interest in another man's hygiene, and it would have been ludicrous to say something like, 'So, you're cleaning your nails these days.'

He had on a pair of new shoes another day. I had always put him down as wanting for money. I put it this way to him when we were walking, 'It must be hard to break in shoes like that.' I said it without affront, just a casual remark in keeping with a long walk. You need shoes that are worn in for walking. He could take no offence.

'I got them a half-size big. That's the secret,' he said. He nodded his head. 'That's the secret.'

'Right.' He had me. 'They must have cost?' I said.

'They were on sale,' he said.

'And where's that?' I said. I looked straight ahead of me, my heart racing in my chest.

'Out my way,' he said.

'They're very nice,' I said.

'Thank you,' he said.

I thought the walk would never end.

We had lunch on me down at the pub. It was Monday again.

43

I had grown to hate Mondays. I even thought about not coming into town any more out of principle, or cancelling our Monday meetings. But what would I do with myself? You've heard of cutting your nose off to spite your face. I didn't want to upset the balance of our friendship. Let him have his shoes. People are bound to get new shoes sometime. I left him at four twenty-five for my bus with the intention of never coming back again.

I had an upset stomach while we were down at the pub about a month later. I'd been in and out of the toilet. I went in again at two o'clock with a bad cramp. I was watching the time for your man. I didn't want to put him off his own schedule just because of my predicament.

The next thing I know, there's a tap on the window above from the street. 'What do you fancy?' this voice says to me.

Jesus! I was sitting there in my hat and coat on the toilet.

'Go away,' I whispered. 'Go away.'

'When's it running?' the voice says to me.

I was up like a shot and pulled the window shut. My legs trembled. I could have been your man's double in my hat and coat. I came out not knowing what to think. The terror of not knowing the man I'd spent the last eight months with on a Monday, Wednesday, and Friday gripped me. 'When's it running?' Was I caught in my own joke? How many times had I said that for a laugh. Even after this, I knew nothing for certain.

'You're better, I hope,' he says to me, and up he got as I sat down, like we were on a seesaw, and off he went to the toilet. I checked the clock on the wall. It was twenty past two. I hated him.

I'll say in my defence that I never stopped picking the horses. I never once led him astray. I couldn't do that sort of thing to a man I called a friend. If there was malignancy, it came from me alone. I told myself that over and over again.

I did, in fact, not bring the paper over a series of days in vague protest. I wanted him to say something. He said nothing about the paper. Instead, he'd tell me about his philosophies and get into a mood. I could understand none of it. 'There are no ideals to realize anymore, do you understand?' He began touching me on the hand. I began bringing the paper again.

He had a new hat some time after the new shoes. Before I had the chance he said that the other one had blown off his head and into the river up by where he lived. Yes, it had been windy the previous day, I had to concede. We went for our walk. I could feel his mild impatience, and he finally suggested we, as he put it, 'adjourn for lunch'. He actually smiled and touched my back. I smiled because it was Wednesday.

He said to me over lunch, 'Man must earn his life, not only economically, but also metaphysically.' He touched his new hat. 'The brain,' he said to me.

I wanted his hat. I ignored him as best I could, tensing my face, looking over the horses for the afternoon races at Leopardstown. I read them out again, what I liked in the second and the third, a sure thing in the fourth. You would have taken him for asleep, but I caught his reflection in the mirror, saw the light in his eyes. He was staring at me. I couldn't move.

He excused himself at ten past two and walked down the passageway to the toilet.

I became demented after that. I began to have restless nights back home, waking up with the image of him standing there with a wad of bills before me, waving them in my face. I saw him climbing out the window and running around to the betting shop.

I remember a man telling me once that he didn't recognize his wife on their wedding night – or, I should say, he couldn't fully comprehend her without her clothes on. He said it was like someone had taken his wife's head and stuck it on another body. Well, that was the way I felt when I saw what must have been him on the back page of the paper with another man presenting him with a cheque. The caption below the picture read, 'Mr James Tierney (left) received a cheque for £20,000 Thursday evening from Mr Patrick Flynn (right).' The brief article below read, ' . . .Mr Tierney has, over the last nine months, accumulated an undisclosed amount on the horses . . .'

Now, like the married man, I, too, couldn't be sure. You see, when we'd been together, he'd always worn the hat and coat. When we walked, I never looked at him directly. I spoke to the side of his face. I knew his profile at best. And at the pub, well, it was too dim to be sure of anything. I was looking at his reflection most of the time. He always sat with his back to the light, kind of leaning over. He didn't like to be looked at. I couldn't put the two images together, the picture of the man in the suit and the man I knew, although they must have been one and the same. I was instinctively certain.

And then there was the name. Surely to God, I'd have known the name of the man who had come and sat with me for nine months on a Monday, Wednesday, and Friday. But I didn't. It was always, 'So how're you today?' 'Grand, and yourself? . . .' Off for the walk and in for lunch, 'What are you having?' 'Same as yourself!' 'Two pints, please, and the lamb for two. Is it beans or peas you want?' 'Beans, please.' Then, 'What do you fancy yourself? You'll have a whiskey?' 'I'll tell you, Thunderbolt runs well in soft going.' Then the first ones would come in after four o'clock for the evening drink, and I'd go to rise. You see, as I have already stated, my bus came before his. 'You're off then?' 'I'll see you. All the best, now.'

On Friday, I waited like an eejit. He never showed up. I admit I got out the phone book and looked up every Tierney there was. But sure, if I called him, he wouldn't even know my name. I'd have to say something like, 'It's me, Mr Tierney,' in some gangster's voice like I meant business.

I went into the pub we'd been at for all those months and went up to the barman and said, 'Do you know my name?' He thought I was having him on. He smiled at me. 'Do you know Mr Tierney?' I shouted.

'When's he running?' the barman winked. 'What are you having?'

'The usual.'

It was useless. I fulfilled my obligation to the end, though. I

46

took lunch as I always did. It was Fish Friday. The barman brought two plates out of habit. 'He'll be here, will he?'

I nodded out of habit. I sprinkled vinegar on the fish and let the butter melt into the boiled potatoes. I ate slowly. His plate steamed, untouched. I almost expected him to materialize out of the dark, to see those eyes, the mechanics of his hands, the way he ate, the way he drank, watching him in the mirror, 'half immersed in nature, half transcending it.' I began to understand his irony.

The plates were cleared. The barman looked at me. I was obstinate to the end. I persisted. I ordered two pints. I set the money down on the table.

At ten past two I got up, steadied myself, and went into the toilet in my hat and coat. At a quarter past two there was a tap on the window. 'What do you fancy?' the voice whispered.

'The Gray to win.' I passed a ten-pound note out the window. My head felt dizzy. I took a deep breath. I went back in to wait and see what would happen when I didn't leave for my bus at four twenty-five.

The Fornicator

Murphy could manage only a cup of tea and slice of toast brought by his wife as he shaved in the bathroom. That was all. He had to catch the boat to England in less than an hour. He didn't want his stomach upset. You could never tell what the crossing would be like.

His wife sat on the toilet seat in her pink dressing gown, leaning forward and touching his thin, white leg. 'I'll miss you.' Her black hair was pulled back into such a tight knot at the back of her head that it stretched and distorted her face.

Murphy knew all about her and held the razor blade steady inches from his face and waited. 'I'll be home on Sunday night.' He stretched his neck forward, giving his throat to the blade with an element of theatrical danger. The blade rasped through the stubble of hair, making the skin smooth.

She smelled of last night's perfume, creating a sense of uneasiness. Anything which hinted beyond the sobriety of their waking hours had this effect these days. By coming into the confines of the small bathroom, she was marking him with a complexity beyond mere animal ownership. She was trying to mark him with the most lugubrious of scents – guilt. 'It's always so lonely without you on the weekends, Tom.'

'What can I do?' He ran the blade under the hot water, looking at the pale blue wash basin which they'd chosen before moving into the house. It had been part of the builder's compromise to let owners have some variation in their homes. She'd picked blue for a boy, an undaunted sentimentalism which Murphy had found attractive at the time, if the truth be known.

Murphy steadied himself. It wouldn't be long now until he was away from her and the aggravation for a few days. He breathed heavily and then shaved along the edges of his emerging sideburns. They were more gingery, the colour of his

48

pubic hair, than the brown hair on his head.

She was saying something.

'What?' he said, distracted. 'What?'

'I said I might take the lads to the zoo on Saturday if it doesn't rain. They love the zoo.'

'Oh, the zoo. They'd like that . . . Do that all right.'

'Do you remember when you took me to the zoo when we were first going out?'

Murphy nodded and once again looked up at the ceiling, seeing the plaster cracked and last year's cheap vinyl wallpaper already dog-eared and pouring off the wall, undoubtedly mildewed from the dampness and bleaching fast. He'd have to get to that early next week, after work. There'd be dampness showing like there was last year, in the kitchen ceiling below, from water seeping along the edges of the bath which hadn't been caulked properly. Was there ever an end to it? One day, he imagined, she'd be up there with the boys, washing them, and down they'd come, 'cradle and all,' onto the kitchen table. It was a legitimate concern. There were reports of it in the paper. The houses were badly constructed. He could go on now like this if he wanted, cataloguing the state of his house, the creak of the stairs, the door that wouldn't close properly in the front room, the condensation around the windows, the putty that had fallen out and made them loose and rattle constantly, and, to top it all off, the indignity of the toilet that took three flushes to get rid of everything . . . As he said so often to himself, 'I wasn't put on this earth to fix the fuckin' jacks!' But this was it, things in the process of breaking, things still not fully paid for, had become the bane of his existence.

Murphy looked into the mirror and raised his chin slightly, making the small crease of fat under it taut.

'That chin of yours.' His wife leaned forward. 'There's nothing wrong with you. If you want to see something bad, look at me . . .'

Murphy felt the timidity of her words, her overture for a morning row before he could escape. The rows always came in the wreckage of the morning, her unwillingness to acquiesce to the daylight and a different reality. A man lies in the dark, it was a simple fact. But she took every caress as a secret compact he was making with her. She was probably right in the long run. But for now, he wanted to get away for the weekend.

'You still look young, Tom.' Silence. 'I love you, Tom. Doesn't that matter?'

Murphy felt the heat of the naked bulb over his head. The hot water in the sink misted the mirror. He closed his eyes for a moment and then wiped the mirror. 'Of course it does, love. I'm just tired.'

She had opened the gown further, moving her legs apart, tentatively showing the fat columns of her legs. 'Why do you always have to get sent over to England? There are others who could go.'

Murphy's eyes moved cautiously. 'Because I asked for it. It's for the weekend only. With the overtime we'll be able to do something next week. Didn't we discuss all this before?'

'It's always next week.'

'I promise.' Murphy turned and gave her a long stare and then looked back into the mirror. 'Do you think I want to leave at this hour of the morning?'

She shook her head. A solitary, mournful, No. 'But we're not really that short, Tom. You don't have to go. Call them up now, and tell them you're sick, and we can go to the zoo. Come on, Tom, it would be a surprise for the boys.' He saw her dressing gown part slightly in what amounted to calculated lewdness. The toilet bowl trembled. She was trying on a pose.

'I can't,' he whispered. 'Next week. I swear. I can't just not show up for the boat.'

'Please.' She set her big body before him, looking away, trying to let him stare at her without her looking at him. Murphy knew she was testing her own sexuality more than his. She had this trick, a sort of self-voyeurism, trying unintentionally to catch a glimpse of herself in the mirror to capture a moment of self-separation. Murphy had caught her at it in town, passing shop windows, the quick jerk of the head. 'What the fuck is that about?' he had said suspiciously.

'To figure out who I am,' was how she tried to explain it to him, but he'd said with the candid felicity of an obstinate husband, 'You are the mother of my children, love.' And this was his trick. Everything should and must be mediated through the children. He had to keep her on the straight and narrow.

Murphy cleared the mirror and gave his hand to her like a man gives it to a dog to lick. And she kissed it.

He held the razor in his other hand, hesitating. She was about to ask him something, no, her reflection was about to ask him something. Her reflection preserved the dimension of space, everything exact except the image was the inverse of what it really was.

'Tom?'

In a slow and deliberate manner, but with imperceptible pressure and pleasure, Murphy let the blade cut into his cheek, right in the fat below the cheekbone, winced, and retracted his hand.

'Tom, you've cut yourself!'

Murphy watched her in the mirror as he used his finger to put pressure on the cut. 'Leave it. I ask for a cup of tea and toast, and you start into a production . . .'

'I didn't mean . . .'

'It doesn't matter what you meant.' A stream of blood ran down his face and neck and into the dark hair of his chest. 'I'm late as it is already!' He looked at her. 'Jesus, get my good shirt, will you?'

She left the bathroom.

This was the last time he was going to get cornered in the bathroom. She always caught him off guard in there, pressing into the small bathroom at the start of the morning. For them the bathroom had held a significance. They'd first had sex in the house in the cold porcelain bath. Two years later though, after Murphy had been booted out of the university and settled for a sales job with Patterson's Foods, he'd come home from work late to find her on her knees before a bath of nappies in brown shite-coloured water. When her eyes had met his, it was the end of something. Now, when she said her life was 'shite', there was an actual image of 'shite', not just a general dissatisfaction, but a bath full of shite in her head. It was a dangerous thing, in Murphy's estimation, that they had shared a moment of lucid deprivation. As far as he was concerned, revelation played no part in marriage, and hadn't she got the new washing machine out of it anyway?

Murphy held a piece of brown paper to the cut, waiting impatiently in his underwear. He couldn't wait to be out of the house. 'Do you have it? And a tie as well, the pastel one,' he called to her. 'Come on, will you?'

She came back in with the shirt. 'Tom, just call in sick this once.'

Was there ever a more pathetic spectacle than to see her shifting her arse around and letting her big legs tremble and part before him, all because she'd heard this was the thing to do these days? A woman was to use her sexuality to get her way. Well, maybe some women had that way about them, but she was a woman more at home with the atavism of scratching a man's back or picking at his scalp in the dark like some sedentary ape. And to tell the truth, his sensibilities lay somewhere in between. Murphy shivered and wriggled away from her touch. 'I'll be late.'

She sat on the toilet seat again. 'I was thinking that maybe I should learn to drive if you'll be away like this.' She said it in a clear voice. 'Delores has been driving for over half a year, Tom.'

Murphy turned his head to the side and looked at the cut on his cheek. It had begun to scab. He'd heard her but ignored her. 'I think I'm set then.'

'Frank doesn't have to do the messages on Thursday nights, and Delores drops him off for the train in the morning . . .' She stood up, blocking the door. Her voice grew louder. 'Delores said Frank says "a woman's liberation is a man's liberation." I never thought of it like that, but isn't it true, Tom?'

'Will you do this tie for me,' Murphy said agitatedly.

'A woman's liberation is a man's liberation.' She rose and

took the silk tie and mechanically began to loop it into a knot. 'I think I should be allowed to drive a car.'

The white lump of her body stood inches away from him. 'I've always found that people who drive cars are more likely to die,' Murphy said, matter-of-factly.

'What does that mean? It means nothing. It means you won't let me do anything . . . Do your own tie.' She made her hands into fists.

Murphy rolled his eyes. He could feel her catching her breath and he knew that nothing was going to distract her. He braced for the onslaught and turned to the mirror again, fumbling with the huge pastel bib of his tie. He'd have left but he was afraid to leave on bad terms, just in case she phoned up his office and kicked up a row.

'I want to look good for you, Tom . . .' He'd heard this song and dance routine before. 'Delores is doing yoga. Remember, you saw her, and you said how good she looked after her baby. You did Tom, and that's because of the yoga! I want to be like that for you!'

'I know you do, love.' Such shite. Yoga. Jesus Christ. Mysticism and calisthenics, whatever the fuckin' connection beat Murphy. As if wrapping your ankles around your neck was going to solve anything. But Murphy nodded his head anyway. 'We'll see.'

'And I want to take the pressure off you, Tom. You understand, don't you? There are things I can do for you, if you'll let me. You will let me, Tom, won't you?'

'I'll be late,' Murphy whispered, touching the crown of her head.

'And you'll think about the driving licence?'

'We'll see.'

Of course the car conspired against him. He pulled on the choke, pumping the pedal. It puttered, revved, stalled repeatedly. He had to wait and not flood the carburettor, or whatever the hell it was that flooded a car.

She looked like she was going to come out to him, but he put his hand up. He must have looked the right gobshite in his hat, banging the steering wheel, muffled curses coming from the car. Finally, the engine caught and, with the sun rising in the cold morning air, he backed out of the driveway, shaking with agitation.

She waved from the door in her pink dressing gown. 'Mind yourself!'

'Go fuck yourself,' Murphy said to himself. She had bamboozled the life out of him.

He drove slowly through the new estate, a grim, grey proletarian dream of poured concrete, little identical houses save for the colour you decided to paint your door or the flowers you planted in your walled-in postage stamp of a garden, or the colour of your hand basin. And the rough pebble-dash facades, like spewed grey vomit. Some great democracy.

And it wasn't even finished. Murphy drove through the debris of broken wood and brick, afraid of a puncture. Cement mixers and pipes lay out on the green, between the two parallel rows of houses, which the corporation had sworn would remain a strip of green for the children to play on. First they lied and said they were laying down sewage pipes, then they began circulating rumours about property tax increases. Now it was the foundation for another row of houses which was going to throw the estate into furrowed rows of shadowy houses. It sent a chill up Murphy's back. All you'd eventually see at the end of it all would be the cross from the church out back of the estate which serviced five other estates exactly like his own.

Misery under construction and still the great big red SOLD signs on vacant facades without windows. Houses identical to his selling for thousands of pounds less, since there was no green. Who the fuck had come up with the design of the semi-detached house, manacling your neighbour to you like this? How many inches were spared by not separating houses? How many bricks were saved by constructing one wall as opposed to two, and what did that even out to over the course of one's life in a house? There were times when he just wanted to knock the shite out of the wall between his neighbour and himself and have this cave-like entrance where he could just grunt and walk into his neighbour's house and vice versa, because that was about the height of it anyway. They were living on top of each other. And with the new houses, you might as well draw the curtains in your house and live in darkness because otherwise you'd be visible from all angles.

Murphy drove down the avenue of houses, down past the post office and the new supermarket that had everything under the fuckin' sun. She'd set him on edge, made him cynical of things he owned, or didn't even own, things he had mortgaged to the hilt. For fuck's sake, he was breaking his arse to own this house with the blue door. It wasn't the kind of lucidity he needed. There was no forgiving her.

Murphy continued to drive slowly, raving away to himself, when there, before him, to top it all off, was the infamous Mr Frank Walsh, Esquire, husband of one Delores – pain-in-the-hole – Walsh, astride the path. The oft-quoted Mr Frank Walsh, bonafide bollocks, purveyor of modern ideas, with a university degree and a silk cravat, waving like you were his best friend because he couldn't get his wife out of bed to take him to the station, after all his preaching how he'd be the better of letting her have the car. Well, let him wave now 'til his fuckin' arm fell off, him along with the other bastards who walked a schoolboy's shuffle down to the train, rain or shine. And the lies of them when he did pick one of them up, out of the goodness of his heart on a rainy day. Lie to your face, and you letting them into your car – something that their wives wouldn't do – of how they enjoyed the morning air, and they were a better man for the early walk, and such shite you'd never heard the likes of before. 'Keeps the weight down . . . Great for the circulation . . . Helps the digestion . . . Gives you time to think . . .' Well he'd decided long ago that he wasn't going to cart this army of fuck-ups anywhere. Let them liberate some shoe leather!

*

Miss Louise Barrett was waiting out at a bus stop on the Dublin road with suitcase in hand.

She had taken the previous two days off work while Murphy had taken only the Friday. There could, therefore, be no overt connection between them. They didn't even work in the same department. Thank God for big companies. Their mutual absence overlapped by one day, nothing out of the ordinary. Coincidence.

Nothing incriminating, was how Murphy worded it to himself. He had actually seen this in a film at home when himself and his wife got their first television two years previous. It was a film about a man who cheated on his wife in Hammersmith for ten years. Before this, an extramarital affair seemed just one of those passing daydreams men have. Who had time to plot a relationship? And, until the last few years, there hadn't been a city in the country big enough for a man to have two women.

But this was the great advantage of television, it provided a repository for tried and tested plans of deception, and the real beauty was that a man like himself, who wouldn't have dared venture into conspicuously reading romance thrillers of seduction and betrayal, who might always have existed in a twilight of sexual dissatisfaction and economic ruination, could find himself sitting before his television with his wife on his arm and see, unfolding, the exact plan of deception that could liberate him from his boring life.

At the exit onto the dual carriageway, Murphy ran into construction and wasted fifteen minutes in a long queue, watching a flag man saunter around waving a green flag whenever he felt like it to let cars past. He was already over half an hour late at this stage. He hoped Louise would still be there.

Murphy saw her standing in a mid-length navy-coloured coat with a fake fox-fur collar, and platform boots which accentuated her thin birdlike legs. She was the height of immodest fashion. As they said back at the office, 'She'd put the women's cause back a fair few years.' She was known simply as 'Chanel No. 5.' Whatever was in season, she bought. She was something of a joke, thin, which was in fashion, but with a bony frailty that hinted at bad health more than anything.

Still, Murphy couldn't afford to be choosy with this one. He'd have preferred her to dress less fancy, although, in a film he'd seen the previous year, a woman spy who was to pass on secret microfilm of atomic secrets had worn a plain old coat to blend into a crowd but was spotted by a CIA agent on account of her stylish hairdo and manicured fingernails. Louise had a stylish hairdo.

Murphy took care of her bag as though he were her brother, shaking her hand and talking loudly, escorting her to the passenger door which he held open with the sort of bustling chivalry of country farmers.

'I thought you weren't coming,' Louise said curtly, and got in.

Murphy pulled away from the bus stop abruptly. 'You have something else with you, I hope?'

Louise said nothing and stared out the window. 'I was waiting for ages.'

The early morning light filled the car. Murphy hesitated. There was no point spoiling the weekend. 'I'm sorry . . . There was construction on the road. I'm sorry.' He leaned over and kissed her on the side of her cheek.

Louise bit her lower lip. 'What's wrong with what I'm wearing?'

'You must have been freezing, that's all. You should have worn something warmer for yourself.'

'I didn't think you'd leave me standing for over three-quarters of an hour.' Her voice was cold and sharp.

Murphy drummed his fingers on the steering wheel. 'Do you want to forget it?' He slowed and flicked his indicator.

Louise touched his hand, feeling it jiggling on the gear lever. 'Keep going.'

'You're sure?' Murphy said sharply.

'I'm sure.'

From his breast pocket Murphy took a cigarette and a box of matches and used the corner of his lip to extract a cigarette from the package. 'Do you want one?'

Louise struck the match, and Murphy leaned over to her, pulling softly on the yellow flame. 'Let's just get away from here.' He inhaled deeply. 'All right?'

Louise settled herself and leaned the seat back and smoked, her small face tucked into her shoulder.

Rolling down the window, Murphy took a deep drag and, leaning to the opening, let the smoke trail into the cool moring breeze, the nicotine beginning to ease him at last.

Outside Port Laoise, a dark green army lorry with a tent-canvas top trundled toward them. Murphy had to pull into the ditch to let it by. He'd forgotten that the prison in Port Laoise was now holding political prisoners. Murphy touched Louise. 'Sit up,' he said softly.

Louise opened her eyes. 'What?'

'Port Laoise. There's a checkpoint up ahead.' The cars came to a halt ahead of him. Murphy fixed his tie and patted his hair down. 'If they ask anything, we're heading down to Limerick on a sales call.'

Louise brought her seat upright and straightened her blouse. She said nothing, only shivered and rubbed her eyes.

'Let me do the talking.' Murphy edged forward on the narrow road into a funnel of traffic flanked by the huge prison walls on one side and by small houses with bricked up windows on the other side. He remembered now that the houses had been abandoned the year before because an old couple with nationalist sentiments had let the IRA tunnel across into the prison.

Murphy eased forward and rolled down his window, the air reeking of diesel. 'Are you all right?' he said quietly.

Louise looked forward impassively. Out of work, in those clothes, she looked like a hooker sitting there in his car.

'You look . . .' Murphy breathed hard. It galled him that she hadn't the head on her to dress properly. 'Just . . . Just act natural. Smile or something if they say anything.' He was going to have a hard job with her this weekend. 'We're going to a meeting in Limerick. You're my secretary.'

Louise turned and tried to smile.

'Maybe you shouldn't smile. Just let me do the talking.' A lorry ahead of them revved its engine and sent a plume of smoke into the air. 'I just hope to Jesus you have something else with you . . .'

Louise continued to stare ahead of her and said nothing. 'Are you using the company's name or a fictitious one?'

Murphy hesitated. 'The real one . . . No . . . Listen, just shut up, and let me do the talking.'

The lorry ahead of Murphy lurched forward. Two guards conferred and took a piece of paper from the driver and then gave the piece of paper back and signalled for Murphy to come forward.

Murphy put the car in gear and edged forward.

One of the guards checked the tax disc on the car, and then his small eyes lingered on Louise and then on Murphy. He said nothing in the end and, with a patent occupational evasiveness, dismissed them with a wave of his hand.

Murphy went through the town, bumper to bumper with other cars. The town had experienced an economic boom, little shop fronts offering tea and scones. A tractor bucked aggressively, riding up on the path, close to window fronts, trying to pass the oncoming cars. The tractor wouldn't back up, and the row of cars facing it was forced to reverse and finally stop while the tractor moved another few inches along the path.

'Can you believe this shite?' Murphy would have bet odds-on that the tractor performed this procedure throughout the day. Whether you liked it or not, you were stopping in Port Laoise.

It was mid-afternoon when Murphy passed through Limerick.

'Can we get something,' Louise said.

'We'll go on a bit and eat,' Murphy answered. He didn't

want to take the chance of being seen in Limerick. Their company had a subsidiary office in the town.

Outside Shannon, Murphy spoke to her again. 'We're safe at this stage. I saw a sign for a place that does chips.' He hoped it wasn't a sign left over from the summer.

But a quarter of an hour on they had passed no restaurants. 'Well, that's that,' Murphy groaned. He was resigned to eating nothing. Later he came upon a van driving slowly, and as he began to pass, the driver, who had his window rolled down, began to shout, 'Fish and Chips!'

Murphy pulled over and parked ahead of the van. 'Can you believe it?'

Louise shrugged her shoulders. 'We might as well.'

'Do you want fish?' Murphy said.

'Yes.'

The van waited, the wink of its yellow indicator light silent in the cool wintry light. Murphy bought two bags of fish and chips and two cokes and came back to the car, shivering.

'Jesus, it's cold.' He handed the warm brown bags to Louise. 'Hold these for a few minutes. We'll park off the road.' Murphy drove on for five minutes or so, turning into a narrow lane and pulling into the ditch with the hedge on either side obscuring any view of the fields.

'Jesus, I'm starved,' Murphy said and shuddered, still feeling the effects of the cold and humidity.

'I feel like we're fugitives,' Louise smiled, curling wisps of her hair behind her ear.

'Your man was telling me he just drives around the roads waiting for cars to pull him over. He has his daughter in the back with the oil boiling away. Can you believe it? Jesus Christ, what a pack of savages . . .'

Louise touched his face. 'You take everything too seriously.'

'I know I do.' She had this horrible expression and way of touching, bringing everything around to a notion of physicality. Murphy ignored her and tore open the brown paper bag and let the aroma fill his nostrils.

'You have to relax.'

Murphy nodded and blew on a chip laced with salt and ate it.

'As long as we're together we'll be grand,' she whispered.

Murphy smiled to himself at the indomitable romanticism of the other sex. He touched her face.

'Can you believe that eejit leaving a young girl with boiling oil . . .'

Louise looked at him and smiled. 'They have to make a living.'

Murphy swallowed. 'It was just the state of her in the back. I'd say she doesn't even go to school. They're out all day and night just roaming around the country.'

Louise tried to touch his hand.

'Not now.' Murphy felt the thick grease coat the lining of his mouth and his teeth. He reached for the coke to cut through the grease. It did no good; the Coke was warm and he could only taste the sugar. Coke was one of those things that needed to be mixed with ice.

'What's wrong?' Louise whispered.

'Nothing.'

'There is something wrong!'

Murphy belched under his breath and turned his head to the side. 'I'm out of it now. Forget it.'

Louise looked at him. 'I thought maybe you . . .'

'If chips get cold before you eat them, they sit in your stomach. Eat them quick,' Murphy whispered. 'Eat.'

Her small frame was hunched. Only her big hairdo seemed to possess any strength.

'We're together now,' Murphy whispered. He might as well get rid of the melancholy hanging over them. He already had the need to be with her.

'I was scared,' she whispered.

'You don't want any more chips, do you?'

She shook her head. 'Listen to me.' Her voice trembled.

'We have the weekend to talk.' He took her chips.

She had that same lugubrious smell about her that his wife had. Murphy knew only too well the biological ambiguity of female repose, waiting for him to react to some chemical imperative that was beyond him. Had the nuances of biological scent been bred out of his species? As far as he was concerned, human noses were a vestigial appendage of a former animalism, existing solely to hold up your glasses in this day and age.

Murphy acquiesced, licked his fingers clean for effect, and rubbed her cheek with the palm of his warm hand only because it was a learned behaviour. 'We have the whole weekend,' he said. He'd have to act the part of the lover for the weekend. The prospect seemed daunting.

Murphy opened the window a little and lit a cigarette. Soft rain fell in a silent mist. He could tell she was anxious, her eyes flickering between her lap and the windshield.

'We should push on,' he said. The evening dissipated in a grey country bleakness. There would be no sunset. The ghost of the moon had already come out.

Louise raised her eyes to Murphy. 'It was her, wasn't it?' she said quietly.

Murphy sat dumb, staring at her, fagged with exhaustion. He took a drag of his cigarette to add some errant action to their solitude and immobility. If he'd have been out of the car he could have walked away from her. 'Come on, will you?' Murphy protested.

'You know, sometimes I imagine what it must be like for her.' She hesitated and swallowed. She was crying without tears. 'At least I know who she is. But she doesn't know me.'

Murphy turned his head toward the window and blew the smoke out of his mouth. He knew she'd been having the dialogue with herself ever since she got in the car.

'I could be more than one person . . .' she continued. 'How many women do you have? She doesn't know. At least I know whose bed you're in . . .' She struggled in her stuttering logic. 'At least I know . . .'

'The solace of the infidel.' Murphy restrained himself, took one last pull and flicked the butt out the window, the muted spiral of the red ash disappearing.

Louise stiffened. 'What does she say to you?'

'She doesn't say anything.' Murphy shifted in his seat. 'Come on, will you?' He squeezed her arm gently. 'Do you want to spoil everything?' He put his lips on her neck.

'Don't.'

He let her brush him away. Her hairdo touched the roof, making her tip her head to the side in an awkward manner.

'You have a romantic notion about love, and now you have one about the estranged wife . . .' Murphy said stiffly.

'You think she's not scared? What else does she have to think about?'

'Jesus, come on . . . What are you talking about her for?'

'Don't you have any feelings? . . .'

Murphy wiped his side window and looked out. 'I can't believe this. What do you want to know about her?'

The deep colour of blood rose on her skin, eyes glossing with tears, small hands tightening. 'You weren't going to come for me, were you?'

'It's not like that.'

Louise shook her head. 'You weren't going to come for me . . .'

'I was late . . .' Murphy looked at her. 'Are you listening to me?'

'You left me out there on the road. I thought you weren't going to come.'

Murphy lowered his head. 'She wants to get a driver's licence. That's what it was all about. She had me cornered at the house. A driver's licence. That's what it was.'

Louise buried her face in his shoulder. 'I thought you weren't coming . . . I thought you'd left me out on that road.'

His mouth caught her words. 'I'm sorry,' he whispered in her ear. Her skin was warm. He felt the small nipples against his chest.

'I thought you weren't coming.' A warm sticky whisper of saliva. 'I was waiting and . . .'

'It's all right.' Murphy closed his eyes. 'We have the weekend.' His fingers unbottoned her top.

63

'Don't ever leave me . . .'

'I won't.' Murphy felt himself blushing.

There was something to be said after all for the cold dampness. His hands rubbed against the cat-tongue coarseness of her nylons. Murphy shifted, lowering his trousers to his knees, big feet pressed solidly against the floor panel, legs sweating rivulets into the seams of the hot plastic seat, and manoeuvred her over the quivering black gear lever. The vents panted on her back. The exhaust puttered outside, the round hole smoking in the cold air. A sudden downpour added to the intimate urgency, rain beating fitfully on the roof as the car rocked gently on the lonely lane.

If Murphy had known more about the country, he'd have known at what time cows are milked. A cow rubbed its snout against the window and mooed. 'Jesus! Cows!' Murphy jerked and Louise fell sideways, buttocks in the air, shoulder and head hitting the hand brake. The car bucked, then rolled backward into the animals. A bawling sound filled the road. Murphy dragged at his trousers, his shaking feet fumbling to find the clutch and brake. Louise tried to right herself.

The cows pushed against one another, the black and white blotches of hides pressing against the car, jostling it as they struggled. They fought to climb the insurmountable thorny bushes flanking the narrow lane, hooves kicking obstinately at the car. 'You fuckers!' a man roared. 'What in fuck's name is going on?' Something solid hit the roof of the car. A dog materialized, shoving its black muzzle into the windshield.

Murphy's foot found the accelerator pedal, but the car shot backward into the thick of the herd. The engine jerked, died. A cow's head crashed through the passenger window, a huge pink snout hitting Louise.

The farmer swung his stick like a madman at the stricken cow, with a heavy dead thud of the stick on the cow's hind. Its roar of pain filled the car. The head thrust up, eyes rolling in terror, into the roof, almost tipping the small car. Somehow it managed to pull back and clawed at the muddy embankment of thorny bushes to get free of the car.

The farmer swung again at the window, hitting Louise on the side of the shoulder.

'My fuckin' cows!'

Louise threw her hands up to shield her face, curling away from the prodding stick.

'Stop!' Murphy roared. He caught the stick the next time it came through the broken window. 'Stop!'

'You've killed my cows, you fuckers!' The farmer didn't let go of the stick as he slipped and slid in the mud. He was an elfin creature with a small weasel face, cursing at the top of his lungs. When he saw Louise with her shirt undone, he fell in a new fury and lunged at her. 'You dirty whore!' he roared, and he pulled the stick loose and swung wildly in the confines of the car. 'I'll teach you . . .' He spat at her. 'Dirty fuckers!'

The farmer wrangled into the car, smashing up against Louise. Murphy grabbed at his head, and Louise tore at the face with her long nails.

'Get your fuckin' hands off me . . .' The farmer thrashed his arms about, hitting Murphy in the throat.

Murphy got the farmer in a head lock. 'Stop. Do you hear me?' The farmer moved his arm with the stick, trying to get leverage to swing it again.

'Get the stick away from him,' Murphy grunted. 'Louise!' Murphy's testicles were still exposed, the farmer inches away from them. 'Louise!' Murphy shouted, raising his arms, taking the farmer's head away from his groin. Murphy spoke in a slow, deliberate voice. 'Let the stick go, and I'll let you go, do you hear me?'

The farmer struggled. His body convulsed as he tried to breathe. Spit drooled from his mouth. His little legs kicked wildly in the air.

'I'll break your neck if you don't drop the stick!' Murphy's arm burned with effort as he tightened his grip further. 'Drop it!'

The farmer's writhing body shook the whole car.

'Get the stick away from him!' Murphy shouted. Louise

struggled frantically to free herself.

Murphy squeezed the farmer's head against the dashboard, and Louise shifted herself free, her chest marred by the coarseness of the farmer's coat. 'Get the stick.'

The farmer clung to the stick, trying to poke it at Murphy. Louise pulled at the stubby fingers.

'Listen to me,' Murphy shouted. The farmer's head was twisted sideways, his face convulsed, his eyes fixed on Murphy's testicles. Murphy flinched and understood, and squeezed the neck tighter until the farmer's eyes looked up at him. 'Listen to me! I'll break your neck!' Murphy looked at the face, hideously aged, deeply wrinkled, and teeth showing in a grimace of spittle. 'Will you stop!' Murphy said, securing his hold on the head.

Outside the dog snarled and scraped the bonnet, hitting its muzzle into the window.

'Stop! I'll let you get out,' Murphy said firmly. 'Are you listening to me?'

The farmer took short fitful breaths, but seemed to ease in his struggle, although his eyes seemed transfixed on Murphy's groin. Again, Murphy had to twist the neck in a precarious manoeuvre to get the eyes to look at him. The farmer's whole body turned.

'I'll pay for whatever damage was done, all right?'

The farmer seemed to acquiesce. Murphy eased his grip on the head. Sensing the release, the farmer stiffened his hold on the stick, and drove it into Murphy's leg with all his force. Murphy faltered and winced, and the stick hit him again on the outside of the leg. 'Dirty fuckers!' the farmer shouted, falling around the car, his legs kicking, wildly, suspended in mid-air outside the window.

Murphy grabbed at the farmer's head and caught the thin stalk of the neck and squeezed as hard as he could, shoving it into the dashboard. The farmer struggled and choked, his hands still on the stick, driving it at Murphy's groin.

Murphy winced and shifted his legs away as best he could, turning the farmer's head as he moved. Something snapped.

The body stiffened and then slackened. The stick fell from the fingers. Murphy struggled with the body as it almost collapsed onto the floor. He had to support the torso and push the head to get the body back out the window. A hairpiece fell off as the body collapsed.

Louise was gasping, shaking, her arms curled over her naked breasts and her knees drawn to her chest. Blood from the farmer had smeared her arms.

Murphy leaned into the steering wheel, his eyes watering in pain. He shook as he tried to pull his trousers up around his waist.

In an awful aftermath of silence, the pouring rain receded into his unconscious, silence except for the injured cow shuddering and breathing heavily behind the car. Murphy's arms burned and shook.

'You killed him,' Louise sobbed.

Murphy turned the key in the ignition, the sudden squeaking metronome of the wipers cutting an arc of visibility, cows plodding in uncertainty ahead of them. Steadying his legs, he eased the car forward. It scraped against something solid. The cows trotted further up the road in the dismal rain, dropping clots of steaming manure.

Murphy turned off the engine and put the car in gear. He cleared his voice, trying to speak. 'I want . . . I want to see.' There was glass around Louise's legs and stomach from the broken window. 'You better get in the back,' Murphy said.

She didn't move. Murphy reached into the back of the car and took her coat and put it around her shoulders. He said nothing more to her. She had her eyes closed.

The sky had already turned a blue grey. Murphy got out of the car, blown and buffeted by the wind. Rain soaked him almost immediately.

The farmer was slumped in a foetal position, a tiny man in a traditional black suit with a shirt and V-neck pullover. A small cherrywood pipe turned on its side still smouldered with its pot of ash. Murphy squatted down beside the farmer and turned the face toward his own, a hideous leathery skin mired with dirt like some corpse exhumed from a bog. Murphy checked for a pulse.

The dim orange of the horizon, almost obscured by rain, turned the air a strange sanguine colour. Murphy depressed the artery at the base of the throat. No pulse. He laid the head down. Rivulets of muddy rain flowed around it.

The injured cow sat in the cold narrow lane with her legs tucked under her huge body like some strange roosting creature, her head low and her snout touching the dirty mud. She had a gash on her hind quarters, nothing else. Murphy slapped his hands together and waved them at the cow. The cow mooed and struggled to rise, dipping her head forward, doubling her front legs as she rose slowly. The back right leg bent at the knee, useless. Murphy whistled and slapped his hands again. They stung in the coldness. A thread of bloody mucus hung from the cow's snout as it turned, looked at him, protested in one long moo, then hobbled back down the lane. He followed her, making her keep moving so she was far away from the broken glass.

Ahead in the lane Murphy saw the front wheel of the farmer's bicycle shyly turned towards the ditch with its dim circle of light. The light would stay on until the battery died. The cow went to the bicycle and stood by it, drawn to what it knew.

The dog, its coat matted and soaked, whimpered in the rain. It moved with its tail between its legs, cowering, watching as Murphy approached the farmer's body. Murphy pointed the stick at the dog. It growled instinctively, but came no closer.

Murphy needed to make the wounds to the right side of the face unrecognizable, as though the farmer had fallen. He found a rock, rose into the pull of stinging rain, steadied his hands and held his breath.

When Murphy turned to the car, Louise was staring at him from the back window with her hands to her mouth. He went up to the car and got in. 'You'd torn his face to bits.'

She looked at her hands and sobbed.

*

Murphy drove for over an hour, afraid to stop, passing desolate town after town. He could not afford to be caught parking in any of them or even out along the roadside. He wouldn't dare turn off on a side road. They were soaked through. It would take them ages to change. They were freezing and their actions would be slow and inept. Murphy slapped his hands against his legs, feeling the sting of numbness, holding them before the vents. He could barely feel the wheel. He put each one intermittently between his legs, trying to get warmth. He needed to keep blood getting to his hands. Everything focused on his hands. He felt nothing else. He had become one monstrous pair of hands, nothing else.

Murphy came to the outskirts of a town with a big parochial hall lit up for a dance, the cark park filled. He pulled into the outer perimeter and turned off the lights and parked. More rain, falling in a slant, windblown, adding to the obscurity, making each car isolated . . . He left the engine running, his hands spread over the vents. The heat burned them. For a moment the full effects of the cold made him shiver terribly. But now they were here . . . They had found a place to change. Murphy was on the verge of collapse.

Louise leaned over the vent in the dashboard like she was performing some religious ritual. Murphy watched her. He could tell she was crying. 'We have another hour at most,' he whispered.

Murphy drove for an hour looking for good places to dump a body, but it was dark, and he had the dilemma of how he would kill her. There was a jack in the boot of the car, but was he going to stop, get the jack, get her out of the car under the pretext of a flat, smash her head, drag her body to a ditch and then escape? The thought of going out in the rain didn't appeal to him. He was only just getting warm again. And would he go to the cottage after he'd killed her? And if he didn't, where could he go, since his clothes would undoubtedly be sprayed with blood and he hadn't another change of clothes? And what if the policemen up at Port Laoise had actually written down his licence number and noted that there were two of them in the car? He couldn't be sure of anything. And then Murphy noticed that the petrol was below a quarter tank, and that effectively saved her life, not that she'd ever know it.

Murphy arrived at a crossroads with a signpost leaning against a hedge. Arrows pointed into the ground and heavenward. There was a village ahead of them. The headlights smoked in the rain as the car sat still. Louise was asleep, or pretending to be asleep. He could go no further. They would have to go to the village. It would be worse being trapped out on the road all night. That would cause suspicion. They'd have to be driven down to the village to get petrol, and God knows what would happen. Someone might look in the boot and find the bloody clothes. For the first time it hit Murphy that they had the bloody clothes still with them. He'd have to burn them at the cottage. If he was to get away with the killing, he'd have to settle himself and make sure there was no evidence left. That, he told himself, was the most important thing, to concentrate, to go over all the details.

Murphy drove toward the village along a road raised out of the bog. 'We have to stop,' he said finally.

Louise looked at him. She hadn't been sleeping.

'We have to stop for petrol.'

She remained curled in her seat, her arms around her shoulders.

'But the window?' she whispered and then hesitated.

'A stone shattered it.'

Murphy eased his foot off the accelerator and brought the car to a stop. 'They know nothing down here . . .' He looked at her. 'Louise . . .' Her frail body had taken on a demeanour of fear, her bony shoulders hunched and her small head set into that hollow of collarbone. She hadn't the capacity to see beyond the killing or even to distinguish between self-defence and murder, and there was no point in him trying to impress that on her. To unnerve her before going down to the town could unhinge her. God only knew what she really felt, sitting

70

there beside him, mute and pretending to be asleep for hours on end, fuckin' imbecile of fashion and unrequited love, the latent guilt of having gone away with a married man staring her in the face. She already believed in her sin. She believed it earlier in the day up in Dublin waiting for him, in the car before they were attacked, the incessant self-doubt. Why had he come with her? What to say to her? Jasus, if he had a hammer he'd have aimed for the crown of her head without a moment's hesitation . . . Fuck a theological debate with her, she'd understand nothing . . . And there was no getting out of going down into the village. There was no petrol. They were stuck. Murphy settled for a modest threat, saying in a sick pastiness of calm breath, 'We'll both be executed, Louise, if you say anything . . .' The words had their slow trenchant effect, mixing with impinging dark all around them. 'There won't even be an investigation into the farmer's death,' Murphy said softly. 'It'll be ruled an accident. The cows trampled him. Can't you leave it at that? You don't want to be executed! Gas us, hang us, or the electric chair,' Murphy persisted in a low voice. 'I don't even know what they use any more . . .'

'Is there still a death penalty?' Louise flinched at the thought of execution. She opened her mouth and began in a tremulous voice. 'He attacked us . . .'

'Is that the way you want to end up, executed?'

Tears ran down her face, her head dipping forward slowly in a gesture of passive exhaustion.

'I don't want to be executed, and you don't want to be executed . . .' The cold effect of his words took the religion out of her for the moment. He had done what he could.

Inside the pub, a line of men sat with their backs to the door looking at a black and white television. Its picture jittered and rolled, casting shadows around in the dark. 'There, that's it. Jasus, hold it steady.' A midget of a man in a black suit with shirt and tie sat holding a pair of rabbit-ear antennae in his hands, moving them back and forth to the exasperated gestures and curses of those watching the television. 'To the left, to the right . . . Steady it, Pat.'

Louise stood behind Murphy as he waited, afraid to advance. He saw the publican in a jumper the colour of oatmeal with a white apron around his thick belly, a huge barrel of a man intent on pulling a pint. Their eyes met for a moment, and the publican signalled he'd come to them with an easy tip of his head. They should not come any further, that was clear.

The publican set a pint to settle on the bar and approached, using his arms to balance as he advanced his weight towards them. 'What's this then?' he said, breathing through his nose and mouth, almost pushing them back towards the door.

'We ran out of petrol,' Murphy said, stepping back.

'Everything's closed at this hour.' The publican's small eyes drifted to Louise, and his head moved with his eyes as he looked her up and down. Dripping wet.

'She's freezing,' the publican said, turning to Murphy suspiciously.

Murphy steadied himself. 'A stone smashed the side window of the car . . . and then we ran out of petrol . . .' There was a gunshot on the television.

The publican turned to see what was going on, letting his gaze linger. He took his time before turning again and raised his fat hand with a tincture of impatience. 'I see then.' He leaned into Murphy with the conniving familiarity of a man about to tell another man something secret, but all he said was, 'I'll see what I can do, but you'll have to wait awhile. Everyone is watching the cowboys.'

Murphy understood. 'We'll wait.'

'Maybe she'd like to go into the house?' The publican raised his eyebrows on his big face. 'She could get a cup of tea and dry herself.' He winked at Louise. 'There's a fire in there, and herself will look after everything.'

'Grand,' Murphy said.

Louise almost buckled and leaned into Murphy. 'I just want to get back home,' she whispered. 'Go in and offer them anything . . . I don't want to go in there.' Her whole body seemed to slump with a deadening tiredness. He felt her knees bend as she leaned against him. 'I just want to get home. Tell them you'll give them anything . . .' An element of fear and hysteria had entered her voice. She clung to him with a trembling intensity.

'Offering them money will only cause suspicion. Listen to me.' He put his lips against her hot forehead. 'When this is all over, I'm going to take you to England.' His lips felt the delicate pressure of a vein on the side of her forehead. She seemed to ease in his arms.

'You swear?'

'I swear. We've come too far . . .' It was a line from a film, or an approximation of a line from a film.

The publican must have had a door which connected the pub to the house because the front door opened and Murphy was caught in the embarrassing and compromising position, kissing Louise.

The publican's wife, a small woman with heavy breasts which moved like two cats in a sack, coughed and stood in the lighted hallway. 'Excuse me . . .' She ushered Louise into the hall and shut the door again.

Murphy sat at the bar on a stool. The publican stood behind the bar, turning a glass silently in his big hands, pulling a pint.

Murphy turned and looked at the screen. John Wayne was sitting with his legs crossed in a circle of Indians.

'Don't do it, John,' the old man with the rabbit-ear antennae in his hands said, and a line rolled down the screen.

'Hold it right, for feck's sake!'

The old man had to adjust the rabbit's ears until the image steadied.

The publican's head bobbed up and down in agitation. 'Cut the messin' out. It's not a fuckin' interactive unit, Jasus. If you left that antennae alone everything would work grand.'

The reception cleared again and the men went silent.

Murphy heard talking at the end of the dark corridor behind the bar and eased off his buttocks, trying to catch what was being said. Louise was in there with the publican's wife. What was she saying?

The publican turned and saw Murphy leaning onto the bar and made a face. 'What are you at?'

'I thought I heard my wife going on. I don't want her to put your wife out.'

The publican looked jaded and waved his fat hand dismissively. 'Leave them to themselves. That's women's talk . . .' He brought his thumb and index finger together, 'Yap, yap, yap. You know the way?'

'Right,' said Murphy. The publican poured himself a clear liquid into a small glass and passed it under Murphy's nostrils. Murphy smelt the stink of drink and the sour nicotine of the publican's thick, discoloured fingers. The publican drank and refilled his glass. 'Jasus, now we're talkin'. Here, have a drop yourself.'

'No thanks.' Murphy raised his hand. 'We have a ways to go yet tonight.'

The publican poured a glass and held it to the light. 'Go on. You're wound like a spring. You need it, wouldn't you agree?'

Murphy took the glass and drained it in one continuous motion.

'And you're married how long now?' The publican swivelled on the heel of his shoes, looking between the poteen and Murphy.

'Nearly a year.'

'And no sign yet?' The publican smiled and made an arc around his own heavy belly. A crude and forward familiarity of an over-sexed agricultural man, the perimeters of life and death punctuated only by a rudimentary education, procreation, Sunday Mass and a hard drink . . . Murphy would have liked to have kicked the arse off the publican, but said, 'She had a touch of pneumonia last year.'

'Sick is she,' the publican said gravely with a shudder, 'and you came down this way though, in the winter and all. Jasus, that can't be good for her health.' The publican shook his head.

'They're putting up houses on our estate. We wanted to get away from it . . . the noise and the confusion.'

'They work on the weekend up in Dublin?' the publican said with a strained sadness and weakly shook his head again. 'That beats all, doesn't it, Christ's sake?' He pulled on his cigarette and used his index finger to pull his collar away from his neck.

Murphy looked at his pint and said nothing.

'Jasus Almighty, it's hot.' The publican broke off with decided perplexity, disappeared into the off-licence cubicle and opened a door to the outside. The fire reddened and roared in the cross-draught of cold air.

'Shut the door!' the little man holding the rabbit-ear antennae shouted. 'The reception is gone to hell.' The entire group of men scraped their boots anxiously, waiting for the reception to clear.

Murphy felt the cold air flowing into the warm crypt of the pub and shuddered. A small calendar behind the bar with a faded picture of John F. Kennedy flapped. The great Irish immigrant Kennedy, the man who dreamt of putting a man on the moon . . . It seemed incomprehensible that in less than a century an Irishman had emigrated to America and had a grandson who became President of America. It was on such dreams that America lived. The philosophy of chance . . . isn't that what had motivated him to go off with Louise? The mere probability of not being caught had reasonable odds. He'd even thought of it consciously that way. A crude mathematics of statistical probability had replaced morality.

No wonder the law had so many definitions of murder – premeditated murder, murder in the first degree, murder in the second degree, manslaughter – a tacit acknowledgment of the degree of chance involved in the act, the extenuating circumstances, everything short of being exonerated by the mere notion of chance.

Murphy shivered as the cold air circulated in the pub.

'Close the fuckin' door!' one of the men shouted with a pitch of anger which suggested a fight could break out if the publican didn't cut out the messing.

'Jasus,' the publican moaned, but the door closed and the reception cleared.

Murphy's elbow slipped out from under him. The little man with the rabbit antennae said something that Murphy didn't catch. Murphy looked at his own face in the mirror behind the bar, his head ringing from the poteen and the unnerving feeling that Louise was telling the woman everything, trying desperately to save herself. He'd put the fear of death into her. Murphy wiped the sweat on his forehead, feeling the pull of skin around his eyes. What was the fuckin' point anymore? Murphy steadied himself.

The publican materialized again from the off-licence, his face shining from the cold outside. 'Jasus, it's warm in here, or is it just me?' Droplets of sweat formed on his receding hairline. The Indians screamed like heathens on the television. 'There are certain people you can't trust,' the publican said gravely and looked towards the television, wiping his forehead.

The thought of escape dogged him. He should have taken the measure to kill her. This was what got them in the films; what they called, 'loose ends . . .' She was a loose end, a woman with nothing going for her, a bleak future of second-rate men like himself coming to sleep with her. She would assume guilt for what had happened. The inevitability of failure would be tied to some sin. Eventually, she would confess . . . First he had to escape the bar; he had to get her away with him . . .

A stocky man in black coat and hat walked up slowly along the narrow corridor with his hands behind his back. 'Evening.'

'Evening, Father,' the publican said from the small off-licence room. He came out and lifted a flap in the counter for the priest to come around to the other side of the bar. The priest tipped his head at Murphy suspiciously. 'We don't often get visitors at this time of year.'

Murphy looked blankly at his half-filled pint but said nothing. The sweet smell of liquor emanated from the priest.

'Car trouble,' the publican said.

'Was that pole ever fixed out there by the crossroads, the one Liam Higgins got his donkey to knock over, so the Americans would get lost and have to come down for directions?'

Murphy could tell the exposition was intended to unnerve him.

The publican made a smacking sound with his lips, 'Don't be codding him, Father.' The publican smiled at Murphy. 'He's a terrible man when he gets started.'

The priest didn't listen and plodded over and stood behind the men. 'John Wayne is a Protestant.'

'It's nearly over, Father,' the publican said. He shook his head at Murphy and mouthed, 'Say nothing.'

'I wonder if he'll live?' the priest said mockingly.

The men remained sullen and said nothing in reply.

The priest turned to the bar with exaggerated effort, using his big arms to give him momentum. 'You heard about the escape, no doubt?' The priest's gaze encompassed Murphy.

The publican pulled the sleek ebony handle and began nurturing a pint. 'I did, on the radio. Three of them out of Port Laoise,' the publican said frankly. 'I'll take your coat and hat, Father?'

'I'm not stopping long.'

'You'll have a pint?' the publican said.

'One for the sake of company.' The priest took the pint, stopped, and said, 'Inside job all the way up, in Port Laoise,' then sipped the creamy head in a satisfying slurp. 'They went out with the laundry, if you can believe that . . .' He wiped a thin line of foam off his upper lip. 'It's a strange thing, imprisoning our own, if you ask me.'

'What would you expect from them up in Dublin,' the publican said in disgust.

'The government is cursing a blue streak over the situation. Embarrassing on an international front. You know the usual, suspicion that we're harbouring murderers.'

77

The publican slung a dishcloth over his heavy shoulder. 'Sure, don't I know it, scaring the daylights out of the Americans. War-torn Ireland. We'll see less of them here this year.' The publican's eyes caught Murphy's, and Murphy felt a sudden chill. The signpost out on the road had been deliberately knocked over, like the priest had said.

'Dublin licence,' the priest said to Murphy, tapping him on the shoulder. 'What are you doing down this end of the country?'

Murphy hesitated and looked at the publican.

'Down on a trip of convalescence. The wife is sick,' the publican motioned. 'She's inside.'

'I was talking to her,' the priest said with ponderous effect, as though he knew more than he was saying, a patent way of priests to elicit more from a situation by the suggestion of omniscience. 'So this is the man who dragged the missus all over the country. She doesn't look well.'

The publican interrupted again. 'He was telling me about the rat race, Father. They're working on a Saturday up in Dublin, and I was just saying . . .'

The priest lifted his paw of a hand slightly in a hint of intolerance, the candid authority of the Church could do that, and the publican obeyed and coughed self-consciously. 'She was sick before you married her?'

'She caught pneumonia after we got married,' Murphy answered stiffly.

The priest gazed at his pint in a feigned meditative way. 'That's a terror. You were probably just shy of the times of consumption. Now there was a horror if ever there was one.' He gave a shudder of memory. 'Women are delicate creatures. Man must remember that.'

The publican stood outside the conversation, stiff and attentive, wanting to say something. The priest kept his eye on Murphy. 'She was telling me inside, her people are . . . from where was it now?'

'Galway.'

'Oh, right. And her maiden name was?'

'Shields.'

'Can't say I know of them. But sure, you can't know the world, can you?' The priest stretched his face in a yawn and showed a broken fence of teeth.

Sweat ran down Murphy's legs. Jesus, had she said something? Was the priest trying to bait him into an argument?

'I'll take a bag of crisps if you have them.' the priest said moving his big head around on his shoulders. 'Cheese and onion.'

The publican rustled under the bar and came up with a red plastic bag of crisps.

'Speaking of women . . .'

Murphy nearly fell off the stool, but caught himself. 'Were we?'

'Well, I was.' The priest's mouth half-opened with a mulch of crisp. When he ate, he brought his lips to the fore like a baboon. 'I remember an uncle who said, if you want to know if a woman has any strength in her, you check the teeth. My uncle abided by that philosophy, because that's what he did with horses and cows, and it proved satisfactory. He was never taken with clothes.'

'That must explain the origins of kissing,' Murphy said. 'A surreptitious dental investigation.'

'Maybe,' the priest said testily, and went into a decided silence for a few moments.

'I can tell you something now, because you're a liberal man.' The priest fingered Murphy's shoulder. 'Listen up. This uncle I just referred to told me that in some parts of the country there's a practical tradition where a woman who is to be wed is taken out to a shed and told to strip off, and then the intended comes up and has a good look at her. She's inside the shed and does a few things, walks around the place, nothing fancy, nothing indecent. I mean she's not going to skip rope or anything but you get a sense of what you're in for . . . That's reasonable enough in my estimation. What do you think?'

'It seems reasonable enough,' Murphy answered.

'Of course it does, because it's an old tradition. All the old

79

traditions had a practicality at their core which was both morally and materially sound.'

'Right.' Murphy steadied himself in the sudden thought that maybe the priest was a sex maniac. This was why the publican had tried to tell Murphy to say nothing.

The music rose in a crescendo, and Murphy turned. The words THE END rose out of the background. He turned again and looked at the publican.

The publican nodded. 'I'll see for you.'

Murphy looked at the priest. 'I need to get going . . .'

'Not on your life, you're not. In this weather, you must be joking? The roads are destroyed with the rain. You have room enough for them.' The priest directed his attention to the publican. 'Let her rest in there. She seems to have caught her death. Poor creature like that, sick and all. Why in God's name is a married man taking a sick woman like that around the country in the middle of winter. That's what I'd like to know?'

Perhaps the priest sensed infidelity. Maybe that was all. That was the priest's tiresome domain, bred like a special breed of dog especially to sniff out sexual misconduct, perverted fucker nosing around women. He thought of them at the seminary in training, scented with a pair of knickers and then set off on the trail.

'Did you know, in Italy, the married couple, after their wedding night have to put the sheets out on the line to prove that the woman was a virgin? There's a grand tradition for you. That's the God's honest truth. That's why it's important for women to take it easy when they're young, not too much activity to break the seal of virginity.' The priest licked the flecks of cheese and onion off his fingers and made a huge O with his thumb and index finger and held it up in the soft light of the bar. He pointed to it with his other hand. 'A thin membrane of blood, what they call "the hymen," dictates the moral limits of what a woman can do before marriage.' He nodded to himself gravely. 'Do you believe that, Dublin Licence?'

'What are you asking me? Do I believe a woman has a

hymen?' Murphy stared at the shaking hand of the priest, which looked like he was giving the OK to a friend.

The publican had his big arms folded over his potato belly, his eyes focused on Murphy.

The priest eyed the publican, stiffening his face. 'You stay out of this here.'

'You seem to want to keep women in a shed away from sunlight the way farmers rear veal, Father. I'm neither a theologian, nor a scholar, but I suppose some evolutionist has a reason for the hymen,' Murphy answered.

'But you seem so much more,' the priest pressed on in an over-familiar manner. 'A caring sort of character, taking his wife off like this for a weekend. Inherent romanticism is unknown in these parts.'

The band of men shifted from foot to foot, swilling their drinks, not understanding the priest, who settled into a morose silence in between talking. He had the luxury of a manic authority where he could dictate the flow of conversation and mood.

The priest stared up again. 'I read this awhile back about the current . . . sit-u-a-tion,' the priest said, putting his pint down on the counter. 'Here is the sit-u-a-tion as I see it,' the priest droned on. 'Although it is sinful for a man to rape a woman, it is also sinful for a man not to have the physical strength necessary to rape a woman.' The priest looked at Murphy, his head moving slowly on his huge neck. 'That's the essence of the current situation as I see it. They have to understand that.' He pointed with his sausage finger down the long corridor.

The publican's left eye twitched nervously at the word rape, muttering, 'Jasus Christ.'

'They're the weaker sex, for the love of Jasus, do I have to spell it out for you?' the priest persisted, knowing he'd unnerved the publican. The bulk of his body visibly puckered and folded in a slow contortion of movement. He had the slothfulness of some prehistoric creature. 'Let me put it another way for you. The threat of violence is the founding stone of civilization. If we'd stick to the facts at hand, with what we've been given by God Almighty, we'd do all right!' His fist banged the varnished counter top and foam poured over the edge of his glass. 'The way you'd train a dog, for the love of Jasus . . .'

The publican rubbed his chin with the meditative fraternity accorded him in these situations. He was obliged to take control of his house and to say something. 'The way you'd train a dog, right. We understand. Point well taken, Father.'

The priest fumed over his drink. 'We have to stick with the facts in the case at hand . . .' His eyes wandered from face to face.

Murphy eyed the publican, who winked at one of the other men, who gave a heavy sigh. 'Right then, I suppose we'd better be, as they say in the films, "moseying along".'

The priest continued to brood, snorting through his huge nostrils. He turned and held Murphy's arm. 'Do you know what?'

'What? Murphy said.

'Here's a queer thing for you before you go.' Breathing heavily, his massive face filled with an uncharacteristic misgiving, almost self-reproach. 'Did you know that there are satellites up in the sky that can spot a penny on the ground?' he blurted into Murphy's face. 'That's a fact.' He squeezed Murphy's arm. 'There's thousands of them up there circling the world. Everything is filmed and stored away and analysed by the Americans . . . It doesn't matter if you're in your bed or out on the street, these satellites can see everything.' He let go of Murphy's arm. 'This is the twilight of the age of Scorn and Ridicule. Fear is going to make a big comeback, mark my words.'

Murphy rubbed his arm, obstinately remaining.

The men had retreated to the door. 'If you're ready for that petrol now, sir?' one of the men said.

'You'd better go on,' the publican insisted, looking at Murphy, pointing at the door. 'This whole thing has gone overboard.'

Murphy got up off his stool, his legs shaking as they found

the floor.

'The Vatican is going to send up its own one soon,' the priest shouted after Murphy, swivelling on the huge rump of his buttocks, his arms extended into two vast fists. 'You'll be held accountable in this world and in the next. We are all under surveillance. Eternity is not long enough, nor hell not hot enough, for the likes of you!'

Murphy drove around to the side door of the pub. The publican stood at the front door. He disappeared and came up with Louise in the yellow light of the hall.

Murphy got out of the car and stepped into the hallway. 'How much do we owe you?'

'A tenner should cover it.' The publican took the note and put it in his pocket. 'So you know the way then. Back up to the crossroads, go left, and it's about fifteen miles down on your right.' The publican scratched his jaw and looked nervously at Murphy. 'You'll say nothing about him in there. He's not a bad sort really. Who knows, maybe he's not far off the mark. He believes in all this spying business. And God, don't we need someone looking over our shoulder.'

'Not to worry,' Murphy said, looking at Louise. She stared at the floor, saying nothing. Murphy could tell she'd been awoken from sleep.

'All the best then.' The publican stood with his arms folded.

Murphy drove away with the simple plan in his head. He'd say to Louise that they were going to London to start a new life together and that she had to write a letter addressed to the company saying she'd quit and write another letter to her brother, Frank. Her parents were dead, fortuitously enough, and how long would relatives stay interested in finding where she was anyway? They had their own worries and children. They'd think she'd got pregnant and left out of shame. They knew her type: flat in Dublin, lonely. The relatives would save themselves the embarrassment of kicking up a racket and declaring her missing. Women went missing from Ireland all the time to take care of situations. Murphy felt fortunate to live in a country where the press had a scrupulous regard for preserving the status quo, where the Church kept truth from people.

'Freak death of Farmer kicked in head by Cow.' It might make page four of the *Cork Examiner*, a mention in the Dublin papers. Murphy reached the crossroads, the broken signpost lit up by the headlights. He turned left and kept the car steady. There'd be the problem of her corpse to contend with, but he'd manage somehow, or maybe she wasn't beyond understanding . . . But he looked at the state of her out of the corner of his left eye. He'd seen some interesting ideas in the films. There was this one about a man who was having trouble with this woman who was blackmailing him . . . how did it go now?

In Hiding

Mrs Feeney hid herself in the cloakroom under the stairs when the bombings started, huddled in with the heavy coats and old shoes that smelt of her husband.

Mr Feeney found her bundled under the stairs, asleep, one morning when he came home from the factory. He went out on his bicycle and came back with wood and rods of steel from some bombed-out buildings.

'Now, we'll sort this thing out.' Mr Feeney was all business, crawling around under the stairs, occupying himself with these brief contingencies where he didn't have to think about things. He hammered reinforcement beams into place to secure the stairs, then came out and made Mrs Feeney go look. 'Let me check this.' Mr Feeney went up the stairs above the cloakroom and pounded with his foot. 'How's that sound? Any creaking?'

Mrs Feeney sat under the stairs. Bits of plaster fell into her hair. 'Stop,' she said. She had her hands around her waist. She felt the feet pressing against her stomach. She didn't know how long it took for a baby to form. Pregnant women always wore loose clothes, so nobody could tell how big a woman got before her baby came. Mrs Feeney hesitated to mention anything to Mr Feeney. She had a terrible fear the child would come when she was under the stairs.

'Well?' Mr Feeney said again. 'How does it sound?' He pounded on the stairs.

'Stop!' Mrs Feeney cried.

Mr Feeney came around to her. 'What's wrong with you? How is it?'

Mrs Feeney nodded from her small cocoon. 'It's grand.'

'There. You're set now.' Mr Feeney raised his eyebrows. 'Right?'

'How much longer will we be here?' Mrs Feeney trembled slightly.

Mr Feeney ignored her question. 'Aren't you set now?' Mr Feeney still had on his hat and coat, a thin figure of a man, a conglomerate of basic human features, although his small fixed blue eyes betrayed years of determined physical exertion. They looked beyond what they confronted, the head always tipped upwards in an enigmatic questioning of a higher authority. Mr Feeney banged the stairs with his fist, forcing a simplicity of character upon himself. 'That's solid.' Bits of plaster fell into Mrs Feeney's greasy hair.

'I'll get some blankets down here and nail them to the wood there.' Mr Feeney staved off saying anything more, placating himself in the shell of his solitary work. The sooner he could get away to the factory the better. He went up the stairs and gathered some old blankets from the hot press.

Mrs Feeney crawled out from under the stairs and shook her hair. She hated him banging his feet the way he did. Mrs Feeney wanted some air. She opened the front door to a desolate sky and a street devoid of humans, houses boarded up and abandoned. The silence calmed her. To think there was a war going on out there. She had only heard its sounds, felt its impact in rumbling nightmares under the stairs.

'Is that door open?' Mr Feeney shouted from upstairs.

Mrs Feeney didn't hear him. The smell of ash lingered from the night's bombings. Mrs Feeney shivered.

Mr Feeney banged things around upstairs, inscrutably allying with noise to obliterate every thought in his head.

Mrs Feeney still wasn't used to the small rows of dirty red-brick houses that stretched down towards huge chimney stacks. The dull layer of soot ingrained itself everywhere, not just from the war, but from the factories off near the river that had belched out smoke since the start of the Industrial Revolution. Mr Feeney had told her that one evening when they had first come to England, from Ireland, before the bombing of London started. 'You see, civilization starts beside a river.' He took her walking down by the river where there were no benches, no flowers or trees or fish.

'We'll be gone out of this before long,' Mr Feeney said

abstractly, coming down. He stomped on the stairs above the cloakroom again, checking his work. 'Come away from there. Give me a hand with this, will you?' Mr Feeney brushed by Mrs Feeney. 'Keep that door shut and don't let the dust in on us.' He shook his head at his wife's ignorance.

Mrs Feeney could see the grey exhaustion in Mr Feeney's face, indelibly marked now by the slight ridge of wrinkles around his eyes when he squinted.

The two of them hunched in the space under the stairs. Mr Feeney nailed up the edges of the blanket while Mrs Feeney held it. She watched him moving around inside the hole, doing what he could for her in his own way. He'd come with her to London from Limerick, to the centre of a World War, to make a living as an animal slaughterer. As he'd often said with a laugh to his wife before they'd come to London, 'There're too many men willing to kill each other and not enough left to kill animals. Isn't that a right cockup of a situation for you?'

Mrs Feeney dropped the blanket out of her hands and Mr Feeney hit his thumb with the hammer and let out a roar, coming out, red-faced, sucking his thumb. 'Jesus Christ! It'll do. I need my hands to work, for the love of Jesus!' He didn't finish the job. The blanket hung in a dark partition under the stairs.

'There's a shirt for you to change into,' Mrs Feeney said as Mr Feeney disappeared up the stairs to put his thumb under cold water.

In the small kitchen, they ate a bowl of stew and dipped it with bread Mr Feeney had bought on his way home from work earlier in the morning. The kitchen contained the only margin of warmth, since the cooker had been on. Mrs Feeney kept the doors in the house closed to contain pockets of air and to keep the dust from blowing up and getting into their lungs. Mr Feeney had learned from some of the men at the factory that it was best to get a bottle of water and spray it around the house, room by room, to dampen the dust which could then be swept up easily. He told this to Mrs Feeney, but she hadn't listened to him. She had no interest in housework.

Mrs Feeney touched her stomach, trying to work up the courage to say something. She got up and took the teapot off the ring, her heavy legs moving under her coarse knit skirt. A constant pressure throbbed low in her spine, her organs pressed by her growing womb. She would have to let out the seams on her dresses because of her increasing size.

Intent upon getting something into him before discussing anything, Mr Feeney continued to spoon his stew into his mouth. 'I'll have a topper.' He held his cup up, and Mrs Feeney poured. 'That's grand.' Mr Feeney put his other hand up like a policeman stopping traffic. 'That's grand, I said.' The tea flowed over the rim of the cup. 'Christ! Do you want to scald me?' He put the cup down and sucked his fingers. His eyes never left her face, resisting her words with his implacable solemnity. He wished he'd not come home to her. Condensation wept on the kitchen window.

Mrs Feeney went out of the room and up to the toilet. Mr Feeney stopped chewing for a few moments to listen to her. What was she at up there? Not that he didn't know. If only they were back home where at least he could keep away from her, or have some women comfort her. He preserved an earnest ignorance when she came back, eating feverishly at his stew. He could smell the odour of the toilet on her. He put the tea to his face, his Adam's apple bobbing in his throat, and inhaled the warm tea. Mrs Feeney shuffled around the kitchen.

When he finished eating, Mr Feeney set his bowl away from him and wiped his mouth with the cuff of his shirt, his tongue skimming his teeth. Her smell persisted, a lugubrious scent that alarmed Mr Feeney by its potency. 'There, now.' He still seemed unsatisfied, tapping his fingers on the table edge.

Mrs Feeney had eaten very little. Mr Feeney let his eyes rest on the bowl for want of something else to stare at, even though he was full.

'I'm not hungry,' Mrs Feeney said.

Mr Feeney hesitated. 'You . . . You need to keep your strength up . . .'

Mrs Feeney took the teapot off the table and put it back on the cooker. 'I don't know . . .' She rested the palms of her hands on the edge of the cooker's warm metal. She sniffled.

Mr Feeney's big boots scraped the floor nervously. He wanted to leave and escape to work.

'I don't know anything about babies.' Mrs Feeney had to stop herself from crying. 'I don't know anything about them.'

Mr Feeney saw her big legs sag with their map of broken veins. He rolled his eyes and took her stew obstinately. 'Is that what's at you? Nature takes its course,' he scoffed dismissively. 'God Almighty.' He laced the stew with salt, shaking his head. 'God Almighty.'

'But how long will it be?' Mrs Feeney whispered, turning to face her husband. 'Will . . . Will we be home?' She dabbed her eyes.

A spoon of stew steamed in mid-air. Mr Feeney hesitated. 'Do you want me to phone up shaggin' Mr Hitler and tell him to stop all U-boats? "Sorry, but meself and the wife were thinking of heading home. Is that all right by you?"'

Mrs Feeney lowered her head.

'Don't start that now. Come on, will you? Nature takes its course,' Mr Feeney said quietly, cutting into the loaf of bread, and yet the faint philosophy of his life had a vaguely discomforting aspect. Nothing had ever taken care of itself, as he knew too well. He tried not to breathe. Her odour had infected him with a strange, desolate melancholy. It tormented him. He tasted it in the butter and the fatty meat he chewed. 'Open the window,' he said, hiding his disgust, pointing with his spoon. The air poured in with a silt of dust that glittered in the cold sunlight. Mr Feeney breathed deep through his nostrils. If only he could abandon her to some women of her own.

Mrs Feeney didn't know if she could believe her husband. She watched Mr Feeney heap the food onto the spoon, his eyes closed as the dark hole of his mouth opened. The cold air blew the steam off his stew. She wanted to ask him more. She didn't want to give birth under the stairs, she wanted to tell him that.

Her whole body stiffened. Her lips muttered. Her husband knew about pigs from his days on a farm, but was it the same with humans? She hesitated with the question. She felt her face flush as the words formed in her head. 'Are pigs the same as humans, then?' she blurted. Her big body made the table tremble.

'No, pigs don't have souls,' Mr Feeney roared. He looked up at her. His eyes had such an innocent way about them when overwhelmed by fear. 'We'll be home before the child is born. Will you trust me?' He blinked and then he blessed himself and rose from the table, ending all discussion. He went out into the back garden, suddenly nauseous from having eaten too much and her inconsolable presence. He came back in a few minutes later without a word.

'I don't want to die,' Mrs Feeney sobbed as he passed. 'I don't want to die.'

'Will you not trust me, woman?' Mr Feeney banged the kitchen door and went into the living room.

Within a few minutes she could hear him snoring. He had turned himself off, a great gift that came with slavish labour at the factory. He had money and work. If he'd come over by himself he would have been the happiest man in the war. He had found an elemental pride in doing something he was good at and which needed to be done.

Mrs Feeney drank from her husband's cup. She staved off tears, breathing deeply, her fingers squeezed around the cup. She felt trapped. After they came to London, she bought worm powder at the chemist's and sat in the late evening on the toilet, but it was too late then. She had grown fat. A child had taken root. She pressed her stomach, squatting on the toilet. It was the air-raid siren which brought her back to sanity as she pulled up her drawers, conscious that she was committing a mortal sin.

The time had passed, six months in London. She knew she was going to give birth under the stairs with nobody there for her. The English had abandoned the other houses on the street:

children and women sent off to the country for the duration of the war. When he left for work, she was isolated. Anything could happen to her.

At noon Mrs Feeney went into the living room and roused Mr Feeney. 'You'll be late.' She'd boiled more tea and cut some bread for him. 'There's a shirt for you to change into.'

Mrs Feeney remained trapped in the narrow street of red-brick houses, her stomach growing big in isolation. She slept under the stairs and said nothing. Mr Feeney stayed away for days at a time, coming home exhausted. He spoke little, going about his routine with forced simplicity. He set his pay packet on the hall table as testimony to his work. He slept on the couch, leaving a few messages on the table and picking up the notes she left for milk, bread, tea, butter, sausages.

Mrs Feeney came out of her house one night, screaming, with blood on her hands. Searchlights roamed the sky. She remembered nothing beyond that. She gave birth during an air raid in a makeshift hospital, down in the Tube. She had to be sedated after the birth.

Mrs Feeney curled in a bed, crying softly. She didn't have her baby. Her body was freezing cold. Paralysis afflicted the right side of her face. When she touched it, she felt nothing, as though her face had been blown off. A nurse had to show her a mirror to prove to her that she still had a face.

There were complications with the child. Too weak to understand, Mrs Feeney wept. A needle throbbed in her vein. When she began to understand, she prayed that the child would die. Her right arm stiffened with the paralysis which the nurse said was part of hysteria. Mrs Feeney was given drugs which made her sleep for a long time. She awoke into numbness so many times, unaware of time, her eyes weeping from the dead mask of her face.

When she recovered from the paralysis, Mrs Feeney feigned a weakness from loss of blood and spoke to nobody. She didn't ask about the child, banishing everything from her memory. It was good she'd never seen it. But then a nurse told her the child was doing fine. It was not as serious as they had thought.

Mrs Feeney said nothing. Her faith returned slowly. She could be thankful that she had not stayed under the stairs, bleeding into unconsciousness. God had sent her into the hands of people who could help her. Cradling the loose fat of her stomach, she brought her knees to her heavy breasts. She felt the damage, the flesh that would never recover. Her nipples dripped fluid, wetting her shirt, making her even colder.

A nurse came and showed her how to squeeze the milk into a small jug.

'You try it,' the nurse said.

Mrs Feeney closed her eyes, ashamed.

'You should have your baby in a day or so,' the nurse said, reaching to take Mrs Feeney's pulse. She waited until the milk reached a mark on the jar. 'That will do,' the nurse said.

Mrs Feeney gave up the jar and turned in on herself.

'You need to do that three times a day. A jar will be sent to your bed . . .'

Mrs Feeney's nipples throbbed, still oozing milk like one of her husband's animals. For once, she wished she had been killed. What was she to do for the rest of the war, alone with a sick child and a husband she never saw?

Mrs Feeney felt the animosity in the voices around her, in the way the nurses and doctors touched her. She should have had her baby in Ireland. They knew her kind, how the Irish came over to make money while the English fought in the trenches. Each prod was for wasting their time, for coming to England.

They wouldn't let Mrs Feeney stay at the hospital. Beds were scarce. Nobody had been able to contact her husband. Someone had gone by the house and left a letter.

Mrs Feeney was helped into the clothes she'd come in. The coarse wool skirt held the memory of birth even though it had been steeped in water, her shirt stained with patches of sweat, the nylons like dead skin pulled up over her thick legs.

Mrs Feeney drank warm milk and a biscuit in a tunnel as her file was recorded. A nurse weighed the baby.

Mrs Feeney ate nervously. Other patients who had been injured by the air raids were bandaged and dazed with puffed up faces. Mrs Feeney felt uncomfortable because she had no visible wounds.

The nurse called her into a small room where Mrs Feeney sat down again. A doctor came into the room and put a tube down the baby's throat and siphoned fluid from the lung. The child choked and coughed, wriggling in the doctor's arms. A nurse had to hold the child's legs. Mrs Feeney put down her tea because her hands were shaking.

'It's all right,' the nurse said severely. 'We have to check the lung.'

Tremors of fatigue still ran through Mrs Feeney's legs, the ankles swollen, her shoe buckles left undone so she could fit into her shoes. Her thighs and buttocks ached as she re-positioned herself on the wooden chair. She waited silently.

A red-faced nurse showed Mrs Feeney how to help bring up the congestion in the baby's lungs. She told her that someone would come and check on the child in a few weeks to see how the lung was doing. If the lung didn't heal, the child would need an operation. She showed Mrs Feeney a small glass dish in which there was thick green phlegm with an almost dark centre. 'You must watch for blood. If the phlegm has traces of blood you must bring the child to a clinic immediately. If the lung is not caught early, it could make the child an invalid forever.'

Mrs Feeney struggled away and went down an escalator and waited for a train on another platform deep in the under-ground. All the tunnels were the same, the clotted odour of dust swirling in the cool passageways, the phantom aspect of other figures with their heads hidden, covering their mouths.

Mrs Feeney's eyes burned. She pressed the sleeping baby

under her coat and moved as though she had her arm in a sling. A train wormed out of a dark tunnel.

At her stop, Mrs Feeney rose up into a cold, wintry mid-afternoon of long shadows. The sky was the colour of wet cement, the air filled with dust and ash from the previous night's bombings. Sulphur burned her throat. Clutching her child to her breast, she walked slowly towards the house. She passed smoking rubble, seeing the strangeness of a living room exposed with its walls blown apart, the colourful wallpaper against the grey sky.

At a corner, Mrs Feeney listened to the hiss of gas escaping from a building with the windows blown out. She moved cautiously; the air could explode at any moment. The anticipation of sound hurt her ears. She walked on, sensing the change in the weather, dust swirling, and then from far into the sky, loose droplets of rain began to fall, blotting everything. Mrs Feeney turned her head to the ground and hurried to her house.

The white envelope from the hospital addressed to Mr Feeney stuck out of the letterbox. He hadn't been back since she'd left.

The house felt foreign. The kitchen window had been left open. It was freezing. Out on the line, the clothes hung limp. They would have to be washed again.

Mrs Feeney went into the living room, exhausted. Physical pain lingered. The weakness fell on her all of a sudden. She would have slept if she had been alone, but she had the child. She stared down at the small head bundled against her rib cage, conscious of her own breathing, trying to control it. She didn't want the child to wake up and scream and add to her misery.

Mrs Feeney struggled off the couch and went to the cloakroom under the stairs to get a blanket. The baby stirred and began to cry. It coughed in such an awful choking manner, the tiny hands squeezed into pink fists as the head shook. Mrs Feeney balanced against the wall, cradling the thin neck, letting the lungs spit up on her shirt the same green phlegm the nurse had shown her. They had destroyed her baby. She had kept it safe for nine months, through the time in Limerick, through the trip on the boat, under the stairs in London, and at the end, they had destroyed her child's lungs.

Mrs Feeney cleaned the phlegm from her baby's mouth with her fingers, wiping them on her skirt.

In the kitchen, Mrs Feeney boiled the kettle and took a mixing bowl out from under the sink. She broke a capsule of menthol and swabbed the base of the bowl with the stickness. When the water boiled, she added it to the bowl. The fumes brought tears to her eyes. She took a towel and draped it over her baby's small head. The baby began coughing immediately, struggling against the whiff of menthol inhaled into its small lungs. The damp cloth writhed, the form of the child outlined, the tiny legs kicking. Mrs Feeney held the baby over the bowl for a few minutes, feeling the chest expand and contract. She kneaded her palm into the fat flesh of the baby's back the way the nurse had shown her. The hacking loosened the phlegm.

When the child went limp and wheezed in exhaustion, Mrs Feeney took away the damp towel and wiped the baby's body. It teemed with moisture. She buttoned up the small shirt the hospital had given it. Then she crawled into the cloakroom, took the weight of her breast from under her shirt and set it at the baby's mouth and slept.

Searchlights still lacerated the sky when Mr Feeney came home. There had been no bombings during the night. A dismal silence persisted. The world had become a filthy place where the worst was expected. Mr Feeney cycled through the deserted streets, one hand on his hat as he turned corners into swirling wind. He put his bicycle into the hallway without making a sound. He smelt the menthol.

Mr Feeney retraced his steps, walking backwards. He turned at the door and went out. He blew into his hands, frozen and shocked at what was in the cloakroom, thinking his wife had given birth under the stairs. A certain giddiness went through his body. Still he controlled himself, maintaining a rigorous silence. 'Nature takes its course,' he said to himself, staving off a sense of guilt, trying to preserve his manner.

Mr Feeney came back into the kitchen. He smelt the menthol in the bowl and emptied it into the sink. He put the kettle down, then stepped out into the back garden, putting a brick at the door to make sure the wind didn't slam it closed. He filled the coal bucket with his hand so the shovel didn't scrape the cement and wake his wife and child.

He made the fire on the old bed of ash, placing each lump of coal softly. He went into the kitchen, dipped a bit of paper into lard, and lit it from the cooker. He cupped the flame and took it to the fireplace, fanning it with the flaps of his coat to get a draught going. He went about his business, but he couldn't help but wonder. 'Is it a boy?' he asked himself.

Mr Feeney hadn't the courage to wake his wife. His defence was that his work had kept him away. His lips muttered because he knew he should do something. He had earned money, and that was important, because his family could not survive without it. Mr Feeney found himself nodding his head as he stirred the tea in the teapot.

Mr Feeney leaned into the hole. Everything smelt of shit.

'I need warm water.'

The baby moved on her breast.

Mr Feeney watched her ascend the stairs and then went into the kitchen. He had to lean against the door to support himself, the ebb of fatigue and shock ringing in his head. He brought up a bowl of warm water and stood on the landing. The smell of the child filled the coldness. He tentatively went into the bedroom, set the bowl down on the side table and left without looking at the child or his wife, averting his eyes to the ceiling. 'I'll warm up the breakfast,' he said outside the door, 'Will I?'

'Do that,' Mrs Feeney answered quietly. She listened to him breathing on the landing, standing still. 'Are you still there?' The child wriggled on the bed as she held the two small feet in her left hand like she did when cleaning the inside of a turkey.

She dabbed the warm wet cloth on the bottom.

Mr Feeney hesitated and without answering went downstairs and looked in on the fire, opened the damper in the chimney, waiting for the draught to take.

The first lapse came over Mrs Feeney. He was home at last. The shock of having given birth without anybody there to console her sifted into her head.

'Are you ready up there?' Mr Feeney said softly when everything was prepared.

'I'll be down,' Mrs Feeney answered. She wrapped the baby in a cotton nightshirt.

Mr Feeney turned and answered solemnly, 'I'll bring this in now.' He swallowed, turned, and stared out the window beading with the trapped heat from the gas cooker.

He wished now that he could leave London. It had been a mistake to move as some neutral interloper into this city whose men were dying every day. Everyone knew he was there for only one reason: to get money. At times he felt the most base creature in all London.

Mrs Feeney came down and put the child into a small box near the fire.

Mr Feeney followed her in and set the breakfast onto his wife's lap. His eyes drifted to the small face tucked into the blanket. A faint smile passed over his face, his lips and eyes tensed, but he couldn't bring himself to say anything. He opened his coat because of the heat from the fire. His trousers hung off his bony hips, held up by suspenders. He retreated after a few futile moments to the current of cool air in the hallway. He breathed deep, feeling the separation between them, the calcified silence filled with half-thoughts.

Mrs Feeney balanced her breakfast on her lap. She could see her husband in the mirror. 'When are we going home?' she said.

'Soon.' He came back into the room with his hands firmly around a mug of steaming tea. His hat was still on his head. He cleared his throat finally, and without looking at his wife, said, 'It won't be long now before this whole thing is over . . . The

Germans can't last forever.'

Mrs Feeney crossed her knife and fork, a bead of grease floating aimlessly with each heartbeat.

'The Americans are waiting for the Russians to wear down the Germans . . .' Mr Feeney looked at the fire. 'You see, it's a struggle between the Americans and the Russians now . . . The war's over for the Germans and the English. It's the Americans and Russians who are fighting for the victory.' Mr Feeney took a deep breath. 'That's the way it is now. One struggle ends and another begins . . .' The war had moved beyond violence, into a realm he did not understand.

He seemed to hesitate for a moment. 'Is it a boy or a girl?' he asked. A muscle twitched under his left eye.

'A girl,' Mrs Feeney whispered. 'A girl.' She smiled faintly.

Mr Feeney let his mouth hang vacantly. He went out of the room and into the kitchen and his face tightened, his nostrils pinched back emotion. Their exile had taken on a seamless monotony, and somehow a child had lived inside his wife and grown in those hours of insomnia under the stairs. It reminded him of how his father used to grow mushrooms out in a dark shed, the eerie grey spores feeding on darkness.

Mrs Feeney heard him banging pots and piling up the cutlery into the sink. She waited for him to ease the pressure of his own mania, the struggle to release his feelings in steady work. She knew he would come in again.

Mr Feeney came to the edge of the door, absurdly incongruous with his hands sopping wet from the sink, and his hat still on. 'What do you think of Mary for a name?'

Mrs Feeney said, 'After Our Lady,' and blessed the baby and whispered, 'Mary, after Our Lady. Yes, Mary . . .'

Mr Feeney nodded to himself. 'We'll have to get her baptized. I'll see about a Catholic church.' He turned and then stopped. 'I'll have to be going.'

'I need some things,' Mrs Feeney said.

Mrs Feeney watched Mr Feeney leave on his bicycle.

The first time the district nurse called to the house, Mrs Feeney was unprepared. She had forgotten all about the nurse.

'The child is sleeping,' she said, keeping the door half-closed. 'I only just put her down.'

'Any coughing or congestion?' the woman asked. She wore a raincoat and carried an umbrella. Mrs Feeney could see by the bluish colour in the woman's hands that she'd been out all day long knocking on people's doors.

'Any congestion?' the woman said again. She wrote things down in a book.

'We're getting her baptized as well,' Mrs Feeney said.

The woman had the small earnest face of a finch. 'Blood in the mucus?'

The woman put the book back into her purse. 'I will have to call again. I have to see and examine the child myself.' The woman gave a look more of a silent plea. 'You do understand that I will have to be back.'

'She's sleeping,' Mrs Feeney said resolutely.

The sky looked like rain again. In an hour or so the night would settle, and then all the electricity would go out. It seemed so futile for a woman like this to have come to her door when the bombs would start falling, wounding and killing new victims.

'I will call next Tuesday at noon,' the woman said. 'You will be here then?'

Mrs Feeney closed the door without answering.

Mrs Feeney washed the stained blanket under the stairs and hung it out to dry. She hid under the stairs the following Tuesday. She heard the woman knocking and then heard her voice through the letterbox. 'Mrs Feeney, are you in there? Hello, Mrs Feeney.' The voice echoed in the cold hallway.

The woman stayed for about fifteen minutes. Mrs Feeney could hear her heels on the tiled front steps. The woman left and came back an hour later. Mrs Feeney was barely able to get back under the stairs in time.

'Hello, Mrs Feeney. We had an appointment today. I know you are in there. Your chimney is smoking.'

Mrs Feeney let her baby suckle. Its eyes looked up at Mrs Feeney.

'I shall have to get a constable, Mrs Feeney, if you do not let me in.' The woman persisted for a long time.

Mrs Feeney watched the seam of light under the door turn dark before coming out. The evening had nearly settled. Mrs Feeney pressed her baby to her.

The electricity and the gas went out before Mrs Feeney's meal was fully cooked. The dark took on an added density. She revelled in its obscurity. She was truly alone for the night. She breathed easily. The threat of bombs protected her, a war within a war . . . Mrs Feeney spooned up lukewarm beans from the pot. She hadn't realized how hunger had stalked her. The night air wrapped around her exposed ankles and curled up her legs. The tea didn't draw because the water had never boiled. It tasted weak and cold, mixing with the sweet milk sloshing inside the terrible emptiness of her belly. She would never be the same again. The tender bruise of her pregnancy still ached beneath her skirt, the melancholy cotton cold between her legs.

Mrs Feeney left the dishes on the table and went up to the toilet, locking the door and peeling away her hidden bandage.

The sky was invaded all through the night and into the early morning. Still the doorbell rang the next morning. The baby was coughing in fits. Mrs Feeney held her baby close to her breast under the covers in the bed. The bell rang again. Mrs Feeney hid in her eternity of torment, using her left elbow like a bellows to let an envelope of fresh air flow through a gap in the blankets. The baby sweated profusely, its body trembling. Even Mrs Feeney found it hard to breathe, but she didn't dare come up out of the covers and have her baby's coughing fill the room.

The bell didn't ring again. The baby stopped coughing and nuzzled into Mrs Feeney's breast. Mrs Feeney surfaced again into the warmth of the room. The fire glowed with a bed of coal. When the baby stopped suckling, Mrs Feeney carefully laid her in the box and covered her.

It rained by noon, a heavy downpour that kept people inside. Mrs Feeney felt relieved. The woman would not come to her in this weather.

Mr Feeney arrived home that evening in a foul mood. He set his bicycle in the hallway and took off his soaking coat, hanging it on a hook by the stairs. He had a bad cold.

Mrs Feeney saw he didn't set any money down on the table as he usually did.

Mr Feeney banged around in the kitchen, the pipes hammering with cold water as he filled the kettle. 'Not even a cup of tea, for Christ's sake.'

Mrs Feeney knew the kettle wouldn't boil in time. She waited silently as the lights went out, ready with two red candles which she lit from the fire. 'I have tea in a flask in here if you want it,' she said.

Mr Feeney appeared in the doorway. 'I don't know how much longer this can last.' He banged the door frame.

'What's wrong?'

'At the factory, they're afraid of us . . .' He towelled his head.

'What do you mean?' Mrs Feeney unscrewed the flask and poured black tea into the steel cup. 'Take this.'

Mr Feeney took the tea and stood with his back to the fire. 'They're afraid that we might sabotage things.'

Mrs Feeney looked up at Mr Feeney. 'But they know you . . .'

'They know nothing about me.' Mr Feeney interrupted, raising his voice. 'They've never been comfortable with us around the place. You can't stay neutral in all this. They're getting desperate. They want to know why Ireland is staying out of it.'

Mrs Feeney looked down at her baby.

Mr Feeney filled his cup again and drank the black tea, rocking pensively as he swallowed. 'They're slow to pay us now. When the boats are sailing again, we'll be gone out of this.'

'I boiled some eggs. They're in the cupboard.'

Mr Feeney went into the kitchen. He salted the eggs and ate them beside the fire.

Mrs Feeney watched him. He trembled with a fever, his head dripping with sweat. 'You need to rest,' she whispered.

'We need money,' Mr Feeney answered stiffly. He drank the last of the tea and then inched closer to the hot fire. He slept for a few hours, woke up and went upstairs in the dark and changed his shirt and trousers and came down. His mood softened. He stacked the fire into a great blaze. The chimney roared. He went into the kitchen, opened the condensed milk. He brought Mrs Feeney her glass of milk.

Mrs Feeney took the glass and drank slowly.

'I was speaking with a priest the other day. He says he'll do the baptism in a few weeks.'

Mrs Feeney said, 'Yes.'

'You're to baptize her yourself in the meantime with ordinary water. You say, "I baptize you in the name of the Father, Son, and Holy Ghost, Amen." Do you have that?'

Mrs Feeney repeated the words.

'That'll protect her until she's properly baptized.' The talk dissipated after that. Mr Feeney took off his heavy jumper and used it as a pillow, sleeping on the floor beside the fire.

She lay down beside him, the fear of the woman at the back of her head. They wanted her child. She didn't dare say anything to him, though. Mr Feeney put his arm around her. The fire faintly glowing. They stayed that way for a long time, the soothing sensation of darkness assuaging fear, the smell of smoke, the child beside them. Mrs Feeney was glad to have Mr Feeney home this one time. Mr Feeney rubbed his wife's forehead with his nervous fingers.

He left in the early morning, whispering, 'Remember, "I baptize you in the name of the Father, Son, and Holy Ghost, Amen".'

The woman called again a few days later. Mrs Feeney was in the kitchen with her baby.

'Hello!'

Mrs Feeney held her breath, waiting. The sun in the blue sky outside shone with a faint heat that had been missing for days. It didn't seem a day for war.

'I know you are in there!' the woman said through the letterbox.

Mrs Feeney didn't move, listening to the curious insistence in the woman's voice.

'Mrs Feeney. Is the baby alive?'

Mrs Feeney waited to hear the click of the letterbox closing.

'Is the baby alive?'

Mrs Feeney eased away from the table. The woman would see her if she went around the back of the house and looked in the kitchen window. Mrs Feeney crept into the hallway, and up the stairs to her bedroom.

The woman rang the bell again.

Mrs Feeney took her baby from its box. She pulled back the curtain and looked down on the woman. She tapped on the glass, pointing to the writhing baby in her arms. 'You see, she's fine.'

The woman looked up. 'Mrs Feeney! Let me in.'

'Leave me alone,' Mrs Feeney shouted.

'I'm getting a constable, Mrs Feeney, if you don't let me in.'

'Come next week when my husband is here,' Mrs Feeney said. 'You can see her then.'

The woman left.

Mrs Feeney locked the bedroom door and waited until the evening set. Of course the woman would get tired of this sooner or later. She'd seen the baby was alive. Maybe that was all she'd come for. They could not make her do something she didn't want to do. Mrs Feeney took her baby into her arms. She could not stop herself from crying. She would not give her baby up to them. She would tell her husband that he had to take her away, that people were coming to the house to take the baby away. Yes . . . He would listen to her. He was scared too.

The time of hibernation had come. She ate ravenously, cold

beans, stale bits of bread and boiled eggs, washing it down with sweet condensed milk which dripped down her chin as she drank in gulps.

Just before the gas went out, she boiled the kettle so she could take up the mixing bowl full of water and add the medicine for her baby. She went through the same ritual, but this time after she let the baby breath the vapours she rubbed the water into the soft fatness of the back, greasing the torso, tracing a line of hot wetness between the buttocks, down the doughy legs to the cold little feet. Then she took a scoop of water and baptized her baby.

The bombing started in a world full of moonlight. Mrs Feeney descended again to the cloakroom under the stairs, settled herself and let the baby's small lips take the hard nipple.

Mrs Feeney heard the siren outside, its muffled sound caught by the coats against the door. She pressed her baby to her. The abysmal thunder of bombs continued as she slept. She woke with a soreness in her bladder and bowels, crept into the moonlight in the hallway and up the stairs to the toilet. She heard the baby crying.

Mrs Feeney went downstairs to her baby and closed her eyes again and succumbed to the delirium of prayer, time eclipsed in the darkness of her paralysis. Unconsciousness overtook her in the end.

Mr Feeney found her holding a dead candle in her hand some time later, red wax congealed on her wrists.

The baby was a haunting alabaster, a stiff doll. Mr Feeney eased the cold body out of his wife's arms. Mrs Feeney let go of the child. She did not open her eyes.

Mr Feeney knew she was awake. He said nothing. He moved out of the dark hole under the stairs with the corpse in his hands.

Mr Feeney boiled the kettle out of habit, confused and afraid to do anything. He set the child in its box in the living room and looked at it from the kitchen.

Mrs Feeney came out and went upstairs and changed. Mr Feeney listened to her moving around. Then she came down again.

'There was a woman . . .' Mrs Feeney shivered.

'What woman?'

Mrs Feeney explained.

Mr Feeney put his big hands to his face.

They waited upstairs in silence. Mr Feeney looked out the window occasionally to make sure nobody was coming to the door.

As evening settled, Mr Feeney took a piece of wax paper and wrote in black ink:

Mary Feeney – Baptized a Catholic. RIP

'You baptized her, didn't you?' Mr Feeney stared at his wife. 'Didn't you?'

Mrs Feeney nodded her head.

'Thank God.' Mr Feeney folded up the piece of wax paper and put it between his daughter's small fingers, bringing them together in eternal petition, a father sending a child away with the pragmatism of a note.

Mr Feeney dug a deep hole when night fell, deep enough that his daughter would remain undisturbed.

Mrs Feeney watched him from the kitchen window in the dark. Tears ran into the corners of her mouth. She saw Mr Feeney bless himself.

In the midst of the cold night, Mr Feeney took his wife away from the house. He had his savings well hidden in the lining of his coat. They slept down in the tubes. The next day they went up to Wales until the war was over. They never spoke of England or the baby ever again for the remainder of their long lives.

The Drinker

John McGinty, age 49, of St John's Place died today, Lord rest his soul. The paper said he died of natural causes. He was found in bed by his landlady, Mrs Peggy Doran.

Of course there was the informal inquest around her street. Mrs Doran, having had a dead man of John McGinty's fame in her house, was obliged to give her account of things.

Mrs Doran stated she knew he was dead before she even went upstairs. McGinty had failed to wind the grandfather clock and his work boots were still on the mat inside the door.

Mrs Doran felt McGinty had died at around 4:45 a.m. It seemed odd that she was so sure of the time of death. It even hinted at some impropriety, which did not escape the attention of those who came to listen to Mrs Doran tell her side of it. But Mrs Doran's reasoning went like this: When she found the body, two bottles of stout had been consumed, the empties placed back on the small dresser table beside a third unopened bottle. According to Mrs Doran, it was customary for Mr McGinty to have three bottles of stout before rising from his bed at 5 a.m. This was common knowledge on the street. Therefore, since the two bottles had been successfully placed back on the table, it was to be assumed that Mr McGinty must have been alive and well as he finished the second bottle of stout, and that the suddenness of death must have overtaken him before he reached for the third.

From the brown, sud-coloured vomit on his striped pyjamas and the blood that covered his pyjama bottoms, it appeared to Mrs Doran that Mr McGinty had been in the process of belching when something must have ruptured inside him, poisoning him almost instantaneously, or maybe he'd suffered a massive heart attack. Since the bottles of stout had not been toppled off the rickety little dresser table, Mrs Doran assumed that Mr McGinty had felt nothing. He must have passed out with the shock, 'Thanks be to God.'

And so went the great drinker McGinty into oblivion, the man of whom it was said that he had consumed thirty pints a day, and mind you that was the average, including of course those first years of innocence when he did not know drink (which some have suggested may have ended before his ninth birthday). He told a friend down at his local with a certain nod of sombre dignity, not a boast mind you, that he'd peaked at around forty pints a day in his mid thirties but had then settled back to a modest thirty, due to a combination of financial and medical reasons.

The estimate of total pints consumed, although roughly figured, comes out somewhere in the region of 383,250 pints over a thirty-five year period of full drinking, not including leap years. The average of a pint over those years comes to around seventy pence, which tots up to £268,275.00, or over a quarter of a million pounds. Accounting for inflation and other cost indexes, this quarter million might be worth who knows, in today's terms. But how did Mr McGinty manage the time so as to pour almost a quarter of a million pounds down his throat?

Mr McGinty's routine was unvarying, his life a testimony to stolid drinking principles. He awoke, as has been mentioned, at 4:43, plugged in a small kettle beside his bed to boil water for a wash and a shave, and then commenced to relieve his thirst at 4:45. In the winter he'd drink in utter darkness, feeling for the bottles on the small dresser table. Often he'd even keep his eyes closed, his movements seemingly carried out by some unconscious part of the brain. He had the measure of the distance from the table to his mouth. He'd down the three pints of stout before his feet hit the floor at 5 a.m. And it wasn't his feet that hit the floor first, but his knees. McGinty would slip out of bed and kneel in a minute of prayer.

Despite there being no light in the winter months, he'd know where the kettle was and take it to the sink and begin washing without seeing his face. For some peculiar reason, he never turned on the light in his room in the morning. He'd dress in the dark, taking his work clothes off the brass ornament at the end of his bed, and his shoes out from under the bed.

Throughout the winter months, McGinty didn't shave until he arrived at his work. When spring came, and the sun began to brighten his room, he'd add this one action to his routine, never really adding time to the overall scheme since, with the light coming through his window, he moved, unknown to himself, at a slightly faster pace. And so he found in autumn, winter, spring, or summer, he was always leaving his room at exactly 5:10 a.m.

McGinty started at 6:30, half an hour before the departure of the first Cork train. He could have stayed in bed until 5:30, risen, eaten something light, dressed and cycled the fifteen miles in time for work. But McGinty had his priorities set differently. At exactly 5:40 a.m. on Tuesdays and Thursdays the Guinness lorry pulled up at Mulligan's Pub, on Mondays and Wednesdays at O'Dwyers, and on Fridays at P.J. Clarke's, to collect the old kegs and drop off the new ones. The publicans would be up sorting through the barrels when McGinty'd arrive on his bicycle and give his patent drinking salute, taking his left hand, as though he were holding a pint, and tipping it to his mouth. Not that he didn't know the drink was already pulled, three creamy-headed pints of stout settling on the counter inside. McGinty had come to some unspoken agreement years before with these establishments regarding his drinking practices. He liked the complicity of gestures which he felt were all part of the secret society of drinking men. Horse men had their ways, spitting on handshakes and the like, so he had his way. Drinking was not the mere consumption of stout, but an affectation of both the personal and social aspects of life.

The ponderous affair with the bottles at 4:45 a.m. was now a more rigorously executed manoeuvre. Sitting upright on a stool in proper drinking posture, McGinty'd tilt his head far back on his neck, hold his hat with one hand and pour an entire pint into his stomach without swallowing – what was known as 'down the hatch' in the trade.

McGinty never let the rim of the glass touch his lip. The glass remained an inch or so above his lower lip, turning on an invisible axis at a steady rate until it reached an angle at which only the creamy foam would be left in the glass, the rest having been successfully delivered to the stomach. McGinty consumed three pints of stout in this efficient manner, listening to the background thunder of steel kegs rolling into the cellar beneath him. It was a sound he loved more than any other in his life, apart from the slow, almost silent whispering suck of stout being pulled by a barman and then left to sift into blackness. If there was a heaven, it had a small bar that never closed, set down near the sea.

With the three pints consumed making a total of six, McGinty had sated his thirst and settled his nerves and would begin the remainder of his journey towards work. As he sat on his bicycle in hat and coat, he seemed to defy gravity. His arse literally engulfed the seat as his great sloping back leaned into the hard cycle. McGinty had a way of pushing into the pedals which made his forward motion erratic, and the front wheel wobbled precariously. It seemed McGinty was on the verge of falling off, either because the drink had affected his equilibrium, or because of his massive bulk. When the wind picked up and the rain lashed down, McGinty would tuck his head into the upturned collar of his jacket and, without actually looking ahead, pedal furiously towards his work with the strange felicity that no harm would come his way. It was only the grace of God and the early hour that kept him from a major collision with cars and pedestrians alike.

McGinty had a cushy job at the railroad, although he managed himself with great conscience and, before he dared to venture onto the platform, took himself into a toilet to comb his hair and straighten his tie. He took his job as seriously as he took his drink and could not have lived without either of them. The work and drink created a perfect balance to his waking hours.

His duties consisted of sweeping up the debris on platform

two and opening up the gates for passengers. And McGinty was responsible for hosing away the dirt and waste that had accumulated on the tracks. He'd put on big wellingtons and drag an enormous orange hose from the storage shed down onto the tracks. It was a disheartening sight: a track filled with human shite. The passengers who rode the train didn't have the common decency to refrain from using the toilet while the train was in the station. It formed McGinty's general conception of human creatures as pigs who needed a good dose of religion and the stick to keep them in line.

Once McGinty'd dispensed with this unpleasant duty, he settled himself nicely inside a small office with a kettle, a toaster, and a small heater. It depended on the morning, but if it was cold McGinty'd make himself toast and a cup of tea and take off his work boots and let them dry before the heater. He read the early morning newspaper from cover to cover. The drink from earlier in the morning gave McGinty a lucidity which was quite uncanny. He was a voracious reader of the paper. Nothing else, mind you.

Whatever McGinty read in the newspaper sank into his head. It was as though he had a photographic memory. He could almost repeat what he'd read verbatim. So when the regulars for the morning train finally arrived, McGinty was up and about with his hands behind his back, ready for a chat. Since he'd bought himself a stationmaster's watch years earlier, McGinty had inadvertently added a certain gravitas to his demeanour and exuded an air of authority as he moved around the station. And having also had the advantage of digesting the morning paper, McGinty's talk had a great command of current affairs. He seemed to have an almost prophetic sense of what was going on in the world and arrested people with his sheer insight and candid summation of pressing political or economic issues. And of course when the regulars boarded their trains and began reading the papers, didn't they have the strange sensation that they'd heard all this said before. But the damnedest spectacle of all was that it wasn't that McGinty's words were attributed to what he'd read in the paper, but the other way round. The paper was giving a reasonable account of what McGinty had already stated back on the platform.

By half-nine the first batch of trains had departed for the country, and trains coming up from the country would not be in for another hour and a half. McGinty was due a drink. Others took tea. McGinty crossed over to Tom Foley's bar, The Whistle, a little pub that had been done up like a train with private booths and glass doors that opened and closed, giving a sense of privacy for each party.

It was the only pub McGinty ever went into in his life that had casters under the chair and table legs. It gave the establishment a queer domesticity, the presentiment of a woman's touch. McGinty could never figure it out. 'You didn't know if you should wear slippers or boots,' was how McGinty summed it up.

McGinty came in unnoticed and sometimes saw nobody at all. He'd smell the cabbage and potatoes that had already been put down for the lunch. These few drinks were often the hardest to swallow as the years went by. His liver had become bad. The thing was to keep from going for a piss as long as possible. Once he started, he was up and down for the remainder of the day. There was even a slight hint of incontinence, and by his mid-thirties McGinty had begun a fumbling routine with his hands in his pockets, checking to see that he was dry.

Sometimes McGinty unwrapped an egg or cheese sandwich and ate in slow ponderous bites, looking blankly at his pints of stout. He gave an impression of complete and utter mental vacuity as he sat at the bar, preserving an element of restraint, creating an attenuated ritual between each gulp of stout.

There was no real rush back to the station. The paper had been read and McGinty was not one to ally himself to the paper just for the sake of looking at ease. Boredom broached the stagnant grey light of a winter's day, or a strange longing fell on him during the summer when the sun came through the window and made him hot and his arse sweat. He seemed to be always longing for a cessation to something deep and agitated inside his head, and drink was the only thing which settled him. If he didn't know better, he felt he might have had a slight case of madness, but the drink kept him level, reasonable, and above all amiable, which was the trick to moral sanctity.

Tom Foley was a non-drinker and a fastidious businessman, and when he appeared he set McGinty on edge. His body squeaked when he moved behind the bar. He was forever talking about the demise of the country. McGinty said little and listened with indifference, making a face now and again or rubbing his chin and saying, 'Is that the way it is now? By God, you have it well figured, Tom.'

Their talk hinted at mutual dislike. When Foley saw crumbs on the counter where McGinty had eaten his sandwich, he'd say, 'Do you know we do sandwiches, McGinty?' And McGinty'd answer, 'You've all the angles covered, Tom,' and then repeat it.

But with ten pints in him by half-ten, McGinty had the upper hand on life. McGinty was in fine form once he found his feet and the door and continued where he'd left off with his assessment of current affairs back at the station. His face shone like a polished apple and he was forever rubbing his hands together, which meant he was all business. But since the passengers had already read the papers by then, McGinty's comments were taken as rehashed, inarticulate tripe. McGinty was aware but talked on all the same. He'd reached a plateau of stupefaction that could be masked by a smile. He'd even untuck his shirt tail to further his comic effect. McGinty was conscious that he was the first or the last thing people saw, depending on whether they were coming or going. His presence defined the city for literally thousands of people. This was where McGinty took meaning from his life. It heightened his sensibility to the things around him, and he lived, not as himself, but as a caricature of his city.

Once the passengers left, it was countdown to the noon dinner, and over the course of the next hour McGinty would flick open his stationmaster's watch, edgy to get on with things. He continued to pace the station.

McGinty had what was known in the trade as 'a feed of drink' for his dinner down at Johnny Donovan's. He arrived with his coat under his arm and his shirt untucked, his tie loosened and his hat set far back on his head. A table remained reserved for him next to the window, and, with the bustle of life around him, he felt in his element. The pub had a low ceiling supported by sagging crossbeams where subdued bulbs glowed faintly in a soft constellation of light. Dampness lingered everywhere, and when the rain fell the sawdust on the floor clumped and stuck to patrons' shoes, and everything smelled of horses.

Two pints awaited him in the interim before the dinner appeared, the first of which he drained in one gulp even before taking off his heavy grey coat.

McGinty then sat himself down to interrogation by those around him. He was, to all concerned, 'the man himself', 'no better man', 'a gas man', 'a desperate man', 'a sound man'. He shook hands like a politician, rising from his small table to greet them with a great bib of a handkerchief tucked in at his neck to protect his work clothes from the onslaught of eating. 'And how are you keepin' yourself?'

'Not bad, and yourself?'

He made full effect of his great weight and displayed a physical marauding prowess, letting his fat hand slap down on the backs of men, making them both nervous and glad to be associated with him.

'How many has it been this morning, McGinty?'

McGinty was well aware that suggestion and not facts added to his mystique. He'd cast a dismissive glance at whoever'd asked him and say, 'Ah, sure you know yourself. The usual, the usual,' then take the second pint to his lips and pour half of it into himself.

'You're a terrible man. It's a wonder you're still standing at all.'

'Leave McGinty in peace,' Johnny Donovan shouted on cue

from behind the bar as he brought out McGinty's dinner. 'He has a schedule to keep. There's people that work for a living in this world.'

McGinty'd smile and rub his hands together and say with feigned seriousness, 'McGinty'd better eat, I suppose.' Before commencing his meal, he first lined his stomach with a glass of lukewarm milk with ceremonial resolve. This added to the mystique of his drinking, the small provisions he needed to incorporate into his routine.

Then McGinty cut out the messing and got stuck into the pints along with a slap-up meal of potatoes, veg, a cut of meat and a dessert. He divided his drink into battalions, two pints, one on either side of the dinner, which he guzzled in quick succession before and after eating. He reserved two more pints, which contained stirred up eggs and milk, for the dinner, and mixed this in with the potatoes, turning them brown and runny. These curdled pints he considered medicinal. Then he scooped up the peas and studded the whipped potato with them.

People usually glanced at him as he ate alone at his small table, orchestrating his dinner with fork and knife, his big feet planted firmly on the ground as he proceeded to top up his drinking glass from the other pints surrounding him.

'Is is true youse were found abandoned down at the Guinness Brewery and they raised youse, McGinty?'

McGinty looked up and cocked his head, and when he winked his whole face folded into a series of ruddy puckers.

After a dessert of custard and stewed apple, McGinty had one final pint with a splash of raspberry for good measure, which was pulled fresh and brought to him with the compliments of the owner. McGinty would hold the pint up and nod towards the bar, holding his hat steady on his head as he cocked it back and murdered the pint. He finished the gesture with resounding finality, banging the glass on the table and wiping his mouth with the sleeve of his coat, and finally blessing himself. There was never a more wholesome summation of life's pleasure than McGinty after a meal, or so people believed. McGinty's eyes took on a myopic glassiness, and his teeth, which were always too big for his mouth, showed in a grotesque false laugh of mashed potato and spittle. It went on for years in this manner, and over the course of time people began a pilgrimage of sorts to see the great drinker McGinty in action.

Despite the visible inebriation of a man burdened with seventeen pints in him, McGinty'd set his huge hands on his knees and rise with exaggerated effort, shirt undone.

Then it was off to the Turf Accountants for the quick bet. Although McGinty took particular joy in the bravado back at the pub, the strain of drink on his insides created a fierce, almost blinding pain which sometimes brought him to the point of passing out, especially as he grew older and his stomach swelled. The dull stupor of the drink finally made him numb. His left leg had taken on the greenish, mouldy colour of sweating cheese. 'Jasus,' McGinty said to himself, shaking inside a stall in the betting shop with his trousers around his ankles. He knew men who'd had to have legs amputated because of the drink . . . Would it come to that? The latter years were spent in the stalls, spitting up his undigested dinner into the foul dirty hole of the toilet. He was passing a pinkish piss and knew his insides were in bits. But he had charted a stubborn course and would see it to its end. On wet days, McGinty found himself watching the horses on the ol' black and white, nodding along with the other men in the pub next door. Some men's penchant was the horses, his was the drink. His eyes wandered from the telly as he gathered his two pints and went to the open door, farting silently beneath his greatcoat, letting the smell dissipate as he watched the mesmerizing rain fall in long scratches in the cold dampness of a Dublin day.

The remainder of the day at work passed with him hosing down the empty tracks again and scrubbing the thick globs of congealed diesel glistening in standing pools of water. When finished with this, McGinty went into the shed, shut the door and stretched out on the ground and slept until it was time to leave.

At 2:45 p.m. McGinty got off work, fifteen minutes before the end of the dreaded 'Holy Hour' when the pubs were closed. The pubs around the area were surrounded by regulars, scarlet-faced with bloodshot eyes, great swayback men with hands deep in their pockets, waiting for 'the cure.'

The White House stood in relief against the grey stone of other buildings. A streak of brown ran down from an upper window, giving the façade a strange human sadness. McGinty maintained the habitual silence of men who are thinking of other things, saluting without words, taking his place against the wall as if sentenced to a firing squad.

The church bell always liberated them, and the heavy bar behind the wooden door scraped on metal as the owner opened the door. McGinty followed a herd of men down a few steps into the dark hold of a sour-smelling pub.

Unlike the other, low ceilinged pubs, the White House had a barren austerity, a floor of uneven polished stone and tall walls that reached into rafters of giant wooden beams. A huge mirror over the fireplace gave the illusion of the pub being bigger than it was. It had survived from the eighteen hundreds and preserved the minimalism of famine times, devoid of chairs, but with round high tables at elbow level fringed with marks from pint glasses. The pub had been part of a big stable years past, and men held the old rings for tethering horses spaced throughout the pub for balance as the night progressed.

A Saint Bridget's cross above the mirror provided the lone reminder that this was a country of Christian drinkers.

The enigmatic symbiosis of drink, religion, and poverty created a subversive and insular world inaccessible to outsiders. McGinty had a presentiment of the history that ran through his and others' blood, all of them bound up in the intimacy of stone encasing a space in which to hide. McGinty drank, as others did, amid a murmuring whisper of words which sometimes settled into silence. The spare word or tacit mute acknowledgement when someone came in might threaten to break into a discussion, but ended abruptly in an uncertain and sullen heaviness of half-closed eyes. There was nothing to say at all, not about politics or religion or the disastrous state of the country. The men felt the burden of tradition in the wake of changing times. McGinty knew he and these other men were the last of a rare part of the city's drinking history.

McGinty's drinking slowed over the few hours he spent at the White House. He stared into each pint, letting it sit indefinitely. He preserved an aura of sombre exhaustion, and pretended, like so many others there, to sleep for minutes at a time. But his hands would be reaching into his pockets to feel for any wetness. He'd become terrified of having an accident. To lose control of his bladder would be the end of him. He'd even gone to the library and looked up a picture of a bladder, just so he would have a mental picture of what he was concentrating on.

As the evenings progressed, McGinty'd turn and face the clusters of standing men and look towards the fogged-over window. Not a sound reached them from outside once the door was shut, except for the slow trundle of a cart which sent a trembling pulse through pints lined up on the bar.

'How's it looking out there?'

A face would turn and lean against the cold glass and wipe away the moisture. 'Holding its own.'

McGinty drank six pints at most at the White House and by seven o'clock stepped back onto the narrow streets.

From there McGinty headed back on his bicycle, settling his heavy body for the long fifteen miles towards his home and one of the bars in which he'd begun his drinking earlier that morning. McGinty liked the circularity of his day, beginning and ending at the same point. It broached some sort of philosophy which McGinty never bothered to articulate, just felt. The long road home rose and fell close to the sea, assaulted by blustering gales and slanting rain laced with salt. McGinty dug deep into the pedals, the burn of fatigue in his thighs, his lungs aching, his legs shaking and his blood polluted with stout. This exertion intensified the tremulous effect of the drink and made his brain spin. By the end he was forced to pedal with one leg, the other had died on his body, gone gammy, swollen almost to twice the normal size, his heavy boot unlaced to allow for the massive toes with the blackened nails. He was seen wobbling all over the road, using only the good leg, raising his arse up off the seat absurdly with a hideous effort on his giant face.

On stormy nights, McGinty had to dismount and push his bicycle up the steep rises until the road split away from the sea. Then he veered inland along the small hedged roads, almost sheltered from the force of the wind.

In the pubs out his way he found a final security against the night. The long strain of the day's drinking ended among another breed of silent men: farmers who regarded drink the way McGinty did. He liked to watch the grimacing pleasure of these men in suits and ties taking a pint to their mouths.

McGinty'd sit close to the fire, leaning on a stool, the bad leg stretched out, the flaps of his coat hanging on either side. Another day coming to an end. He stared out at those around him, his eyes moving slowly, fagged with tiredness, the pasty yawn of terrible fatigue, his insides gone to bits. Over the last weeks the slow poison in his leg palsied the left side of his body. His head flinched and his eye began to twitch uncontrollably like a man edging to tell a dirty joke. McGinty battled on though, following faces and conversation, feeling the intensity of shadows, men moving unsteadily into strips of light, faces and eyes strained and wrinkled, ruined faces and strange blue eyes.

McGinty breathed softly. He'd see things to the end. He was moving slowly towards immobility, he knew as much. He turned his tongue inside his mouth, the amber glow of flame caressing his face. In these moments, McGinty felt he'd lived the happiest life a man could ask for and drank the last five pints of his day slowly, savouring the dark flavour, listening to the wind whistle and pull on the door, the fire crackling softly. He had a few whiskeys in the end, Power's and Paddy's, no better medicine for a quick departing. He let it burn the bag deep in his stomach.

The sheer inertia of sitting in these hillside pubs filled him with contentment, the slow unfurling of time measured in the moments of waiting for a pint to settle. There was never a minute's complication, the repetitive nature of life most comforting. Literally years of his life had accumulated in this way, and he could honestly say that during those moments he'd thought of absolutely nothing.

McGinty's life progressed in this unfailing manner without incident until the morning when Mrs Doran, upon rising and going into the hallway, saw the clock unwound, and, blessing herself, knew before she went upstairs that McGinty was dead in his bed.

The Inheritance

The vague solipsism of my father's latter years ended in melancholic inevitability, a quiet death beside the fire, the morning paper tucked in beside him. I flew home to sort things out and bury him.

I had the unenviable position of arriving after a long absence, with the eyes of relatives and distant associates of my father watching me. I insisted my wife not be there. There is an essential animosity underlying these funerals.

There were two kinds of people at the funeral. The first contemplated either hell or heaven, looking down at the grave or heavenward. They had ceased to live among the living. These were the infirm, in varying stages of decrepitude. Many of them used canes to help them move about.

The second had a more gregarious earthliness. They talked in tight black circles, easing apart in a hideous blossom of cunning faces when I came with my hand extended. I knew they were speaking of my long absence with furtive bitterness, how I had abandoned my father and mother. I was the exile. Still, I disarmed them by calling them by their names, a trick I'd learned from a man who told me that was how to confuse a dog.

To tell the truth, if I could have got away with it, I would rather have sent flowers and been done with it. However, prudence prevailed; there was, after all, the modest inheritance of the house to consider.

During the funeral, Mrs Bennet, the woman I'd paid to take care of my father for the past few years, began this keening noise, something which I thought should have been left as the prerogative of bereaved relatives. I was reduced to the silent provocation of making eyes and faces in her general direction as she continued to whinge and sniffle. I actually had to circle the grave, tipping my hat at two gravediggers, having them move. I took the woman's shaking hands in my open palms. I felt the bones in her fingers, stiff and cold like brittle twigs. 'We will go to the house after the funeral and talk,' I whispered.

She recovered her senses after the invitation to the house, and reverted to a more docile demeanour.

By the time it was all over, I had upstaged my father, the corpse, and made a magnanimous speech about faith and eternity, of transcendent love, looking directly at my accusers who shied away.

The affair ended with a yellow tractor spluttering out of a shed to bury my father. The gravediggers had only been props.

I travelled with Mrs Bennet in the company of a distant relative who had to get back to work, but who had obliged and taken me home. He mentioned something about another mutual relative who was not doing so good. It seemed my distant relative was regularly attending funerals, signing registers, securing what I felt must be a solid turnout for his own death.

My relative spoke about the weather. Apparently it had been a particularly wet winter.

Mrs Bennet preserved a dignified silence, staring out the window, stiff and compact. I could see she was waiting to say something.

She wanted me to know how it had happened, to put me at ease, that is what she said when we entered the house. She began with the over-anxious disposition of someone accused of a crime, exuding an obsequiousness that can only be dismissed in the aged. I would have stopped anybody else from proceeding, but I could do nothing with her.

Using her hands in an almost pleading manner, she put them to her lips, touching her temples, raising them in the air, and of course blessing herself at every mention of my father's name and appending it with 'God rest his soul'. I could see she had been rehearsing what she would say to me.

I tried to interject, to stop her again. I touched my head with a subtle hint at a headache.

She persisted. She seemed to be accounting for and justifying her own actions on that grim day. I had the strange feeling of being some impassive inquisitor. I didn't know how to put her mind at rest and dismiss her without a scene so I stood there, presiding over my own indecision.

Mrs Bennet explained how she'd been boiling potatoes out in the kitchen at noon on the fateful day. It had been raining, on and off. She'd been watching for showers since the clothes were out on the line. She pointed to a fogged window over the sink. I dipped my head and acknowledged that one would have to go out the back to see if it was raining. We even stepped out to the line, through the small passageway at the back of the kitchen.

The garden had the unsettling smell of decaying onions. It almost brought tears to my eyes.

Mrs Bennet kept talking.

Seeing my father's shirts and socks still on the line sent an unnerving shiver up my spine. This last baleful task would be left to me. I would take them in under cover of dark.

Mrs Bennet continued with her chatter, pointing to the disadvantage of the small window and the constant fog on the glass which prevented her from seeing the sky overhead. 'You see, I have to go back and forth. Back and forth, you see.'

I bit my lip and made a face that approximated concern. The tedium of her explanation gave me a dull throbbing headache. I had not slept in two days since the news.

The door slammed behind us when we came in from the yard. 'We had more broken windows with that wind. I had a man put in a plastic window in the door last year.'

I knew she said this to everyone; her words gave a somnambulant impression of *déjà vu*. I have this feeling that there are only so many words and sentences allotted to each individual; a repetitiveness sets in after a finite number of years. We are all limited creatures.

'I sent you the bill for the window last year,' she continued. 'You remember?'

'Yes, I remember.' I didn't. I conceded she earned her money though, obliquely acknowledging the contingencies in her routine. She got things done, she had conceived of plans, of schemes, she was no different from anybody else. Her life existed within the confines of my old house. Part of my life had existed here. I had learned how to walk and talk, to read and write, within these walls.

Mrs Bennet reminded me of some rigged-up machine which somehow miraculously keeps going. She deserved credit though. She'd maintained the house, my inheritance.

For that, I endured further elaborations, if only to allow her to exorcise herself, supposing that death for her kind possessed an essential mysticism. She was performing a personal ritual. I followed in her wake, out of place, feeling the marginalizing effect of so many years away. She even showed me the pot in which the potatoes had been boiling, and the gas ring on which the pot had been set when my father died. She actually transformed the nondescript pot into an artifact which would forever be associated with my father's death. I feigned an appropriate civility. I conceded these things to her. After all she'd been with my parents the past six years, there at my mother's death, and with my father at his end. I actually touched the pot in a most affecting manner, running my fingers over the steel handle, and smelt potatoes and my father's death.

'He'd even begun the crossword puzzle,' she said, taking up the folded newspaper in the sitting room.

I lagged behind, then offered up some dismal attempt at conversation, 'He liked crossword puzzles,' but broke off at that. I had only seen him once in the last two years.

I excused myself and trudged upstairs to the toilet. There were small tubes of ointment lined up at the end of the bath, some with the handwritten directions still on them from the chemist. It was my money which had bought these things. I washed my hands in freezing water, opened the window, felt the air fill my nostrils and then went down again.

Apparently, there were no words passed, no shout or cry for help from him when he died. She assured me of his peaceful death. Only a stain where the tea had fallen from his dead hands marked his passing. She pointed to the stain. She even sat in his chair, and re-enacted what must have happened. The fidelity to detail had a macabre quality. She was acting my father's death in the very chair in which he'd died. I could see her groping for words, for an expression. I remained steadfast in silence, indolent witness to this mimicked requiem. I had a heaviness in my chest. The incense from the funeral and the dampness out at the grave seemed to have settled in my lungs. I found myself shivering again. My clothes bunched at my crotch. The cold had not left my hands from the freezing water. I needed to strip off and curl up under the blankets and sleep for a long time.

'. . . like that,' Mrs Bennet said softly. Her hand stiffened on her lap, and then her wrist turned. I had not caught what she'd been saying before that. 'It fell like that, you see. The cup, it fell like that. He must have been holding the cup and then . . .' I traced the invisible fall of the cup. Tiredness conspired to predispose me to this sort of attenuated nostalgia. I stared at the dark stain in the rug and had to sit down.

I closed the door behind her after we had tea and bread, but not before she had asked me what would become of the house. She said it in a most suspect manner, almost expecting me to have known something. Her watery eyes set on me and blinked. She seemed set like stone for a moment, something immovable.

I gave some evasive answer. No, I yawned, then stood up, resolute on escorting her from the house. I had conceded enough to her. Thanking her for her services, I bent forward and put my cheek to her cold leathery cheek, in what must have resembled the kiss of Judas, for she flinched at the finality of this gesture and threw back, leaving me pouting at thin air. 'I'll be there for the reading of the will,' she said obstinately. 'Your father asked me to be there for the reading of the will.'

You can't be aggravated at those who mind the infirm, those who take over the vigil of your dying parents while you stay among the living with your own wife and children. Money cannot adequately compensate: the feeding and bathing, picking out the clothes for another useless day confined to a chair. They say the infirm talk constantly, or demand things at least, enforcing their presence in any manner they can find. Their life only affirmed through the action of others who must be paid, which must make it all the more horrible.

'Your father asked me to be there,' she said again. She was standing before me. 'I thought he told you?' Her small bony hands gripped the back of the chair, the shrunken aspect of her face chicken-like, jerking on the stalk of her neck. She said, 'He told me he wrote to you.'

'I received nothing,' I answered. I yawned and tears came into my eyes. 'You must forgive me. I had a long journey.'

She remained resolute, though she shifted her legs and made a movement with her lips. Her head moved slowly toward me, the eyes straining. She had a thin skin over her eyes, as if she suffered from cataracts.

'I received nothing,' I said again, putting up my hands. 'Nothing.' I shook my head. What other gesture did she want. I lingered in this dreary immobility, wanting to wear her down with my own melancholy.

'He told me he wrote to you,' she insisted, an evocation of fear and animal stubbornness. I had the strange notion that she was not going to move from the spot, that I could go to bed and get up again and she'd still be there. I could do nothing to prevent her. Things that I was not even aware of had been set in place and would prod me into predetermined action.

I acquiesced in a most deferential manner. 'If it was my father's wish, I see no reason why not.' It would be somewhat uncomfortable with her present at the reading of the will, but the whole death needed a point of discernible agitation. She would serve that function.

She showed herself to the door.

My wife arrived a few hours later by taxi. I had only sterling on me. I had to go next door and borrow the money from a neighbour I'd dated over twenty years earlier, part of that inevitable pairing of neighbours' children. She'd been a sort of training in sexuality. I had always managed to avoid her on my visits, checking at the window before going out, but here she was before me with sagging breasts and greying hair. She offered her condolences, took me into the hall, went upstairs and returned with the cash. I saw what I assumed was her son peering at me from a door leading to the kitchen. 'If you need anything, milk or tea . . .'

'Thank you . . .' I hopped the hedge in a sudden moment of athletic exuberance, a reflexive action at seeing how old she'd become. We were all aging, all of us.

My wife took the hop as part of the funeral-induced numbness. I dispatched the taxi man without a word.

Only the tips of my wife's fingers touched me when we went inside and shut the door. 'The children are staying with my mother,' she whispered. 'I have a few days off work.' She had brought down a loaf of brown bread, tomatoes, and ham, which she set on the table. It reminded me of when we were first married. It was good that the night's provisions could be still carried in a plastic bag, it took away the unbearable weight of the day's obligations. There are journeys which must be undertaken without possessions.

We had tea and bread in weightless silence. My wife got up and answered the phone and told someone that my father had passed away. I hesitated and scanned the table for crumbs with my finger, turning a poultice of bread with my tongue. She was dressed in a navy business suit, with a tight skirt down to her knees. Despite the skirt's formality, it preserved the beguiling shape of womanhood. My eyes lingered on her. I knew other men stared at her in this way, but only with those sidelong glances which are allotted the sexes these days.

My wife turned and looked at me, and frowned at the phone and gave the full address of my father's house. I listened to the authority in her business voice, a voice she never used with me.

She put down the black receiver and came in and touched

me again on the shoulder. 'You must be tired.' Her hair brushed against my face.

I stiffened. 'I am.'

She produced two miniature bottles of whiskey, the kind you get on planes. 'It will make you sleep.'

I looked at her and nodded. She had imagined it just as it was unfolding before her now.

'Don't you want me to warm it?'

I shook my head. She poured the contents of both bottles into a glass.

It was custom to have the curtains drawn, which Mrs Bennet had done, and when the night fell, the house went into utter blackness. My wife got up and turned the light on in the hallway. I let her do these things for me, looking out at her from the dark of the kitchen, imagining her looking at the outline of my body holding the glass of whiskey.

'I should call the boys.' I didn't see her mouth move.

'Yes,' I answered. 'I'll speak with them tomorrow. Tell them I'm sleeping.' The whiskey burned my throat.

My wife touched me with this ephemeral tenderness again as I passed, like someone touching bruised fruit. I could hear my son's voice in the receiver.

I went upstairs, my fingers finding the railings, anticipating the creaks in the stairs, the subconscious memory of distant years retrieved from the recesses of my brain, as though this knowledge would be needed again, as it was now, for this one last time that I would spend in the house of my birth, the house of Mother's death, the house of Father's death. Then it could be forgotten forever.

I felt a twinge in my left buttock as I reached the landing. I would no doubt be limping tomorrow for that sudden bravado of jumping over the hedge.

I stood still in the uninhabitable landing space. It had been left undecorated. Even my parents, who had packed the house with little pictures, frilly curtains, lamps, chairs, small porcelain figurines, and a sideboard filled with two full china sets, had abandoned this cold boxed space to nothingness. There had been no attempt at transition between upstairs and downstairs, no slow metamorphosis.

The sheet smelt damp and vaguely of detergent. The faded wallpaper was coming unstuck at the corner above the window.

My wife drew the curtains back. I could barely make out her shape as she moved softly. I felt her lie beside me in her slip, leaning softly into me with the timid expectation that is shown to those in mourning.

I closed my eyes tight, almost holding my breath.

She had this unflagging romantic ideal about love. She believed you came through life by premeditated action, a good plan. I had the strange suspicion she was acting out something she had read in one of her romantic novels or from an article in one of her eminently practical women's magazines, 'When your husband has suffered a grave loss.' I felt her breath on the back of my neck, her warm hand touching my stomach and then settling further down.

I found myself erect, flinching, almost embarrassed like a schoolboy. I have always contended that the body does what it likes. This was a sad case of the tail wagging the dog.

I swallowed and turned over, mumbling something. She took this turgid impropriety as a moment of ubiquitous longing, tugging gently at my lose sack of testicles. They churned of their own accord. The romantic novels were right, quote, 'a man in the wake of death has an almost sub/ unconscious longing to procreate. It is part of his evolutionary nature.' The women's magazines confide that 'You should be attentive to your partner's needs.'

I could do nothing, a prisoner within the didactic sway of romantic fiction. And the whiskey had its incapacitating effect. I had taken it like a good child takes its medicine. I had been primed for this moment. Our lives are dictated, not by philosophy, not by great literature, by Shakespeare and Milton, but by pulp fiction where even the authors prefer to remain nameless because this is no one person's story, it is life.

My wife put her fingers to my lips. We stayed like that for a few moments. I couldn't see her face, then she moved delicately, drawing her slip up to her waist with her other hand. I felt her legs part, trapped hot air rising in the darknes from between the heavy blankets, and did, if not what comes naturally, what was expected of me, letting her tongue enter my mouth while I eased into another space.

When it was over she eased away, taking back possession of her tongue, and I slipped from her. She hesitated, then without a word went out to the toilet to clean herself. I listened to the wheel of the toilet-paper holder turning.

An unnatural yellowish light drifted into the darkness. I lay on my side, looking up at the faded, indecipherable wallpaper, dog-eared above the window, vaguely conscious of this monstrous page set before my eyes. My neck craned to make sense of it. I drew myself up in the bed, and then the light in the bathroom went out again without a sound.

The Rain in Kilrush

It had been raining for over a week when Maguire kicked his wife in the back and threw her down the stairs. He stopped himself after that, shut the bedroom door behind him and slept.

It was dark by the time Maguire heard the knock on the door. He tasted the tears in his snot, brought up phlegm from his chest and held it in his mouth. He waited for a moment, laid out on his back in his grey suit. Wind whistled through the windows, drains spluttering outside. He stayed quiet, feeling the invisible damp web of humidity that followed the long downpours of the cold winter months. The fresh smell of rain had disappeared by the third day.

Again the knock on the door. 'Dad, are you awake?'

It would have been better if he'd been left to sleep through into the morning. Maguire heard the feet on the stairs. He closed his eyes.

A timid head looked in through the dark. 'Dad?'

Maguire turned his head and let the phlegm into the sheet and wiped his heavy lips. 'Where is your mother?'

The boy came into the room and hesitated. 'Downstairs.'

Maguire heard the fear in the voice.

'She's sick,' the boy said softly, the words subsumed by the dull static of rain on the corrugated roof of the animal shed.

Maguire broke the rhythm of the rain. 'You're an awful cunt, you are.'

The boy stopped. Darkness coagulated in the corners. Then he spoke again. 'She's hurt.' His voice cut through the pure cold in the room.

'Are you making tea?' Maguire said, to gain control of the situation.

'She's sick,' the boy repeated.

'Are you making tea?' Maguire raised his head as though

about to get up.

The boy instinctively moved back. 'If you want it.' The boy had a face that inspired pity, like a creature half-formed. A prominent belly stuck out above his thin legs, making him look like a little aged man.

'Well, go on with the tea then,' Maguire said finally.

The boy disappeared and closed the door.

Maguire lit a cigarette and stayed on his back, smoking. He inhaled the cigarette and curled the hot smoke with his tongue. 'I only pushed her,' he whispered to himself, making the motion with his hand. The dark consumed the gesture. 'It was nothing at all.'

It wasn't the first time Maguire had hurt his wife. But he had never touched her face. He had that much restraint and judgment. All her injuries were covered by coarse wool jumpers. Even he had never seen his wife's injuries.

It was the boy who started it. Ah, yes, he remembered now how it had started – her siding with the boy as usual, the two of them down there. The little cunt could do nothing right, running under the tails of his mother's skirt. Wasn't he lucky enough to have only the one? Thank God for small miracles that a flying kick had served as a crude form of contraception years past. Imagine being stuck with a pack of cunts down there after him now, and there were fathers he knew, right enough, who couldn't lay a hand on anyone for fear of being beaten up in their own house. Now there was a shocking state of affairs for you . . .

Maguire heard noise downstairs. He strained to hear her voice. God knows what she was about downstairs, conspiring as usual for sympathy with the boy. They should have let him sleep.

Something scurried across Maguire's ankle. He gave a sudden start and felt whatever it was moving toward his knee. He sat up and brought the glow of the cigarette to the leg. Insects crept across his ankle. Maguire grabbed his leg, crushing them underneath his trousers. 'Cunts.' Maguire looked up and saw spiders on the ceiling. The heavy rains had

131

driven the insects to seek the shelter of his house. It had rained like this only one other time in all Maguire's life, when he'd been a boy.

The stairs creaked, a cup trembling on the saucer. The boy put his head into the room again.

'I'm coming down.' Maguire steadied himself, drew down the last of the cigarette and stubbed it out on a saucer by the bed. 'I'll take the tea downstairs.' He gave a sigh of dissatisfaction, showing that he wasn't going to be bamboozled into getting up in the night to say sorry. He sat up into the threshold of the light from the landing.

The boy's face stayed in shadow as he stood in the doorway, his hands drawn together with the saucer like someone in prayer.

'I'll have it downstairs. Do you hear me?'

'Vomiting, she is,' the boy said, almost defiantly.

'Go on down, I said.' Maguire caught the tone.

The boy went downstairs reluctantly, stopping to look back at his father.

'Vomiting.' Maguire muttered the word to himself. He knew as much. A concussion – that was what she probably had. That's what the doctor called it the last time. Ignorant ol' bollocks who'd dared to put questions to him about what had happened to her. Jasus Christ. 'She fell down the stairs, can't you see for yourself, Doctor?' Thank God he had the boy primed beforehand to parrot the 'fell down the stairs' business. They rehearsed it going down on the tractor. Maguire threatened to kill the boy, to drown him out in the well if he didn't say what he was told and nothing else. Of course, the doctor saw the imprint of Maguire's size elevens on her back, but Maguire stood there with the conviction of ownership and brazened things through. The doctor wanted to keep her in for 'observation.' There was one for the books for you, 'observation,' if you don't mind. 'By God, Doctor. We couldn't leave her here. Meself and himself would starve without her.' It had taken all of Maguire's farmer's gall to get out of that one, his big brown coat cinched above his hips, the dirty wellingtons, his knotted stick for herding animals like an extra appendage to underscore his persistence. But Maguire didn't fancy another standoff with the doctor. He wasn't one to run against a stone wall. And of course the wife had the brothers in the area who'd have to be contended with if he ever came under suspicion. Though, who'd want her back? He took solace in that at this stage. Still, it was a delicate situation all round. Maguire knew he was too quick with the fist. Too bloody quick, his own worst enemy . . .

Maguire let his eyes adjust, hesitated at the top of the stairs. Two sandbags were pressed up against the front door, but the rain seeped into the house around the edges of the walls and where the concrete floor had cracked. The fire in the grate turned the flowing water to a strange, shifting, sanguine pool.

Maguire's wife was far enough away from the fire that the light didn't fall on her. Maguire moved close. She had her head down on the kitchen table. The plates were still on the table from the dinner. A red basin for the dishes was set beside her. Maguire could smell vomit in the basin.

The boy stood with the tea steaming on the far end of the table. 'Here, Dad.'

Maguire took the cup and moved away. The cold rain ate into his bones. He gave a bewildered shudder and went over to the window. It was clotted with flies drawn to the weak light inside. The animal shed was barely visible. He could hear the animals inside, though. He knew they had been locked up all day and left unfed. Wanting to grab at the boy, he said nothing, waiting for a few moments.

'Arrah, come on with you now, woman.' Maguire said softly, turning from the window, smiling, his hands up in a manner of forgiveness. 'Sure, you're all right, love.' He went over to his wife and stretched his hand out across the dimness to touch her.

His wife said nothing.

Maguire withdrew his hand and squeezed the cup nervously. 'Come on, will you? For the love of God it's over and done with now. Don't make a production out of this.' He tried to laugh it off. 'What more do you want? Amn't I sayin' sorry to you?'

Again nothing. Maguire moved, sending ripples through the rainwater that seeped silently in under the door.

The noise of the animals in the shed aggravated Maguire. 'They weren't fed, were they?' Maguire looked at the boy.

The boy hesitated, 'I was watching her . . .'

'Anything to get out of a day's work. Should they pay out there for the ignorance inside this house? I've a mind to throw the both of you out with what you've done to me, do you hear me, you ungrateful pup? And to leave those animals out there with nothing to eat . . .'

'It's her head,' the boy said meekly.

'Will you shut your face! If you'd the mind to take care of what concerns you, you'd do better. Don't think I don't know you're a pair in this together. Neither of you would work to warm yourselves if there wasn't a boot up your arse!' Maguire let his voice rise, casting a look at his wife to see her reaction. She hadn't moved. He knew he had damaged her at that moment. It had been hours since he went at her.

The boy stood silently in the stale yellow light.

'Let's see you then.' Maguire went over and touched his wife's shoulder. She didn't move, inert, slumped forward on the table. He pressed his enormous head before her. His big hands found a lump behind her left ear. He eased her back in the chair. 'Let me see you, woman.'

Her eyes rolled, her head lolling on her swollen neck, bruised in patches of blackness the colour of potato blight. Maguire's face tightened. 'Can you hear me?'

She half-looked at him and then leaned forward. Maguire held her chin with one hand as she vomited into the red basin.

'How long has she been like this?'

The boy began crying.

'How long?' Maguire insisted. 'Come here to me, son.'

The boy moved through the pooling water, disturbing its colours.

'How long?' Maguire could barely speak.

'Dad, she's not going to die, is she, Dad?'

'Now listen to me.' Maguire could barely speak, his heart racing under his coat. 'How long?'

'She's not going to die, Dad, is she?'

The boy gave out a rat's squeal as Maguire grabbed him by the hair. 'How long has she been like that?'

'Since you went up,' the boy spluttered.

'Christ al-fuckin-mighty! And you left her there all this time, you ignorant cunt! It'll be on your soul if anything happens to her. Do you hear me? Mark my words, it'll be you they'll be after for this.'

'I didn't do anything. I didn't know . . .'

Maguire raised his fist but stopped himself.

'I've medicine out in the shed for her!' Maguire said, putting on a heavy coat and pulling the sandbags away from the door. 'Watch her.' He took his torch and went out. A tide of sediment rushed around his legs, almost sucking his left boot off his foot. He felt the dull insensible death of millions of things all around his mountain. The deluge from the stream further up the mountain roared in the dark, pouring images of uprooted trees and smashed bridges into Maguire's head. The entire darkness of the mountain seemed to be rushing down to vanquish his small farm.

The cone of light from his torch illuminated a monotony of sizzling rain. Dead mice floated in the yard. Maguire slogged toward the shed, to the dark claustrophobia of dankness and hunger. The animals sensed him, bawling out in the humiliation of captivity, tethered in the freezing hole of the shed. They recoiled, shocked in the sudden beam of his torch. A stream of insects poured off the animals' heads as the light shone on them. Maguire dropped the torch. Holy Jasus . . . He took the torch again, pointing the beam of light into the quagmire of mud and shit, seeing the hesitancy of scraping hooves, his eyes drawn to the plague of insects scurrying around the nose and eyes, into the ears, the anus of the animals, any warm passage away from the flood . . . Maguire felt the horror of what nature had reclaimed in so many days of incessant rain. The animals' legs had become afflicted with fungus. That cunt of a son of his should have let them out and fed them in the light of day. Was everything left for him to do?

Maguire found the box where he kept his supply of animal medicines. He found the smelling salts for his wife. This should do the trick. He tried to push his way through the animals again, their cries filling his ears. There was nothing for it now. He'd have to let them out into the night. There was no grass with the flood, but they needed to get out of the shed. They'd become demented in the dark enclosure.

Maguire took a knife from his pocket, cutting into the heavy ropes. He shouted, slapping the hot hinds of the animals, brushing away worms and dark insects. The animals pressed towards the small doorway. A cow slipped, frantically trying to regain its footing. Its huge belly knocked Maguire against the stone wall. An ooze of green shit poured onto Maguire's coat.

Maguire recovered and slopped his way back across the ruined yard filled with frightened animals, the torch slashing the dark.

'Hold her steady,' Maguire said. 'Jesus, can you do nothing right?'

The boy held her head close to his chest.

'I'll sort you out later, don't you worry.'

Maguire uncapped the small vial of salts. Its pungency burned his eyes. He placed it under his wife's nose. Her head jerked back.

'Can you hear me?' Maguire looked into his wife's eyes.

'Are you OK, Mam?' the boy whispered. His eyes moistened.

'It's us,' Maguire said. 'Me and Thomas.' He brought the salts to her nose again. Her head turned sideways, her arm rising instinctively, saying something, an incoherent stammer.

Maguire was at a loss. An animal always licked the hand or came to its feet, and that told you everything was fine. Maguire waited impatiently, his head tilted a bit like a perplexed dog. 'How many fingers?' He held up three fingers and shoved them before his wife's face. 'How many fingers?'

'How many fingers, Mam?' the boy repeated.

'Shut up, you.' Maguire glared at his son. 'How many fingers?'

His wife made a sound through her split lip.

'Three, is that it? Three.' Maguire said, answering his own question. He showed the three thick fingers to his son. 'She said three.'

The boy nodded, 'Three, Mam.'

Maguire stood up, felt the blood rush to his head and had to grip the table. His eyes closed in a moment of reprieve, muttering, 'Thanks be to Jesus.' He raised his head and flinched. Spiders hung in tight balls over threaded webs, waiting to descend and eat the insects.

His wife recovered enough by midnight to take a sup of milk. The animals returned, drawn to the monotonous surroundings of the house. A cow rubbed its nose against the window, mooing. Maguire was beside himself. They had found only the saturated earth, everything edible uprooted or submerged in the icy water. His wife was still vomiting every so often in the red basin beside her. She'd said little, her eyes fixed on nothing, staring blankly. Maguire forced her to keep getting up every few minutes as he harassed her with the salts.

'I'm fine,' she said, waving her hands at the salts. Maguire took it as encouragement. He stood up and sat down as the time passed, the thread of his own harried argument going through his head. He'd not touch her again . . . This was it, done and over with, end of story . . . He took the brush and knocked the spiders from the ceiling.

The boy watched quietly in the background.

Maguire couldn't take it. He got up and opened the door,

seeing the cows silently going into the shed again, like creatures drawn to some abandoned ark. There was no let up on the rain, the sky stuffed with clouds. 'We'll have to stir some mix for them,' Maguire said gruffly to the boy, breaking the tension. 'There is nothing in the fields for them. Well, go on then. Look lively. Get the mix.'

Maguire stayed with his wife, sitting down before her, saying plaintively and simply, 'How many fingers?' He held up the same three fingers. 'Come on now. Don't do this to me, love. Come on.'

Her heavy head moved slowly, almost falling to one side. He could see her perceptibly catching herself. He waited until the boy was out of earshot and whispered, 'I'd me eye on somethin' down in the town for you.' He leaned forward, the crack of his arse showing, his voice close to her swollen ear, 'Somethin' you've been wantin' this long time.' He held her gnawed fingernails.

'I'm sorry,' she wept, slobbering over his hairy hand.

'I have the mix,' the boy said, coming back with two buckets.

Maguire averted his eyes. 'Well, go and stir it up,' then he smiled into his wife's eyes. He spoke in his softest voice. 'Sure, who knows, but maybe we'll head up the Dublin way for a weekend. What do you think of that now?' Maguire let his fingers scented with the salts secretly feel for the lump behind her ear.

She drew her head back slightly. 'I need the doctor,' she said in a hoarse voice, her lips on the back of his hot hand.

Maguire squeezed her arm, the smile leaving his face. 'Don't talk nonsense and scare the boy. You're fine as long as you stay awake, love.'

Maguire stood up and put on his coat. She was still fighting him.

The boy worked in the periphery of the fire, mixing the grain meal in a steel bucket.

'You'll have a sup of cocoa with a powder, that'll do the trick.' Maguire leaned over again with a tinge of agitation.

'You have to stop feeling sorry for yourself. There's work to be done.' Her eyes were glazed. Concussion it was, he was sure. She'd have to be kept awake. He knew that much about concussions from his hurling days. The injured had to keep themselves awake. Maguire filled the black kettle and set it in over the fire, heating the water to add to the mix.

One of the cows hit the window again, nearly breaking it. 'Jesus Christ!' Maguire went over to the window. The cow was still there. Maguire whistled until the cow moved away, but it stayed close, defying him. Like the insects, it wanted the sanctuary of his house. Maguire opened the front door and took the sweeping brush. The cow stood obstinately still in the dark, its head bent. A writhing tattoo of earwigs clotted its huge eyes. 'Get away, you cunt!' Maguire shouted. The cow defied him. Maguire could see it was stricken with some sort of dementia. There was nothing as unpredictable as a frightened animal.

He'd have to go out there himself and take care of things. 'I'll have to feed the animals,' he sighed, feeling the burden of so many things falling on him. He felt a weakness inside him as he closed the door.

The boy held up two fingers, 'How many, Mam?'

Mrs Maguire had managed to stand up. She was taking the red basin off the table to the sink, moving in a slow shuffle on her big legs. She looked at her son and whispered, 'Two.'

The boy smiled and Maguire hesitated. The best thing was to leave her alone at this stage. He was only acting the maggot, adding to the fuel with his talk of going into the shops and trips to Dublin. To make an issue out of things was a dead loss, to be bribing a wife, for Jasus sake, I mean, what the hell was he at? 'You come on with me and lay some straw down outside,' Maguire said to the boy. It was best to have the pair separated until things settled down.

Snail shells broke under Maguire's feet as he went across the dark yard. In the shed he poured the steaming mix into cold metal troughs. The coarse tongues of the cows scraped against his hand, feverishly lapping at the hot watery meal. A flutter of wings startled him. A string of birds had taken sanctuary on a dark perch above him. Maguire took a shovel and dug into the streaming shit, slopping it out the open door. He came into the yard, panting. A cold drizzle blew in his face, the night transforming all sense of human contact into the biblical solitude of Noah.

The boy came outside with more meal. 'Go on in with it.' Maguire leaned against the shovel. Insects encircled his wrist. He dropped the shovel with a scream in a moment of panic.

Inside, Maguire's wife had boiled custard and opened a tin of pears. The fire burned strong, the water on the floor alive with the flicker of flames. She moved slowly, holding an exposed paraffin lamp to the cracks in the wall where the insects silently poured in from the outside. There was the soft crackle and hiss of things burning.

'That's them settled for the night, thank God.' Maguire caught his wife's eye but remained serious, shrouded in duty and obligation. 'I was telling Thomas here that we'll have to dig a drainage ditch off to the side if this rain keeps on.'

The boy took the bait. 'Can I help, Dad?'

Maguire gave a sardonic grin. That was it now, as long as he could manage this pair through the night, just as long as she stayed awake and pulled through till morning when he'd be sure she was grand.

Insects fizzled and dropped in flaming beads into the water on the floor.

Maguire's wife spoke for the first time. 'We should sweep the floor.'

'We should.' Maguire eased his mood. Thank God, she was out of the worst. He opened the door and brushed the tide of creatures outside, feeling a sudden lightness in his head from hunger and other things. He stopped in the open doorway, his broad back outlined against the dark of the exile rain.

Maguire and his son ate hot custard and pears, their shadows half-submerged in the still water on the floor. The moon appeared in the sky outside.

'It's letting up,' Maguire said, pointing to the window.

His wife's face turned sheet-white again as she sat still, the web of broken veins on her cheek, a dark bruise showing under the left eye.

A sudden shock passed through Maguire. 'We'll dig a drainage ditch off to the side if this rain keeps on the way it has,' he continued as he slurped the thick pear juice off his spoon. He got up after that and burned more insects off the walls. He was fagged with exhaustion but afraid to go up to the freezing bedroom creeping with earwigs and spiders. And he had to keep vigil over his wife, make sure she didn't succumb to sleep.

Maguire tuned the radio on to the BBC to kill the silence. Through the crackling wheeze of the reception, a man read Shakespeare at three o'clock in the morning. Maguire knew the poem from his years at school. 'I know that one,' Maguire yawned and sat down again, patiently waiting for the first light of dawn. He fought sleep as he sat still, but his head drifted with the dull sensation of being dragged under. In the end he fell asleep with his head on the table.

His wife turned bad soon after that – convulsions that nothing could stop, the dry heaves from an empty stomach. Maguire struggled and tried to hold her, her limbs jerking as though jolted by electricity. Her chair toppled over, the cup of cold cocoa smashing. The boy screamed, 'Mam!' She stopped after a few moments and went limp. Maguire set her against the table. A trickle of blood came out of her left ear.

Maguire struggled with the tractor out in the big shed, revving the engine, a thick plume of diesel filling the shed. The animals kicked and moved away as the tractor lurched into the yard. He stormed into the house again and up the stairs to change into his Sunday suit and tie, dragging his heavy coat off him.

'Dad?'

'Will you wait?' Maguire roared. He'd leave the house

respectable and show that he was serious. He could play the supplicant or whatever was needed. He washed in the small toilet, dragged a comb through his hair. In the bedroom he fumbled with the knot in his Sunday tie. 'I swear to you Jesus, on my word, this was the last time!' He spoke to his reflection with morbid intensity.

Things ran through his head. In a moment of stark practicality Maguire took a box from above the dresser. 'Yes . . .' He went to the black table board and began in a simple, earnest manner, holding his breath as he wrote. He took an envelope.

The boy screamed downstairs. 'Come on, Dad, please!'

Maguire searched in his wife's drawer for a round pale-blue tin of face powder a sister in England had given her the previous summer. He came down in his Sunday best and set the cups in the sink and rinsed the basin, abiding by an insane logic of cleanliness as though it could grant a level of impunity. But what else could he do to defend himself?

'She's going to die!' the boy screamed.

'Will you shut up?' Maguire opened the tin of powder and dabbed the left side of the face, considering it for a moment before doing the other side.

Maguire and the boy took the body out to the tracter, the boy holding her legs as Maguire lifted her up into the small cab. The tractor lurched away, leaving the house to the spiders.

'You saw she was better, didn't you? Weren't we just eating there, the three of us?'

The boy sobbed as he held his mother. His eyes gleamed in the errant light reflected in the flood waters outside. It had stopped raining for the first time in days.

Maguire rocked on the springs in the worn leather seat of the tractor, rubbing mist off the window. The tractor's lights washed over an apparition of gleaming water. 'Is she breathin'?'

'Yes.' The boy was sobbing again.

'Give it over, do you hear me?' Maguire's arms spread out over the big steering wheel. He was silent for a moment, then the scheming came back into his head. 'Weren't we eating, the three of us?' Maguire blurted. 'Weren't the three of us just eating?' his big head turned in the cab. 'No, that'll not do at all. You were in bed. You saw nothing. Are you listening to me, son? Nothing!'

The boy's head bobbed in the semi-dark of the cab, his small body up against the cold metal interior, his hands holding his mother's head.

Maguire stopped the tractor. 'Can I trust you, son?' Maguire whispered. He looked at his wife, still unconscious. The tractor spluttered in the still dark. 'It'll not happen again,' he said softly.

A laconic, 'Yes . . .' finally came from the boy.

Maguire turned and put his fingers at her throat and felt a faint pulse. Then he tore at the gears. The tractor moved off like some prehistoric creature across the land.

A light flicked on up in the priest's house when the tractor pulled up. The boy had not understood until it was already too late. 'What are you doing?' he cried.

Maguire turned quickly and spat. 'Would you have me go to a doctor before a priest, and her in that condition? She needs to receive a sacrament.'

The boy could say nothing, trapped.

'Is she breathin'?' Maguire said again.

'Yes.'

'In God's name, who is it?' The priest had his head out the window.

'It's Sam Maguire, Father.'

'Maguire! What do you want at this hour?'

'If I could have a word with you?' Maguire climbed down from the tractor.

'I'll be down,' the priest said, banging the window shut with an exasperated gesture.

143

Maguire would have a job with the priest, but he had the letter in his inside breast pocket as insurance. The priest had a head on his shoulders; he'd see the prudence in taking the land. Maguire would make . . . 'a donation,' that's what he'd offer. That was the right word to put on it, 'a donation'.

The priest wore a long dressing gown and unlaced black shoes. 'Is there someone with you?' he began testily, trying to go out into the freezing night, but stopped and looked at the cut of Maguire in the suit and tie. 'Have you come from a dance in that get up, or what?'

The tractor was still going, shuddering in the cold.

Maguire stepped into the hall, stopping the priest's advance. 'Who's there with you?'

'Father,' Maguire said, leaning forward as if to whisper something more. 'I've to talk to you.'

'Don't you pick the fine hour?' The priest made a face of disapproval and went into a dark room off to the side of the hall and turned on a cold hanging bulb.

It came to Maguire. He could make a confession. That was it. He'd confess he'd hit her. That would be the priest's hands tied if it came to it . . . the ideas poured into his head. There was no point being too hasty with the letter. She might come out of it, and if he got the priest to go down with him to the doctor there'd be a level of implication with the Church, and certain matters of decorum would have to be abided by. Leave it to them powers to sort it out among themselves. Morality would come down on the side of power and practicality.

There was a succession of oppressive pauses. A picture of the Pope on the wall presided over the silence of shining brass fixtures. The priest turned his back on Maguire and took a cigarette from a side table beside a decanter of ruby port. He went over and peered out the window at the tractor with sombre indifference, giving Maguire time to say something. Maguire could sense the priest's calculated reserve, part of his training, no doubt, years of experience with callers in the night.

'She's not dead?' the priest said, his back still turned.

'What do you take me for, Father?' Maguire half-laughed to break the tension.

'It's no matter what I think, now is it?' The priest turned, and smoke poured from his mouth and nose. His grey hair stood on end, but he still cut a heavy, dignified figure in the stark light. He wore the starched bib of his cleric's collar around his neck, signifying his position.

There was a knock outside the door. 'Will you be wanting something, Father?' the old housekeeper said. Only her wizened head poked in through the door, the neck laced in the ruffles of her night dress.

The priest waved his hand dismissively. 'No, go on up, Mrs Hanlon. We're set here.'

The priest looked at Maguire with a contemplative expectancy, drawing things out until he heard a door close upstairs. The smoke of the cigarette hung in the air. 'So tell me, what is it that has you out at this hour, Maguire?'

'A confession,' Maguire answered, bowing his head in a penitent way, his eyes roaming in his head.

The priest rolled the cigarette between his thumb and index finger, nodding slightly. 'A confession, is it? Don't make a mockery of confession.' He came forward, taking hold of Maguire's arm, speaking with an inflexible weariness. 'I'll hear no confession. We'll speak man to man.'

Maguire swallowed. He began hesitantly. 'We've had the weather and all up above, and, sure, you know the way it is?'

The priest kept his hand on Maguire's arm, staring at the floor. 'Indeed.' He brought the cigarette to his lips again, making a kissing sound as he pulled. 'So go on.'

'It's her head, Father.' Maguire began his pantomime of subservience.

The priest applied pressure to Maguire's arm, his eyebrows upturned. 'And she's not dead?' the priest repeated.

'No, Father,' Maguire said. 'The head got banged up a bit is all . . .' He drew a long breath and then went on. 'While she was out with the cows, you see. They've sort of gone peculiar with the weather and kind of, you know, they went at her . . .

She got a hit on the head.' Maguire pointed on his own head. 'And the ear a bit as well.'

'Where is she?' the priest interrupted.

'I've her outside with me, Father.'

'On the tractor?'

'Yes, with the boy as well.'

'God Almighty.'

Maguire stopped and put his hand into his breast pocket. He felt unsure of himself, preferring the naive passivity of letting things be done to him. He wondered what the Keenan father had said when he came to the priest with the story of what had happened to that big pregnant daughter of his who never produced any child in the end. 'Father?' Maguire said.

'What?'

'I was thinking of my land.'

'What are you on about?' The priest saw the envelope and withdrew his hand cautiously. 'So what's this, now?'

'. . . 'Tis a letter.'

The priest took the envelope over to the bright bulb and opened it. He read slowly, holding the letter close to his face. The cigarette hung at the side of his lip.

'It would be a donation,' Maguire began tentatively, about to advance, but stayed put. 'I was thinking of going up Dublin way, for good like . . .' His fingers pulled at the collar of his shirt.

'Will you stop?' the priest muttered, not looking up.

'It's signed there, Father. Legal and all.'

The priest scratched the grey bristle of shadowy growth, a meditative awareness of what Maguire was up to. The cigarette throbbed as he breathed. He finished the letter and made a sour face, bringing the cigarette to the centre of his mouth with his tongue before removing it. 'You've a nerve coming here.'

Maguire stiffened, a flush of fear on his cheeks. 'What's that, Father?' He put his hand up in a pleading manner. 'Sure, I was saying to the boy, it's a priest's blessing she's in need of, not a doctor. That's why we come up to you, Father. That's God's honest truth! There's many that would go to a doctor before a priest, but I'm not one of them.'

'Don't blaspheme in my presence,' the priest said. But even as the circle of cold light washed over Maguire, the thread of complicity began to be woven between them.

''Tis true, though, Father. You can ask the boy yourself. I says to him, "We'll take her up by Father O'Donnell and have him give her a sacrament".' Maguire knew he had to bring up mention of the son, make sure the priest knew that the son was ignorant of any conspiracy. He could sense the priest's apprehension, though he saw he was baited by the promise of the land.

'You're the dirtiest sort, do you know that?' The priest paused in a sublimated indecision, nervously brushing ash off the front of his dressing gown. 'It's the likes of you who take their filth out into the open to shame the lives of decent people.'

Maguire put on a forlorn ignorant look, letting his mouth hang open. A hiss of rain distracted him.

'And you have her with you?' the priest said finally.

'I do, Father.'

The priest put the paper down on the table. He went to the door. 'Mrs Hanlon?' he said sternly out in the hall. 'I'll need some things.' He faced Maguire, clearing his voice. 'We'll take my car.'

'As you wish, Father.'

Maguire and the boy brought her into the cold light of the room. She'd recovered enough to open her eyes. Maguire had done a bad job with the face powder, caked unevenly on the left side of the face. She looked like a cheap prostitute. Maguire put the three fingers up before her face again and did the old routine.

'Three,' she said quietly.

Maguire spoke in a rushed, consoling whisper. 'We're going down with the priest. Now, listen to me. You fell out with the cows in the rain . . .' He had his arm around her. 'Isn't that it?'

Her voice was pasty. 'Yes.' She had the boy beside her.

'You fell out with . . .'

The boy finished it, '. . . the cows in the rain.'

'I'd me eye on somethin' down in the town for you. Somethin' you've been wantin' this long time,' Maguire whispered, patting her shoulder.

It was a concussion, no doubt. The eyes were still glassy. Maguire moved the hair back behind the ear, seeing the clot of dried blood. He licked his fingers. 'Hold steady.' He wiped the blood off the ear. His wife let out a sigh.

Maguire stood up and breathed hard. He rubbed his face in exhaustion, and it was then that his eye caught the letter on the table. His ears picked up the muffled talk of the priest. He leaned over and stealthily slipped the letter into his pocket. For a moment he had a mad idea of eating it, envelope and all. He had to catch his breath, a chill of fear making him shiver. 'We're ready here, Father.' Maguire helped his wife out into the hall.

The priest came down the stairs dressed in a dark officious coat and hat, along with a small leather bag containing holy water and a Bible. 'I heard you had a fall out in the rain,' he said by way of co-ordinating stories.

'A cow, Father,' she answered.

'I see. So it was a cow?' The priest's nose twitched at the smell of the powder. 'What's that?' He looked closely at the face. 'She looks like a banshee, you eejit.' The priest shouted up to the housekeeper. 'Mrs Hanlon, we'll need some warm water.'

Maguire nearly died of anxiety as they went back into the front room. It seemed ages before the basin of warm water arrived and Mrs Hanlon got the powder off. The priest kept fumbling around as though trying to remember something. Maguire almost fainted, but the priest only said, 'Where are those cigarettes gone to?'

'The mantelpiece, Father.' Maguire pointed with a weary, painful face, holding his son close to him, looking as miserable as hell.

The priest instructed Mrs Hanlon to call the hospital, to tell them they were bringing in a patient. 'Come on, we should be off,' the priest said finally, turning to Maguire.

The rain lashed down as the car pulled out into the dark. Maguire couldn't stop himself from smiling in the back seat. He'd the priest tricked. The priest could fuck off for himself as far as Maguire was concerned. 'We'll speak man to man . . . No confession, my arse,' he said to himself. You'd have to be up early in the morning to catch Maguire out. There'd be no giving up the land. Maguire had to resist the urge to slap the priest on the back. He stayed still in the back seat, his whole body trembling with an excruciating excitement, the letter next to his pounding heart.

The Football Field

When the Corporation broke ground on the football field out back of the Talbot Projects, there was a great ceremony. The mayor came in a black limousine and said, 'The discipline learned on a playing field carries into life.' The old and the young gathered. The mayor described the features of the field: an all-weather surface, complete with a modernized drainage system, spotlights, a six-lane athletics track. A dormitory-style facility and weight room were also set for construction at a future date. 'Revenue from school and city leagues' usage of the facility, plus the training camps in the summer, is estimated at over £200,000 a year,' the mayor continued. 'We are committed to reinvesting in our people, in our cities.' There were even jobs associated with the field. Eight people from the estate who might have emigrated to England or America were to become professional groundskeepers, their training to consist of an intensive programme with an English Premier club for one season. The celebration came to an end with the ribbon cutting and the mayor heading a ball thrown by a fat woman in Nike track sweats and a Sony tee-shirt.

It was the fat woman, Mrs Fitzgerald, who had mobilized the Talbot Projects into fighting to get the football field. Her husband had died of lung cancer years earlier, leaving her with their only son, Franky. The boy, now a twenty-year-old, hadn't amounted to anything. Mrs Fitzgerald made him go with her wherever she went. Franky was slightly touched. He'd been kicked in the head at school when he was young, and that ended that.

Mrs Fitzgerald had become one of those socially-conscious women who was involved for no better reason than she had nothing for herself at home. She bore no grudge about what had happened to her. There were people worse off. As she said herself: 'Sometimes when you slide down the banisters, the splinters don't all go the same way.' Before she had started into the football field crusade, she was considered a formidable woman with not enough to do. But, in a pinch, she was there for anybody.

How Mrs Fitzgerald had become embroiled in the football field crusade was a mystery. It just happened. She couldn't tell you in what division Liverpool played, or explain the offside rule, but when she set her heart on something, there was no stopping her. 'Fooball field this and football field that' was her kick for weeks. Her son Franky stood vacantly by her side, mouthing the words, 'football field'. Mrs Fitzgerald got the whole place tormented with her constant calling at flats in the Projects, explaining how a football field was the answer to their depressed state. 'Franky would have been the better for it,' she said, obliquely referring to Franky's condition. 'Boys with too much time on their hands.' Finally, she organized a band of women into appealing to the newspapers to do stories on the state of the Projects, the crime and pregnancy, the lack of motivation and pride, the unemployment and the drugs.

Mrs Fitzgerald enrolled herself and three other women in a city tech course in film and collected money for a Camcorder to make a documentary about the human story within the Projects. The camera scanned around the little square flats, crammed with sagging sofas used for children's beds, squat televisions set in corners, antennae hanging out the window searching for channels.

The film used the ongoing metaphor of the wasted field out the back of the red-brick Projects, juxtaposing innocence with the horrible state of the overgrown field. It was there that the children encountered all the bad elements of inner city life. Franky made the tea and buttered bread for the women as they went around the place filming everything. He even made a cameo, like Hitchcock did in his films, a silhouette staring through the iron railings. RTE pandered to social-awareness films. It was cheaper than making real programmes.

When things were in full swing, the women were doing all

the morning chat shows. They had heart-wrenching stories of youth gone wrong. AIDS and other diseases were common. Youths shared needles and died in the small bedrooms of the Projects. Mrs Fitzgerald wanted to make it known that she wasn't looking for handouts. She emphatically stated that the football field would bring respect and dignity back to the inner city.

The Projects' central location on the edge of the city, its proximity to both the train and the buses, was cited as its principle advantage. Studies were conducted by Mrs Fitzgerald into how long it took to walk from the various bus stops to the field. Franky did the walking, timing himself with a stopwatch and using a trundle wheel to measure the exact distance. Mrs Fitzgerald took another course, in desktop publishing, at the local technical school. Her final portfolio for the Football Field Project was a desktop success story. She produced a series of newsletters which culminated in colour pie charts relating to the feasibility of the different 'transit corridors'. She even appeared in a Macintosh television commercial.

Committees from other districts couldn't compete with Mrs Fitzgerald. All they could do was argue that the Talbot field's location was unsatisfactory. The entire region was plagued with high unemployment, prostitution, and drug-related violence. Even the infamous film, which Mrs Fitzgerald had called *The Field*, showed the true deprivation of the area. 'Imagine having a team of convent girls going into Talbot Projects for a workout? How many virgins would come out?' It seemed like a riddle, but it was a deadly serious issue.

Mrs Fitzgerald was up to the challenge and countered with a Neighbourhood Watch programme. A campaign to clear graffiti was organized. The local scout master declared on television: 'My unit will protect any young woman's honour, providing an escort if need be, to and from the complex.' But this ineffectual bravado nearly ruined everything. The tenor of the proposal took on an ominous militaristic aura.

Mrs Fitzgerald had to intervene, assuming full control of all media-related events. She made another quick film showing the clean-up, which appeared on the national news. Sony donated a more sophisticated camera this time in exchange for Mrs Fitzgerald and Franky wearing Sony tee-shirts throughout the campaign, which they did.

Uneducated as she was, Mrs Fitzgerald had a natural rhetoric which capitalized on her amateurish approach. Her hair was dyed a vivid carrot colour and often set in rollers or gathered in a net. This allied her with forces beyond the realm of fashion. She was impervious to insult. She had a hard city accent which bordered on pantomime. Some people said it grew thicker as the fight over the field grew into a full-blown media event. She propped her integrity up with her city tech certificates. She had brains. 'Not bad for a woman whose husband went to an early grave and left her with an unfortunate creature . . .' Mrs Fitzgerald had everything down to a tee. It was political suicide to argue with her. She would say or do anything. 'She is more Dublin than Molly Malone,' one columnist reported.

All sorts of interest groups solicited Mrs Fitzgerald, and she embraced them all. 'She embodies the inner city woman's struggle for personal identity,' a speaker announced as Mrs Fitzgerald sat with her big legs crossed, smiling out at an auditorium of women. As usual, Franky was by her side, dressed in a black suit and white socks, peering nervously out into the darkness. She accepted membership of the 'Sisterhood of the Historically Enslaved', tipping her head to accept the fake shackles which were put around her neck. Franky became hysterical and had to be pulled off the woman. He was a protective son.

The Projects finally won out by reminding the government of election promises to revitalize urban slum areas. It was a true victory for the ordinary people. Social theorists scrambled to document the cultural phenomenon, to show how cameras and computers had brought the immediacy and poignancy of the Talbot Projects to life. It reflected a new age in democracy. A cry of despair could now echo throughout a planet. A new level of social consciousness was upon humanity.

To put it another way, the government had the shite scared out of them. Old women with cameras had tracked them down, showing old footage of election promises, hassling like seasoned reporters.

On the Monday following the ribbon-cutting ceremony, a team of men came in lorries and carted off all the carcasses of rusting cars, their broken windows like sad eyes, the yawning bonnets closed once more and dragged off. A huge crowd of unemployed cheered them. Two bulldozers were brought in by midday. Mrs Fitzgerald and Franky were there with tea and buns. Mrs Fitzgerald had a camera set up to film the work. She was going to see this through to the end, an enigmatic wholesome techno-knacker who could discuss 32-bit video, 68040 processors, and the price of cabbage.

After the first day, less attention was paid to the field as the bulldozers worked from morning to night, digging away the top layers of soil. A small hut was erected for the workers and barbed wire laced through the railings around the perimeter of the field to keep people from trespassing.

The work stopped on a Wednesday morning in the second week. The Corporation called a meeting with Mrs Fitzgerald. Something strange had been discovered. All the Corporation could say at this stage was that some artifacts and the skeletons of horses had been dug up by the bulldozers. Radioactive carbon-dating techniques would have to be used before anything could be agreed upon conclusively. The corporation hadn't the expertise to make any statements.

Mrs Fitzgerald went wild with excitement. 'It's another Viking settlement! I'll bet you anything it is!' Up at the other end of the city, a Viking settlement had been uncovered a few years before. During the Dublin Millennium a cultural centre had been formed, including a living museum showing the different aspects of life under Viking rule. There was no stopping Mrs Fitzgerald, despite the Corporation saying that 'nothing was certain'.

'All the bones have to be verified,' Mr Taylor insisted.

'Vikings,' Franky smiled.

'I felt it in my bones all along that this was something more than a football field.' Mrs Fitzgerald's whole face grew red, and her eyes watered.

Franky gawked at her in a frightened way. 'Mam,' he whispered.

'It's all right, love. There's Vikings down there, Franky. The fellas with horns from Norway.'

'Like the fellas in the Harp ad on the telly!' Franky laughed and put his hands to his head and pointed two fingers up in the air, wiggling the horns. 'Like this, Ma.'

'Stop messin' around, Franky.' Mrs Fitzgerald looked at the two men from the Corporation in their navy suits, striped ties and polished shoes. She could see the condescending smiles that she had accepted for so long on these waxy faces. She detested them, the rates men and collectors coming through the Projects, knocking on doors, serving notices for evictions. So this was where they ended up at the end of a long life.

'We called you here in confidence,' the fatter of the two men said, smiling softly. 'We don't want to release any information prematurely. Now if we could have your word?'

Mrs Fitzgerald calculated that this might be an even greater source of income. She had to act on the spot. The football field was one thing, but to be associated with a lost city, to make tea for archaeologists . . . Well, one thing was for sure, she'd have to check with the local tech to see if they had courses on archaeology. She didn't want to be caught out not knowing all the right terms and dates.

'Please, can we have your word, ma'am?' the older said, approaching with his hands out. 'You will be the first to know anything, I promise. We just need time to investigate.'

'I think that maybe I'll see if the Projects can get a twin city alliance with some place up in Norway. What do you think of that?' Mrs Fitzgerald brimmed with resourcefulness, the idea of calling up a foreign country and telling them, 'I think we have some of your Vikings down here on our football field.'

The older corporation official blew out his sagging cheeks. He was beyond words, twiddling his fingers before himself.

'If we could just wait a day or so, please,' the fatter one said.

There was no time to waste. She and Franky ate at the chipper down the road, battered sausages, cod and chips, light on the salt on account of her blood pressure. Then it was down to the library. Franky piled up every book on Vikings. His idea of secrecy was to go around saying, 'I know something you don't know,' which led him to blabber the whole thing out to a girl at the desk.

Mrs Fitzgerald, for her part, wasted no time at all. She was listening to a tape about Viking exploration. She looked up carbon-dating to see what it was all about, in case she could go out there into the field with some of the women and test the place herself, not that she didn't know already that the place they lived on was really the home of a great settlement of Vikings, and to think that it was herself who had got the ball rolling, so to speak, on the whole thing in the first place . . .

An attendant came and touched Mrs Fitzgerald on the shoulder to stop her from tapping a pen on the oak table.

Mrs Fitzgerald gave a jerk and looked up. 'They should build a monument to me,' she said in an agitated way. How dare someone interfere with her work!

The next day she scanned a picture of a Viking warrior which she included in a press release to be broadcast on all the morning radio programmes. She had culled and memorized some information from the books about Viking settlements in Dublin. Since this site was closer to the sea than the one up along the Liffey, she was sure that the settlement on the edge of the sea would be of much greater significance and size. She said a committee from Norway's Viking Institute was flying into Dublin and provisionally accepted the idea of Talbot Projects twinning with some place up in Norway. Mrs Fitzgerald then went on to explain radioactive carbon-dating to the general public on RTE 2.

The evening papers carried a picture of Franky in a Viking

outfit, standing beside his mother who wore a long golden wig which hung in two braids. They had got the attire from the people down at the Guinness brewery who had made the Harp ad.

The Corporation remained close-lipped about the whole affair, saying that any announcement was premature. However, they had uncovered a disconcerting record which showed that the field in question had been owned by a glue factory up until the late thirties when the factory had burned down. How a thorough investigation of the site had not been carried out by the corporation was still in question. How many animals were buried there? Some portions of public record had been erased for security reasons. The originals were being sought down in the archives. It seemed there had been a stipulation against building on the field, because, when the Talbot Projects were erected, the field remained untouched.

The two Corporation officials were glad to see Mrs Fitzgerald on the verge of making a fool of herself. Nobody could want to build a football field on top of an old glue factory. She would now be seen for what she was: a raucous crow filled with hare-brained schemes. It would show that giving people access to technology, allowing them to interrupt other people's lives with their senseless drivel, letting them harass politicians and virtually hold the entire city hostage, was a grave mistake. The word of the glue factory was passed up to the ministry at the Dáil. The ministers gave a unanimous sigh of relief. Mrs Fitzgerald would get what was coming to her. They were ready to lambast her schemes.

But it wasn't that easy. If it was proved that Mrs Fitzgerald and her son Franky had taken the city by the horns, so to speak, then what would that say for the credibility of the government? It might cause the opposition to call for a general election. The entire affair might backfire on them. The initial fervour against Mrs Fitzgerald abated as the ministers met behind closed doors. During the discussions, updates on the activities of Mrs Fitzgerald and her son were monitored and relayed to the ministers. Apparently, Mrs Fitzgerald had spoken live to a Norwegian official in Oslo, who greeted the nation with, 'Dia Dhuit, a cara', and Mrs Fitzgerald thought he was speaking Norwegian. The ministers were on the floor laughing. If there was ever a time to throw caution to the wind, this was it. Mrs Fitzgerald, patron saint of Dublin, didn't know a word of Irish. They could undermine her on that point alone, arguing that she had made an international spectacle of herself and Ireland. The absurdity of the entire matter would now be seen as part of Mrs Fitzgerald's sickness, and of the media's insatiable desire to cause controversy, even at the expense of national interest. There was talk of the Ministry of Health declaring her a schizophrenic and committing her.

In the field, a team of archaeologists from Dublin university worked into the cool night with small trowels and brushes, exposing the remains of literally hundreds of horses. A generator powered a rack of lights which lit up the excavated holes. The archaeologists didn't need carbon-dating for conclusive proof that these animals had been slaughtered in the last sixty years. Decapitated skeletal remains were uncovered. It seemed as if the horses had been decapitated and discarded and never used by the glue factory. Some of the bone still had putrid dark flesh and spots of attached hair. The hooves were still intact.

Word arrived up at the Dáil. The Corporation had secured a censored document which gave a detailed account of what had happened up at the field. In the late thirties, many of the local businesses and merchants within the city had opted to change their stables of horses for motorized vehicles. Records showed that there were over two thousand horses within the city at that time. It was estimated that over a two-year period some of the biggest firms completely phased out horses. The animals were reported to have been shipped to the country. But many of them had ended up at the glue factory. Literally thousands of horses had been butchered by companies to avoid the expense of putting them out to pasture. The place had burned down mysteriously following the transition from horses to cars. The Corporation had planned a clean-up, but with each successive government the problem had faded, until it had been forgotten.

Some ministers asked how many horses would be discovered. The information from the archaeologists was that they were finding full skeletons at a depth of twenty feet. The Dáil went into turmoil. Possibly the underground water supply was already flowing through the horse grave, and the stench from exposed flesh would fill the city. At all costs, the situation must be concealed. Mrs Fitzgerald had to be neutralized. There was a fervour of emotion, the possibility of government collapse. Things were desperate at the Dáil.

As with all scandals, there was a leak. Mrs Fitzgerald was up late, sitting at her kitchen table, drinking tea and leafing over Irish phrases of welcome. She wouldn't be caught out again. She was still in the Viking wig. She had forgotten to take it off. Franky had fallen asleep with his arms on the table. He was snoring. She could see the red scar where his head had been cut open. She wiped her eyes, finding tears there. Even when her husband had died and Franky had been injured, she had accepted it, because she could do nothing else. Now here she was at an age when she should be looking back on her life, looking forward to putting her son into a job. She closed the book and put her head down on the table and closed her eyes and said her prayers. It was all too much.

A friend of a friend came round, a small man in a grey tweed jacket, knocking on the door. He said he couldn't stay, but that the Corporation had discovered that the field was filled with horse skeletons. It was very serious, an embarrassment to all concerned. He told her of the huge slaughter.

Mrs Fitzgerald stood impeding the man's entrance. 'We'll get the football field though, right?'

The man said he knew nothing about that. He was just here to warn her that it was going to get worse before it got better. The government was running scared. Someone had to be accountable.

Mrs Fitzgerald shut the door and put her hands to her face.

She wasn't thinking of the horses, but of her field. Franky woke up and said, 'What's wrong?'

Mrs Fitzgerald dabbed her eyes. 'Nothing.' She looked distracted. She boiled the kettle and stood over the blue flame. The generator puttered off in the field. It wasn't her fault that the place was filled with horse skeletons, and what if it was anyway?

The man hadn't mentioned anything about the Viking artifacts. She felt a flush of embarrassment at all the things she had said on the television and radio. The evening paper was beside the cooker. She saw herself in the wig and suddenly became conscious that it was still on her head.

The two of them drank the tea in silence. Franky fidgeted with his hands. 'Did I do something wrong, Ma?'

'No, love,' Mrs Fitzgerald whispered. She had to stop herself from crying. 'You have to promise me . . .'

'What, Ma?'

'Promise me that if there are any people who start shouting at me, that you won't do anything. You see, I made a mistake about . . .' She swallowed. 'Just promise me that you will be good.'

'Yes, Ma.' Franky went into the living room and lay down on the old sofa and went to sleep again. Mrs Fitzgerald turned on the gas heater and tried to sleep.

When Mrs Fitzgerald came in to him, she was smiling and nodding. 'I've got it, Franky. Come on.'

The McDermots had an old Toyota van that the husband used for carrying vegetables to and from Moore Street. Mrs Fitzgerald put on her hat and coat and went up and spoke with Mrs McDermot on the eighth floor and said she was up against a wall, the whole football field was at stake. Mrs McDermot was half-asleep. 'What?'

Mrs Fitzgerald told her what had happened. She even mentioned that the government was thinking of bumping her off.

'Holy Jesus,' Mrs McDermot whispered, huddled in her

pink dressing gown. 'I'll get Tom and the boys.'

A group of men gathered down by the McDermots' van. They were smoking and talking among themselves. Mrs Fitzgerald came down in full costume along with Franky dressed in his Viking skins. The men looked at one another and shook their heads. She was at the end of her rope. They drove up along the Aston and the Aran quay, and then up around Christchurch Cathedral. The Viking Centre was down the back of a stone building, away from the street level. The gang piled out of the car and went down to a barred window. One of the men was an electrician and went off looking for wires that were connected to an alarm. He gave a whistle, acknowledging that he had found and cut the alarm. Another fellow jimmied the bars loose and pulled it out of the brick. Mrs Fitzgerald orchestrated everything.

They went in through the front door. Mrs Fitzgerald had a flash lamp which she had bought for emergencies when the ESB went on strike. The four men followed her, carrying coal sacks. The cone of light scanned the dark crypt. They found the Viking artifacts stored on shelves in a cold room.

It was over in a matter of ten minutes, and then the Toyota drove away, leaving three of the men to reset the place so that a burglary might not be suspected for a few days. Mrs Fitzgerald sat up front and talked frantically about what the government was trying to pull on her and the people. 'We'll have that football field, you mark my words,' she said, gritting her teeth. Franky sat in the back, smiling.

Mrs Fitzgerald went up to the guards with the offer of tea and bread. The rack of spotlights was turned off at this stage. The place was deathly still. The guards said they couldn't touch anything while on duty, but Mrs Fitzgerald badgered them until they accepted and went into their tent to warm themselves. Mrs Fitzgerald stood in the doorway, talking about what a great thing the football field would be when it was completed. She kept them talking for a bit, while the men from the Projects in black clothes and dirty faces went around trying to bury or throw some of the Viking artifacts into the holes around the field.

As Mrs Fitzgerald talked to the men, it began to rain on the canopy. She knew that, if it kept up, the place would be too mucky for anything to be done the following day, allowing the artifacts to sink in the sliding mud holes. 'Well, good night then,' she shouted, to alert the men out in the field that she was leaving.

The limbo of rain dragged on. The field remained un-touched, the artifacts wallowing in mud. The government said they wanted to talk compromise. Mrs Fitzgerald said she would meet only in a public place. The meeting was arranged for Bewley's.

It was days before anybody could go out into the field to continue the excavation. The place was waterlogged. Mrs Fitzgerald was mum on the Viking settlement and went into a seclusion of sorts. The rumour of the robbery up at the Viking centre was all over the Projects, and the Corporation caught wind of it. Soon the whole city was whispering about it. It wasn't like Mrs Fitzgerald to refuse to comment like some old politician. Her closed door said it all. It was a milestone for the people, the great Mrs Fitzgerald, the voice of the common people refusing to be among her people.

The meeting at Bewley's took place. A government official said that many of the establishments who had sent their animals to slaughter were still prominent within the city. There would be a public outcry at the manner in which the companies had slaughtered animals that had loyally served them for generations. How could a city that had lived amid the sour dung odour of the city streets not have asked, 'Where did the horses go?' How could they not have recalled the clip-clop of hooves that echoed in narrow lanes, the horses that delivered everything to their doors, the coal and the milk and the bread? What arguments could the government and the people raise? It had all happened in a time of world struggle, a time when so many things disappeared. Nostalgia and senti-mentality were post-World War II inventions.

Mrs Fitzgerald agreed that the horror of the burials could

not be revealed, not for those reasons, but because she wanted her football field. But what about the Viking artifacts? It was agreed in principle that the robbery up at the Viking Heritage Centre would never be acknowledged, that neither Mrs Fitzgerald, Franky, or the McDermots would be prosecuted. The government agreed that, since Mrs Fitzgerald had made such a commotion about the Viking settlement, one of the archaeologists from Trinity would have to be contacted in an appropriate manner and bribed to come down and authenticate that, indeed, a band of settlers from up at the major Viking settlement at Christchurch had stayed on the field for a short period of time, but there was no lost city or any great significance to the finds.

In exchange, Mrs Fitzgerald went on air and called up the Norwegian Viking Institute to say, 'I regret that inclement weather has interrupted work on our site presently. We will inform you of further developments.' She ended with an Irish blessing. The words had been written by the government.

Mrs Fitzgerald never really got over the surreptitious nature of the meeting with the government ministers, and how they said that Franky could have been committed to a home and taken from her, because, as far as they were concerned, no woman in her right mind would have implicated her son in such a barbarous act. Many of the artifacts that had originally been uncovered up at the Viking museum and were eventually recovered from the field were smashed to bits, lost treasures of Dublin's past. The government finally prosecuted the McDermots on charges relating to other crimes the police had known about, but the government knew that everybody would assume that Mrs Fitzgerald had sold them out to save herself and Franky.

The media blitz surrounding the football field receded as Mrs Fitzgerald resigned from the committee associated with the enterprise, citing 'ill-health' as advised by the Corporation. She had done what she could for her own people. Now it was in the hands of the Corporation. She did not leave her house so much or go into neighbours' houses and pester them. And they didn't come to her either. Like Parnell and Collins, embraced and then rejected, how could she tell her own people that the government had tricked her into submission? The threat of jail loomed for Franky. If she had made a mistake, she was sorry. She had done everything in the name of the Projects, getting the government to commit to urban redevelopment. For months she took the bus into the city to do her shopping so she wouldn't have to listen to people talking about her, how she sucked up at the end to the Corporation. Rotten fruit and stones were flung through her window, her door was painted with four-letter words. Franky got his head kicked in.

A general election was called, as it always is when blame skulks about in governmental politics. Rumours of how the government had plotted against Mrs Fitzgerald began to circulate. Nothing was carried in the media, but the issue of free speech became a political football. Who could blame Mrs Fitzgerald for leaving the public eye with her son threatened with jail? A government official revealed that Mrs Fitzgerald had not sold out the McDermots.

Mrs Fitzgerald was reinstated in the community. Still, there was a sour note to the whole thing. Even when the field was unveiled, it wasn't as it should have been. Mrs Fitzgerald was invited along with Franky. They stood by the mayor as he made the same speech he had given at the groundbreaking ceremony. Mrs Fitzgerald just nodded, her lipstick smeared on her face, her hair the same carrot colour. Everyone could see she was a beaten woman.

At the end of the ceremony, Mrs Fitzgerald got up out of her chair and went before the microphone. Her voice was weak and quivering. She was out of practice. Franky stood beside her. People turned their heads away. She thanked all those she had worked with through the early parts of the project. She remembered her husband and blessed herself and she held Franky's hand and said she was proud of him. Then she turned to the mayor and said, 'We don't have a name for the Talbot Projects football team, your honour.'

The mayor smiled and looked out at the crowd of people,

the cameras flashing in the bright April morning. 'No, that's right. We'll have to come up with something. We could sponsor a contest in the papers?' the mayor said, nodding at his own suggestion.

'How about the Talbot Stallions?' Mrs Fitzgerald said. Her eyes were filled with tears.

The government ministers looked pensive, but Mrs Fitzgerald left it at that. She let her son work on the grounds. Whatever the horror of the past, and the cruelty of the people around her, she was willing to forget everything. The field had been a grave of horses, then a grave of burnt-out cars and rusted washing machines, then a grave of children. She was glad for the children who would not inject their first needle out in the old field.

The Walking Saint

Once a year, Mr John McManus made obligatory contact with his past. Choosing the most dismal of Sundays in late winter, when there were no sports to settle him in for an afternoon of hooting and cheering, he announced the trip to see his great aunt, a nun, commonly referred to as 'the walking saint' by McManus. He began in earnest meditation at the table. 'I've an idea now for what we could do with ourselves for the afternoon.' The *we* gave it away. 'We're dressed to the hilt, and there's no better time than the present,' McManus said.

'You mean there's no football matches on the telly,' his son Johnny groaned.

'That's enough of your lip.' McManus listened to no protests, nodding with practicality as he gnawed on a piece of fat. 'How many people can say they're related to a walking saint, tell me that?' He pointed menacingly with his fork. 'You'll need the saint's prayers when the Leaving Cert comes around, and if you want a good job. Do you know that when I came up here to Dublin I had to sit an exam against over a thousand others for my job? And do you know what?'

'They chose only twelve men,' Johnny said with a mocking guttural country accent. 'And you were one of those twelve apostles of the Gas Board. Hallelujah.'

'We'll have enough of that, walking atheist.' McManus rolled his eyes at the brazenness of his son but did nothing. He knew his son would get into the university by himself. His son didn't need the intercession of faith or walking saints.

While the girl cleared off the table, McManus went upstairs and parted his hair with oil and a comb. Dabbing on after-shave, he whistled away to himself, participating in a long standing ritual that went back to his boyhood: the yearly visits to the walking saint. There was always a reverential tip of the head when the words 'walking saint' were pronounced. Not that much had come of her, really. When he'd first come up from the country to Dublin for the job interview with the Gas Board, the walking saint had arranged for him to stay at a priest's residence so he wouldn't have to waste money on lodgings. But of course, you couldn't get out of a priest's clutches without dropping a fair few bob for Mass offerings, which added up to what a boarding house would have cost and more. That was usually the way of it. The walking saint cost you more than she gave you. Her mission was not of an earthly nature. She had the commission of eternity. Still, she'd blessed his pencil box on the morning of his exam.

'Right, have we got everything – the communion and confirmation medals and the wedding ring?'

Mr McManus's eldest girl of seventeen, Martina, with long stringy black hair and a rat's twitch of anxiety for a face, held a pen in her hand. 'Do you think she could bless the pen I'm going to use on the Leaving Cert?'

A pen! It was a shock to McManus that such stupidity had been inherited so completely. But thank God it had afflicted the girl and not his son. 'Jesus, I don't know about that, Martina. It's . . .'

'It's vulgar,' Mrs McManus said from the kitchen.

'Yes, that's right. It would be vulgar all right. Do you have your confirmation medal? She'll bless that for you.'

Martina made the horrible reflexive twitch, the eyes watering. 'I don't have to tell her what the pen is for. I'll just tell her to bless it for . . . for a special intention.'

'I wouldn't have her bless a sneeze,' Johnny laughed behind her back.

'I'll make sure she gives you a good blessing, walking atheist,' McManus said severely, but there was no conviction in what he said. The walking atheist was a bad bastard, no doubt, but McManus took an edifying pride that he was rearing the sort of creature who would grow up to badger other men the way *he'd* been badgered and looked down upon in his years of service at the Gas Board. McManus couldn't figure how he had managed such a son with the likes of himself and his wife, but accounted for it simply: 'The whole is greater than the sum of its parts.'

The Sunday afternoon rain had the roads desolate, how the earth would be if everyone died. McManus was in good form since there was the odds-on prospect of getting a good afternoon tea up at the convent. His rheumatism acted up though, and he managed to keep the leg warm by depressing the clutch erratically, changing gears more than was necessary, which kept everyone's head rocking forward slightly as the car moved along. His wife eyed him cautiously. McManus raised his index finger off the steering wheel to indicate silence. He would endure his suffering alone. His solace was simply that, without speaking of it, his family was aware of it. They knew this was the hazard of walking the streets, rain or shine, to read gas meters.

The teeming humidity of the rain made McManus sweat profusely, and the damp turned the windows misty. McManus had to keep wiping the window with a handkerchief. He finally stopped off at a small sweet shop. 'Martina, go on in and buy a few lottery tickets, a bottle of Lucozade and a box of Rose's chocolates, and a pack of Sweet Afton.'

And a bottle of holy water,' Mrs McManus insisted.

'Jesus, wait a second. Didn't we buy holy water at this very shop last year, and it's up in the bathroom untouched? We should have brought that. Does holy water have an expiry date?'

'It does, Dad. Celestial disclaimer. Miracles are not guaranteed after date of expiry.'

'Listen here, walking atheist. I don't give a shite if you damn yourself to eternal oblivion, but have the common decency not to do it in a moving car with your family in it.' With a flourish of his handkerchief, McManus cleared the window, waited for his daughter, then bucked away from the small sweet shop as a spasm of pain ran the course of his right leg.

*

The car proceeded through the old part of the city, along a great wall behind which lay a succession of great old structures, a maternity hospital, a jail, a convent for the aged and deranged and a graveyard. It had a strange effect on McManus, for wasn't it the sum of human existence set in brick? There must have been a great municipal and philosophical presence of mind in days gone by, a fixity to the simple things, before it all got complicated. McManus wanted to give the walking atheist a good puck for himself.

Dwarfed by the wall, the black car crawled slowly along with McManus looking for the small entrance to the convent cut out of the brick. The convent had the look of an eighteenth-century prison, but had actually been erected by the Sisters of Charity for the care of the infirm, the deranged, and the plain old.

McManus checked his face in the mirror, mechanically licking the tips of his fingers and patting down the parting along the exposed thin line of his pink scalp. In a way he felt slightly ashamed of what had become of himself. To present his own mediocrity once a year had a humiliating effect now in his later years. His own job at the Gas Board approximated to what one could expect of a competent nine-year-old, since all he had to do was go around to the sides of houses and read the gas meters, jotting down the numbers and submitting them to the accounts department. There was an unspoken accountability in his visit to the walking saint, the small-talk and chat. It was as much as to say, 'Is this what's become of you, my favourite nephew?' For all of her spirituality, that was the way the walking saint must have felt. There was a knowing practicality behind the walking saint. She had a way of quizzing the children when they came to see her. Questions in their sums and trick questions about percentages. 'If there was a cake there on the table, and someone said to you, "Would you like one sixth of the cake or one third of the cake", which would you take?' And she had a certain smiling sympathy for the one-sixth takers, and a wink for the one-third takers who might then get a question from their catechism on the Trinity:

'How many persons in the one God?' A certain logic with numbers seemed to be her way of judging character and future prospects. McManus's grandfather said that when the walking saint was a girl she only talked about land and money. She'd a great head for figures.

McManus brought the car to a stop. The great outer walls had long since turned a grimy black from the soot of coal fires and car exhausts, adding a gloom of overbearing antiquity. 'I'll ask you now to be on your best behaviour.'

Johnny shrugged his shoulders.

'Everyone agreed, then.' The flood of years, of his own dead parents and the times they came up on the train for this pilgrimage, filled McManus's head. He had to catch his breath.

Mrs McManus, wearing a bit of crocheted white knitting on her head, bowed her red face. 'We should say an act of contrition,' which they did in sorrow for their sins.

Mr McManus knocked on a heavy iron-studded wooden door.

A small man opened the door and stepped back. McManus entered the small enclosure, followed by his family. They entered into an ill-contrived purgatory, a sort of dark stable crowded with old men in ill-fitted herringbone tweed suits. These were the sane (or at least non-violent) residents who had the privilege of going to this makeshift room to talk among themselves. Most of them sat quietly with half-open mouths, gawking into space. McManus looked at a small group seated at a table. 'Good day,' he said congenially, assaulted by a smell of distilled whiskey. He could see there were piles of matchsticks for betting and steel tumblers for whiskey before each of the men at the table. The cards had disappeared, though.

McManus announced that he'd come to see his aunt. The men began murmuring, civil war medals on their suits jiggling.

The attendant on duty, with his big belly bursting through a buttoned cardigan, wavered in obvious intoxication on his stumpy bow-legs. He had been sleeping on the job. Only a ridiculous black cap he wore, with a silver badge saying porter, distinguished him from the patients. In McManus's estimation, the attendant looked like an overgrown school bully.

Clearing his throat before speaking, the attendant balanced himself by holding the back of a chair. 'Were you called for, sir?'

'We never needed an appointment before.' McManus leaned forward. The attendant smelt of whiskey. 'Is there something wrong?'

The attendant jerked his head back. 'Ah no, sir. I was just wondering, that's all.' The chair scraped against the cold floor. He showed a set of cracked teeth that looked like they'd been glued back together. 'If you'll have a seat now, sir, please.'

McManus rolled his eyes and shuffled his family onto a church bench pushed up against the wall. He was used to this sort of bravado down through the years. The attendants were of the lowest order, fiddlers who were always 'on the make' as they said, bringing in whiskey and taking bets for the men. Sin, it seemed, had been recognized and allotted its own room out by the walls of the convent. This was what McManus loved about the old days, the unspoken pragmatism. Evil was a living creature which had to be cordoned off and contained.

The attendant picked up a black phone receiver, cupped his hand over his mouth and waited anxiously. He motioned to one of the old men to open the front door to clear the air in the room. McManus watched as the attendant inserted a Silvermint sweet into his mouth.

Martina and Mrs McManus had the same perplexed look. The smell of the men scared them. The girl was the slim image of her mother. Mrs McManus seemed on the verge of saying something, but Mr McManus gave her a severe look.

A mildewed dirty skylight had turned everything a ghoulish green in the small waiting room, and the men looked like etiolated stalks with heads craned towards the failing light. This was the first defence of a cloistered medieval insularity, the small darkly-lit rooms preparing the penitent for entrance into another realm. Everything about it said that sanctity could only be ensured by a removal from vice, a retreat from the vicissitudes of earthly existence. Beyond lay the domain of a walking saint.

McManus touched the oily sleekness of his hair. He caught Johnny's eye and saw the sombre mood the place had brought onto the walking atheist. The boy had his head partially down-turned, the eyes averted from the old men. McManus wanted to say, 'You see now, walking atheist, we weren't such eejits as you thought.' Faith propagated itself like moss in the small enclosure of dank walls.

The attendant crunched away on the mint. He took his cap off, exposing a shining egg head which he wiped before setting the cap down again.

'We need some air in here,' he said gruffly to one of the men. 'Fan the door, will you?' His eyes looked uneasily at McManus. 'Mother Superior will be along presently, sir.'

A man looking over rounded spectacles smiled at the family.

McManus gave a knowing nod in the men's direction. He was always struck by the strange affability of old men who wanted to tell you something, men who had been abandoned within the walls of a convent to die. As a boy it had terrified him that old age could bring this on. His mother, and even the walking saint, had made mention of what happens when men have neither family to care for them nor money to keep themselves. It had provided the unconscious push in his youth, the phantom room of dying men reminding him of what can and does happen to those who go astray. Most of the men had been manual labourers all their lives, earning little, and now abandoned by their children who had fared just as badly. The demon of ignorance and, no doubt, drink had done its damage, but the sorry end of it was simply that without money you could depend on nothing and nobody. This was what these men, in their inept gesturing and agitated winking, were left to contemplate, until death, which awaited them just one hundred yards away in the cemetery.

An old fellow breathing quickly through his lips as though blowing on a spoon of hot soup rocked back and forth as he sat. 'Could you spare a cigarette, sir?' he shouted, making everyone jump. Obviously he was partially deaf. The words had a nasal slur. He pulled at McManus's arm. 'Just one cigarette, sir. Just one.'

McManus reached into his pocket for the extra package of Sweet Afton, knowing from experience that you couldn't give just one man a cigarette. The men became agitated, coming out of the gloom like curious cats. McManus distributed the cigarettes. In a minute the room was choked with smoke and coughs. It hid the smell of whiskey.

'I'll tell you something for nothing there, sonny,' a man winked at the walking atheist. 'I know your sort through and through. You'd do well to follow this advice to last as long as us here.' He pointed at the other men who took a particular pride in their age, straightening up and looking at the walking atheist. 'If you don't have to run, walk; if you don't have to walk, stand; if you don't have to stand, sit; if you don't have to sit, lie down. And remember this: Always eat whenever you can.' He punctuated everything with a blink of his moist eyes. 'That should see you through life, sonny.'

'I'll remember that, sir. To paraphrase: Sit around on my arse and do shag-all.'

At that the old fellow faced McManus and grinned. 'You've a job with him, I'd say.'

'Don't be talking,' McManus concurred.

The crunch of gravel and the jingle of keys announced the approach across the no man's land between the convent and the guard house. The heavy attendant put on a black coat with a theatrical flourish, raised his cap, wiped his forehead, and munched down on another mint. As he pulled back a heavy bar on the door he was already shouting, 'And aren't you looking great, Mother Superior.' His silhouette merged with the Mother Superior and they exchanged some words. A wave of cold, grey light poured into the small room.

The men instinctively rose, and a low reverent hiss of 'Ssssister' filled the room as the Mother Superior came in.

She acknowledged them with frank condescension, a dismissive movement of her sleeve. She saw the men at the table and the matches. 'There wasn't anybody playing cards out here, was there?'

'Not at all, Mother,' the attendant answered, waving his hand over the men.

The Mother Superior had a huge jailer's ring of keys tethered to a string that disappeared into her pocket. 'Well, there better be nothing going on out here.'

The men stayed silent. They waited, the cigarettes pinched between the thumb and index finger, glowing in the cup of their hands.

The family sat lined up like dismal convicts before a firing squad.

Mother Superior moved toward McManus, who winced as he stood up. He touched the fastidious knot of his thick navy-blue work tie like some earnest schoolboy.

The Mother Superior came within a foot of McManus's face without saying aything. She had a terse leanness about her, a gaunt mannish face with eyes set unnaturally far apart. 'The once a year McManuses,' she said.

'The very people,' McManus smiled for lack of anything else to say, trying to take a step back, but found himself wedged against the church bench.

'The McManuses from down the country always write us a fortnight in advance to let us know they are coming.'

'We'll do that in future, Sister,' McManus managed, retaining a level of decorum and subservience, enduring the galling spectacle of having himself shown up in front of the walking atheist. This was all the walking atheist needed to make a show of things, which he did, emerging from the smokiness in the room to brazen the Mother Superior with a strange defiant stare, saying out of the blue, 'Father, Son, Holy Ghost, boiled some ham and burnt some toast.'

'Johnny, please,' Mrs McManus beseeched.

The attendant pulled on his cigarette, glad to have attention drawn away from him and the men.

The Mother Superior took account of the walking atheist's words and gave a nodding gesture of silent scorn, but meditating all the same on what she'd have done to him if she'd half the chance. With her usual frankness she stared at McManus and said, 'Your aunt is very sick.'

McManus hesitated. 'Sick . . .'

'Sick, Mr McManus. Yes, very sick.'

The smoke curled, drifting towards the open door. The old men strained to catch what was being said. McManus felt the stifling quiet of the small room as the Mother Superior hesitated.

In the end she took a step forward and wheeled McManus away by his elbow. Her face was inches from his. Her breath was horrible. McManus stiffened in a way that made his joints crackle. 'It's a situation of a delicate sort.' She was trying to manhandle him into a mutual complicity. 'You understand of course, Mr McManus,' she persisted. She showed the inflexible resolve of a creature who got her way.

McManus didn't, but he felt the pressure of her fingers on his arm. 'The children would be better served if they stayed here.' Her thick caterpillar eyebrows moved on her forehead.

McManus nodded obligingly with a simpering religiosity.

'I'm taking your husband up to the house to talk,' she said, turning to Mrs McManus. 'I'll have tea and sandwiches sent out to you.'

McManus added, 'It'll only be a short while.'

'The pen,' Mrs McManus said hesitantly, egged on by Martina who held the pen out.

McManus averted his eyes to the Mother Superior's face, and she dismissed the gesture of the pen, leaving the girl holding it sheepishly.

The walking atheist spoke loud enough to be heard by the men, 'They've probably buried her already,' which made the men issue a hiss of consternation and cross themselves with their cigarettes.

Again, Mrs McManus pleaded, 'Johnny,' while Mr McManus rounded out the pantomime of dissatisfaction by compressing his lips, making a clicking sound of an agitated insect.

The Mother Superior vented her frustration by leaning down and brushing the small piles of matches onto the floor. 'I'm not a fool, Mr Bennet.' She glared at the attendant. 'Shame on men who can't even keep the Sabbath.'

McManus caught the grinning face of the walking atheist and the bewildered men scrambling for their winnings as the bar slid across the door once more.

In the cold narrow corridor McManus sullenly followed, in tow, with a perceptible halting gait, his right leg scraping the cold tiled floor in which he could see his reflection. Everything was meticulously polished and smelt of carbolic acid.

McManus drew the stares of old men and women gone in the head who were held in chairs by leather straps. He smiled at them. There were others who stood looking bewildered at the walls or the ceiling.

The fervour of the visit was long since lost. McManus's odds on the afternoon tea had drastically diminished, and there was nothing ready back at the house. Still, McManus instinctively picked out the clank of pots from some distant kitchen on the lower floors. A strong smell of meat permeated the cold air as they moved into the desolate recesses of an old passageway with little rooms off to either side.

'If you will, Mr McManus?' The Mother Superior led McManus into a small windowless room with an empty fire grate, a plastic bowl of fruit on a round table, a single chair and a lone light hanging from a high ceiling. He had just been directed to sit down when the Mother Superior began in a dramatic, yet sombre manner. 'Your aunt's condition, Mr McManus, concerns the very foundation of this order.'

McManus tensed his face in a manner which he thought was necessary under the circumstances. 'What's wrong with her?'

he offered.

'She suffered a stroke that has left her partially paralysed.'

McManus leaned forward in his seat, sensing something more.

The Mother Superior took her cue and proceeded. 'With the shock of something of this nature, there is a, how shall I say it, a fear of death that sets in. Mortality has a way of . . . of fixating itself in the brain . . .' She touched her head, intimating the brain.

'I see,' McManus said when he didn't see at all, pressing his knees with his hands. The bulb cast a clinical starkness, making him uncomfortable.

The Mother Superior pushed on. 'You see, Mr McManus, your aunt's faith was tested in . . . the ordeal . . .' That is what it had come to be called, as McManus was to learn, 'The Ordeal.'

'But she's the very rock of faith itself.' McManus puffed up his cheeks in a show of exasperation. 'She's . . . She's a walking saint.'

The Mother Superior's eyes looked heavenward, her hands following in the way the religious do, invoking space, shaping the unseen into something real. 'That is the mystery of His ways, Mr McManus.'

McManus extended his right leg as a twinge of pain ran to his big toe, making him bang the floor with his boot. His face reddened. 'How has her faith been tested?'

The Mother Superior seemed to hesitate, as though she'd gone too far, but then saw the copper bracelet on McManus's wrist that he used to stave off the rheumatism. The tight cowl around her face pinched a taciturn expression. 'She wouldn't sleep without the light on,' she finally said, with a level of self-consciousness that made her cough slightly and blink anxiously.

McManus looked up and wanted to have a good laugh. What the hell did wanting a light on have to do with anything? He showed his teeth to register a moment of contemplation and hide the laughing inside his head.

'It's not a laughing matter, Mr McManus,' she said severely, with prescience. 'I'll have you know she screams if the light is turned off. Everybody knows about it . . . the other sisters and the residents and . . .' she straightened herself. 'And the Cardinal has been informed, I may tell you now.'

McManus had the sudden foreboding notion that the Mother Superior had done something to his aunt. She was after all the keeper of women and men out in the hallway who were restrained with leather straps on their arms and wrists. She had a capacity to immobilize and detain, a staunch defender of the faith with the resolve of the inquisition. 'This is not the Dark Ages for God's sake,' McManus burst out. 'Maybe she's deranged from the stroke. That can happen when someone gets sick . . .' McManus found he was half-shouting. 'Yes . . . You . . . You can't test the faith of someone who doesn't have their senses about them.'

The Mother Superior raised her hand in protest, the loose arm of her dress flapping like the wing of some restless bird. 'Mr McManus, this convent will not veer from its duty no matter what the circumstances or the consequences. In her final hour your aunt has abandoned the Almighty. A life of charity and poverty has been undone in her last hour. God came and tested her faith and she was found lacking.' She pointed heavenward with her long finger. 'Lacking!' She broke off for a moment and then began, 'I am talking of her salvation, about her soul and where it will spend eternity.' She trailed off into a whisper.

McManus looked distraught, making a clumsy gesture with his own raised arm. Trying to point to where his aunt was, but of course he didn't know. His extended hand took refuge on his brow and then slipped quietly into his right trouser pocket where it found his leg trembling. He felt the jingle of change in his pocket. It suddenly struck him: maybe it was money they were after him for?

The only reason the walking saint got out of the convent once a year was to participate in a national collection campaign, to extort money out of decent people who couldn't refuse. Well, if that was the way, he'd set them straight there and then. He persisted, though less resolutely, feeling it was really the money she was after, but disinclined to broach the subject. 'But there are insane people who can speak all sorts of gibberish and they're not accountable for what they say. She's had a stroke, and that made her lose her senses. Any doctor would say that she is suffering from the effects of the stroke.'

'We do not hide behind doctors, Mr McManus. The word of a doctor is nothing to the word of God. We will not lie on her behalf, we will not let her die without begging God's forgiveness . . .'

'But wanting a light on . . . Surely to God . . .' McManus shook his head in a venerable posturing, feeling the burden, that he was fighting an abstract philosophical battle. After all, he hadn't seen his aunt in a year. There was no point of reference, no sense of what she'd become. He drew himself out of his chair.

'Surely you understand, Mr McManus?' The Mother Superior seemed to stalk him, her head thrust out of the habit, the eyes following him. 'What is the greatest fear children have?' she whispered.

'Wetting the bed.' McManus said, as a point of goading.

'Fear of the dark, Mr McManus, that's what. And why? Because children have no faith in God, in the Almighty's ability to vanquish darkness with the light of faith.'

McManus could see there was nobody who believed in the Devil like the religious. It was as though the Devil slept in their very beds, whispering into their ears. As McManus sat there he began to see through the fixed look in the Mother Superior's face. It was more than likely that it was her faith that had been tested by the walking saint's ordeal. How could she reconcile it with her faith when the walking saint was off in some room screaming if the light was turned out?'

The Mother Superior was saying something . . . McManus looked up.

'Make no doubt about it, your aunt's faith has been tested by the ordeal.' There was a moment of apprehensive quiet. A trolley rolled somewhere out in the hallway. McManus pricked up his ears like an alert dog.

It was in this moment that the Mother Superior slipped in slyly, as though in mid-thought: 'Why indeed was she picked out for the ordeal by the Almighty?'

McManus drew himself back to the issue at hand.

'That boy of yours perhaps . . .' Her thick eyebrows came together in a desperate, pensive way.

'What?' McManus saw the way it was now, the insufferable indignity of it that she should even dare to think she could get away with the likes of that. His face became imbued with blood. The leg twitched violently. To think that she had casually offered up the possibility that his son was in some way to blame for what had happened to the walking saint . . . And yet McManus hadn't the outright conviction to speak his mind. He had been sized up well, trapped in the religious fear of his upbringing. Hadn't he set up his son as an evil solace against the world? Indeed, there was the dark notion that what she was saying made some sense to McManus. After all, this religion was one of retribution. That was how it had been handed down to him and his kind, and from the stories in the Bible, the blood of lambs splattered on doors, plagues delivered unto the oppressors . . .

The Mother Superior whispered softly, 'God works in mysterious ways, Mr McManus.'

A knock at the door interrupted further discussion. A plump nun in white brought in a tray with tea and sandwiches along with slices of brandy cake and a bowl of whipped cream. With silent discretion, the Mother Superior directed the nun, putting her body in front of Mr McManus to obscure his view.

They thought he could be bribed by food. He was being made the right eejit and yet he remained steadfast. The tray emerged again on the table, and McManus was left staring down at the usual delicate triangular sandwiches of cold meats, ham and roast beef with the peculiar extravagance of salad dressing, a layer of taste unto itself. His eye finally fixed on the depression of the nun's thumb print on the soft white bread.

The Mother Superior stood back as the nun leaned over the table, arranging the solitary meal for McManus. Of course, he obliged, but not before he said in his stern voice, 'I should like to see my aunt,' as a sort of vague but commanding protest.

The door closed behind, and McManus was left like an ignominious Hansel stuffing his face at the witch's gingerbread house.

Twenty minutes passed before the Mother Superior appeared again.

McManus, satiated by the brandy pudding, looked up from his seat, holding the ear of a cup of tea. He'd licked the bowl of cream clean in a moment of bravado to offset the tension, even though he had a condition when he ate dairy products.

The Mother Superior eyed the bowl, understanding his intentions. What was not said was important. The clairvoyance of the subjugated had occupied the time of the walking saint when the country was under foreign control and everything was said in silent subterfuge. As his father used to say disparagingly about talk, 'When all is said and done, there'll be more said than done.'

'In circumstances of this nature years ago you would have been sent away, Mr McManus.' She hesitated. 'But this is the time of the doubting Thomas.' She was a creature who had not reasoned with anybody in years, ill-equipped for inconsequential gentleness or diplomacy, as was McManus himself. But in that moment of expectation, McManus felt a bout of indigestion rumbling inside himself, and finding the need for the relief of open space, forced the point curtly, 'If I could see my aunt?'

Silently, McManus followed the Mother Superior at an appropriate distance. They went down a staircase, along a windowless passage that held the coldness of interment. The quarters had the stark lunacy of a saint's mortification, a place of pure cold, everything conceived to make the body useless and infirm, to rob it of heat, to let cold enter the marrow of bone. A diffused reddish glow emanating from beneath the bleak representation of the twelve stations of the cross provided the only light. McManus passed the eighth station, and shuddered, seeing the wounds on Jesus's feet had been worn away by the silent adoration of lips.

A smell of fresh-cut roses drifted out of the small cell which contained the walking saint. The walking saint was on her back. McManus had to assume a reverent stoop to keep his head from touching the low ceiling. He crossed himself, his eyes filling with tears for a moment. McManus hesitated to move, afraid to cast a shadow.

The left side of the walking saint's body had died in paralysis, the flesh the colour of aged, jaundiced leather. Her tiny hands had been joined together. The left eye, half-closed, floated aimlessly in its socket. A perpetual tear flowed down the withered cheek and into the ear. The other eye, transfixed, stared at the light. This eye was the only source of life on the face. Existence had come down to this one solitary sense, to this solitary image of light.

McManus collected himself soon enough. He could see the walking saint understood nothing.

The Mother Superior instructed McManus to a chair. It was warm. Obviously, someone had been keeping vigil. McManus's big rump spread out on the chair as he looked at the walking saint, too afraid to touch her. A collection of rosary beads, a bottle of holy water and a prayer book were set on a small side table. They'd been at her to repent and offer up a good confession.

To McManus, the walking saint looked like one of those disinterred doll-faced mummies that are stuffed away in the recesses of side altars in Cathedrals.

'Can you hear me?' McManus whispered, inhibited and self-conscious of the Mother Superior behind him.

The walking saint had passed beyond pain and recognition. It was as though God had forgotten about her, as though she was so far removed from the real world down in this crypt, that she was hidden from God's eyes. Or at least, that was the impression that came over McManus at that moment. He even found himself wondering why the dignity of death had passed over her . . . The walking saint had spent her life in the service of the aged and infirm, given up a life in the outside world. She had endured the decrepitude of others' old age and dementia, subjected herself to the grotesqueness of what human flesh can emit from its orifices.

The Mother Superior turned off the light.

McManus had to catch his breath as a sudden strange crying filled the pure silence of the cell. 'Turn it on,' McManus shouted. Sweat turned cold on his flesh.

The light filled the room again.

'Jesus, what are you trying to do to her?' McManus managed, getting his breath again.

'There is no light in eternal darkness,' the Mother Superior answered stiffly.

The small lips of the walking saint had parted slightly from the screaming. McManus took a glass of water and a cloth from the table. He gently poured a trickle of water into the small hole of the mouth and waited. The walking saint's body jerked, but the water disappeared. McManus dabbed the lips. His face was over the eye, which seemed to see him for a moment. Then silence returned to the walking saint, the right eye again fixed on the light.

The Mother Superior had not calculated the effect of the screaming on McManus, who had become afflicted with shivering. He got up but there was nowhere to go. He had to almost back up to move away from the bed, turning slowly to face the Mother Superior who had a horrible look in her eyes of disquieting despair. McManus could see the look of madness. The Mother Superior had become unnerved and resentful of what the walking saint was doing to everyone. McManus could imagine her coming down at all hours of the night and turning out the light only to hear the sudden screaming. The walking saint had become incidental in a way. Really, all the Mother Superior was concerned about was herself. She wanted her personal faith restored.

'She should be under the care of a doctor,' McManus said softly.

The Mother Superior shook her head. 'A doctor comes and sees her . . .'

McManus was aware of his own limitations. He hadn't the power to have her removed and there was no point causing a scene and disgracing both the church and his own family's name. Maybe it was better to leave things as they were? What would have happened if he hadn't have come today? But of course he had, by the grace of God or coincidence, who knows?

'You will have to leave her now,' the Mother Superior said.

'One more minute, please . . .' McManus turned again and sat down. He touched the walking saint's icy fingers, feeling the small wedding ring of her vocation: a bride of Christ for over half a century. Everything that was said and done amounted to nothing in the end, only death . . . And hadn't that been why the care of the old, the infirm, the mad, had been committed to the care of Christian charity through the years, to nuns who gave up their lives in this world for the glory of some other world?

McManus could see his own father in her face, the same McManus face that the walking atheist had inherited. He put his lips to her wet ear, tasting the salt of the perpetual tear.

'Mr McManus . . .' The Mother Superior's voice rang anxious, afraid that McManus was whispering something into the walking saint's ear. 'Your family is waiting for you, Mr McManus . . .'

McManus hesitated, and then, in his most pure moment of atheism, committed his most religious act. He raised his hand to the light and whispered. 'Don't you see . . . Mother?' The shadow of his extended arm ran the length of the walking saint, bisecting her. He was working with very little, light and dark, yet wasn't it after all the essence of religion? 'She is staring at God,' McManus whispered . . . 'Staring at God . . .'

The Mother Superior stepped back, afraid that McManus

had gone mad as he began to shout. 'Don't you see it?' Tears streamed down his face. He was taking no chances.

The Mother Superior stepped back to the door and then her hands came together in a shock of revelation or a moment of uncanny pragmatism. It didn't matter, what mattered was that McManus saw the effect and kept up the waterworks of tears and the shouting ... 'The light of God,' McManus shouted. He knocked the jug of water off the table, stumbling forward.

'The light of God,' she whispered, nodding her head as recognition broke on her face. She stared at the light, McManus at the dark of the shadow.

'She is staring at God,' the Mother Superior cried, and went out into the passageway weeping. They had not understood, that was all. 'She is staring at God.'

That was how McManus the gas meter reader, father of the walking atheist, saved the walking saint from a sorry funeral on a rainy Sunday afternoon in early December.

The walking saint died a fortnight later in the contemplation of the light. The cardinal offered up prayers in the graveyard next door on a glorious winter day with a pale yellow sun and the wintry stars up in the clear blue sky. The herringbone-tweed men acted as pallbearers, decked out in their war medals. Their breath showed in the cool light.

McManus, as surviving relative, read from the gospel up at the church and was fed the usual compliment of sandwiches and brandy pudding afterwards. And there was a barrel of stout on hand. McManus indulged himself, dressed up in his Sunday best and his hair parted with oil.

There was great talk of the walking saint's faith, of her devotion. The word saint, or more exactly 'saintly' was used by the cardinal. Of course, pronouncements were premature at this stage. As it says in the good book, 'lots had already been drawn' for her clothes which had been torn to shreds for the usual relics – the first order of business when you went about getting someone into the running for sainthood. It seems the diocese had the little glass casing with the bit of blood-red backing in stock.

The cardinal was pressed on the matter by a few newspaper reporters. The aura of saintliness was fostered by the honey light of the mid-winter day when you couldn't help but contemplate the glory of God's creation. The reception was held out back of the home in the great expanse of gardens. Off in the distance other men in the same herringbone-tweed suits tilled the land, growing greens and spuds and raising livestock. The bleat of sheep travelled on the stilled air. In an old city tram that had been converted into a sun room sat the industrious women, like fat cats sunning themselves, smiling, glad of the weather, their hands mechanically working away to the click of knitting needles, making socks and jumpers for the residents. Everything had a self-contained efficiency to McManus's mind as he supped at the warm stout and circulated among the throng, receiving the words of those in attendance. Yes, it was a great day all round.

The Mother Superior made herself scarce when McManus roamed the garden. He saw her avoiding him, and sure it was best for things to be left unsaid. They were in agreement on that point. It would only be awkward . . . You answer your own conscience in your own way. That's how McManus thought of it, and anyway the drink had made him mellow and satisfied.

The cardinal was holding court near a fountain of St. Francis feeding birds. The reporters were scribbling away on pads of paper. The cardinal was explaining the process of beatification, canonization, and finally sainthood as best he could. He said the way it worked was that a committee would be set up in the diocese and strange occurrences, cures, or outright miracles due to prayers offered up to the walking saint, or by the placement of her relics on different parts of the body, would be documented and duly forwarded to Rome where a commission would convene to see if the reports deemed the testimonies true and worthy of further investigation. Of course, the cardinal intimated that the process could take centuries, and there were no guarantees. 'You could be an early runner, but what matters is staying power over the centuries. Name recognition is everything in a run at saint-hood,' the cardinal said decidedly.

'As it is with dishwashing liquid,' the walking atheist laughed at McManus. He had really let the walking atheist go to hell of recent times.

The cardinal paid no heed to the walking atheist and continued with his blabbering.

The walking atheist had said to McManus the week before, 'Do you know that human intelligence is limited to the size of what can fit through a woman's pelvis?' It was due to the size of the brain or something, and what could McManus do except wink and say, 'Well, don't tell your mother. She'll be very upset, son.'

Out in the garden a glass of sherry had gone to Mrs McManus's head and was making her cry. Martina was all concerned, leaning into her mother, earnestly shepherding her over to the sun room. McManus watched the two of them. God, his daughter was the spitting image of how his wife had been. Yes, the faces don't change down through history, the death mask is inherited from generation to generation . . .

'There now,' McManus smiled at his wife, intercepting her and leading her into the tram. He took his handkerchief to her stained lips.

'Isn't it beautiful weather for it,' she whispered.

McManus was off again, continuing his rounds, slurping away at the old drink. Port was produced for a final comment from the cardinal. Only time would tell, keep your fingers crossed and all that, and who knows, but the prayers might be answered.

McManus remembered reading stories of the church re-morselessly pursuing prospective saints from the Middle Ages into their graves, prying open coffins only to find scratches on the insides and pronouncing the sin of despair on the corpses. Some plague or other had rendered the victims in a 'suspended animation' of sorts, and they had been buried alive.

Sin, it seemed in McManus's religion, could follow you beyond the grave. But the main thing now for McManus was that the day had been a great success, and he had got the walking saint into consecrated ground.

The Sunday Races

The Sunday morning was silent as always. Emmett hadn't slept well. In his dreams he was moving in slow motion; faces passed him, the earth swallowed him, the dream opening like a wound in his head.

Emmett awoke in his track suit with his running magazines scattered around his bed. He'd fallen asleep reading an article about a tribe of Kenyan runners. Tentatively, Emmett tensed his injured left leg. It was locked with stiffness, numbed from the bandage tourniquet. He grimaced. The dull numbness throbbed under the covers. He uncoiled the bandage, exposing the thin whiteness of his leg, the black hairs matted with sweat. The muscle tear was getting worse, bleeding invisibly. He put his face in his pillow.

Emmett sat up again in the cold half-light of his room. The space was small, encumbered by a bed which occupied half of the room. He let his fingers run over his legs, feeling his ankles, the soreness in the joints. He'd become accustomed to the pains and the injuries. It was part of the game. There were some lads who were on a hundred and twenty miles a week. Emmett was grinding on ninety, but he was the best. His pelvis and kidneys took the worst of it. For over a month he'd been passing blood in his urine. He'd heard that was normal.

It was on the long run that he did the damage, or at least that was what he reckoned. He took a knock against a wall. It wasn't anything at all, yet the constant attrition of the miles compounded the hit. In cross-country running there was never anything sudden like the snapped tendons of sprinters or footballers. The injuries always started as nagging pains, indistinguishable from the usual soreness. A day off and common sense would have been medicine enough, but nothing ever seemed that serious until the morning, when the injury had pooled with blood and swelled over time.

Emmett's thigh was badly torn. He touched the muscle, and a knifing pain ran to his pelvis. He took three aspirin from a bottle on his table dresser, worked up a spit in his mouth, and swallowed. He tasted the arid powder of the tablets at the back of his throat. He took a bottle of menthol rub from his bag and let his leg rest on the dirty sheets. The bottle had a spongy applicator on a wire. He swabbed the muscle in easy strokes. The odour wafted under his nose as the clear liquid trickled down to the tender skin at the back of the knee. The skin stung and turned pink. Emmett worked his fingers down his thigh, letting his thumb bury itself into the unseen injury. The locked stiffness softened, almost acquiescing.

Emmett made tea in the kitchen. The mugs huddled in the cupboard, the sugar hardened by the morning dampness. He set a tray and went upstairs. The silence of the morning blanketed his father's face. His father was getting old. Emmett could see the scalp under the hair. 'What's that smell?' He squinted his face, 'Jasus, what is it?'

'Just some rub for my legs to get dem warmed up,' Emmett said as he laid the tray down at his father's hips. He could see the outline of his father's thin legs under the covers.

On the small dresser, Emmett looked at the grey fingers of ash on a saucer. 'Yer not supposed to be smokin', Da.'

'Are you limpin'?' his father asked.

'No . . . You know, stiff . . . Dat's all.'

His father coughed violently and spilt his tea, leaning forward. 'Take . . . take dis . . .' The cup of tea toppled over.

'Da . . .' Emmett took the tray away. He went into the back room where his mother lay sleeping. She had migrated into the spare room to get away from the coughing. Emmett kissed her on the forehead. 'I'm off,' he whispered.

'You're limping,' Emmett's father said again when he came back into the room. 'Did you see her?'

'Yeah.'

'I hear she's got the church blazing with candles for us, and Jasus don't we need it?' He wheezed as he pulled on another cigarette.

Emmett looked at the rain falling in muted static outside the window.

'Good luck, son.' His father's words were a whisper of smoke. Emmett heard only the coughing. Phlegm floated in the spilt tea on the tray.

There was a laconic sleepiness to the morning as Emmett met up with Mr Brennan. A dirty rain littered the night's rubbish. Pipes spluttered and drains gurgled. Emmett was limping noticeably with the bandage he'd wrapped around his leg.

'How's about this for weather?' Brennan grumbled. His breath had the odour of stout. He could see that Emmett had been crying. Unnerved, he nodded his head agitatedly. 'Gimme that bag there. Grand.'

'Mr Brennan?' Emmett began.

Brennan eyed Emmett with suspicion. He could see the pronounced limp in Emmett's walk. 'We better head off,' he began in a pre-emptive tone.

'It's my leg,' Emmett looked into Brennan's eyes. 'I don't think . . .'

'Relax, will you. There's nothing that a good rub won't get you through. Do you hear me?'

'I . . . I . . . Mr Brennan . . .'

Mr Brennan turned his eyes in his head. 'Hold your horses awhile. You don't have to do anything you don't want to do, right? How many did you get in yesterday?'

'About six, and a couple of sprints.' Emmett stood abjectly in the rain under the town clock. 'Mr Brennan, I'm tellin' you . . .'

Mr Brennan nodded his head. 'Now this is what we'll do. We'll head out there and see who's about and explain that you've had a bit of an accident, right? We'll say you took a knock this morning' on the roads coming down and see what the judges say. It'll be all right. Sure, they know you've been winning everything.' Brennan let his mouth open in a vacuous smile. 'But we should make an appearance. OK?' Brennan said it like a priest, letting a smile mask his anger.

191

Brennan started his car, rubbing his hands together, cursing as usual. Emmett sat silently. He was afraid to touch his leg, tensing and relaxing it to keep the blood flowing. Brennan turned the radio on. The news was the same as always, something sad or terrible from Saturday night. Accidents on the road. Coups in different countries. Everything seemed to happen on Saturdays. Sunday was a day for news, a silent morning of a dead week, a retrospective when priests and politicians made sense of things. Brennan checked his watch. It was coming up on eight-twenty. 'Jasus, we don't want to be stuck listenin' to Mass for the sick.' He laughed in a forceful manner. 'Right?'

Emmett didn't smile. His father listened to that Mass on Sundays.

They had to herd the cows out of the field before the race could start. The week's rain had waterlogged the original course in the lowlands. The farmer who gave up the property was in his wellingtons, driving the cows through a rusty gate. His wife was with him, a plump middle-aged woman past the change of life. The farmer's face was tattooed with the blackness of the unwashed, an ingrained swarthiness. He prodded a stick into the bony shoulders of his animals as the dogs harassed them, cutting betwen their legs. 'What a whore of a day.' The farmer moved about in disgust. He was one of those hard-faced men two generations removed from the great potato famine, a descendant of death. He didn't understand things like sport. His time was lost in the constant attention to his animals and his fields.

'You better get back in the car for a while.' Mr Brennan sighed. 'I don't know what the hell is going on.' He looked at the farmer. 'Do you have a jacks here?'

'Now hold on there. I thought you were bringing a portable toilet. That's what Brother Madden told me.'

'Yeah, he's not here yet.' Mr Brennan turned towards a ditch.

The farmer rapped on Mr Brennan's shoulders. 'Don't even

think about it. I don't want my cows eating your shite!'

The coldness of the morning was clotted with a greyish gauze of threatening clouds. Emmett took a step back. More cows plodded along nervously. Their eyes were huge black lakes, reflecting Emmett's cold face. They had eyelashes which made them peculiarly feminine, almost tender. The distended sacks beneath their hind legs jiggled as they ran. The farmer pushed on, his wife following him in a kind of bovine trot with her buttocks swaying.

Brother Madden drove up in a minibus with his boys. He was one of the judges for the Irish team. Brother Madden was upwards of 20 stone. The young runners were skeletons beside him. Emmett looked on quietly, aware of his own thinness. Brother Madden's elephantine feet plodded through the mud. He exuded the corpulence of the religious, a man who never missed a meal in his life. He ate at baptisms, at weddings, at funerals.

Emmett could feel Madden's eyes watching him. 'You ready then, Emmett?' Madden let his fat hand maraud on Emmett's head.

'I don't think I'll . . .' Emmett looked at Brennan.

'Right as rain,' Brennan chimed.

Rain fell in a cold icy sheet, the mountains obscured in low-blown clouds. It had rained like this for nearly four days straight. The constant rhythm of the rain had followed Emmett for days, at night in bed, at school looking out the window, in the car on the way to the field. The sea itself seemed to engulf the land in this dome of greyness, saturating the whole of the county. The February sky carried with it threats of flu and pneumonia and the deathly skulk of earthy dampness. During the dead season animals went unmilked, stuck in cold rains, while others drowned in lowland fields. The old perished in the grip of arthritis or consumption. It was the limbo season, where darkness reigned its effulgence, claiming the infirm.

Emmett was aware of a coldness and the rain seeping into him, compounding his injury. His body was stiff from the previous night's unrest. His track suit smelt of last night's sweat. The hot tea of earlier on was somewhere in his intestines, but he was getting cold. He limped towards the stony walls. The field was clotted with the prints of animal hooves, the grass churned with mud and cold water. With the loose rain there was no odour or taste to the morning. His body had been numbed to the sensation of life. He kept hoping the race would be cancelled. He wasn't sure that Brennan was going to tell Brother Madden anything. Emmett began crying to himself, first in sniffles, and then tears ran down his face. All he needed was a few days' rest to sort the leg out. If only Brennan would tell them as he had said he would.

A sudden shower of hail began pelting the small huddle of cars, sending people in a scatter for cover. The race was off for now. Emmett hobbled towards the car as the sky grew almost dark. Brennan turned on the engine and revved the car, blasting the heater. 'Christ Almighty!' He opened an egg sandwich and a flask of tea. 'Here, take a sup to warm yourself.'

Emmett was shivering. The car rocked in the cold wind. 'You said you would tell them,' he began hesitatingly.

Brennan chewed his sandwich, holding his tea close to his face.

'I mean it. You don't own me . . .' Emmett began crying again. He put his head on the dash, sobbing. 'You think I don't want to get on the team?'

'Listen here, sunshine.' Brennan quivered with firm solemnity. He squeezed Emmett's arm. 'You can't always think of yourself, you hear me . . . I've given up a year of Sundays for you. And I've asked for nothing ever. So don't you give me this business now. Has your father ever come out here?'

'All you have to do is tell them that I got a knock. They know us, Mr Brennan. They'll believe you. I just need a week to get over this thing. It's next week that counts. Come on, please.' Emmett raised his face from the dash. 'Please.'

Brennan whispered, 'Self-pity is a bad thing. You hear me, Emmett? You get out there today and prove yourself a man, for Christ's sake. I thought you were the boy with the dreams, and here I have to beg a pup like you to do me a favour.'

'It's not like that . . .' Emmett's face was twisted with redness.

Brennan banged his flask on the dash. 'You got some nerve. Now you listen to me. You're goin' to do the man's thing here if I have to kick your arse around that field myself.' His voice bordered on a scream, and then he tempered it with a low pant. 'Have you any decency at all?' Two flecks of froth formed at the corners of Brennan's lips.

There was a claustrophobic air in the car. The windows were fogged with rain and words. Emmett was shaking with nervousness. Running for him had always been something simple, something unshared. Before he'd ever met Brennan, he had gone off on those mornings alone. He had lived his own dreams all those years, not Brennan's.

Emmett closed his eyes. Those runs had been struggles fought both inside and outside the body, conscious assaults on hidden roads, winding hills, a series of journeys, into mountains alone, into the organs of his body, slow agonizing runs that reckoned with the physical animal lurking beneath his skin, journeys elemental yet anchored to the basis of civilization, to biology, the intake of oxygen, the supremacy of the heart muscle, the sinews of lean flesh, all those things that trapped prehistoric animals but let man live, eat, and reproduce.

Nobody knew his secrets, the long runs that took him on roads untravelled, passing the crumbling ruins of roofless cottages haunted by cows, running along hidden animal trails. These runs bred a kind of mystifying euphoria, a self-containment removed from the company of others, something beyond the vulgarity of medals and trophies. The fifteen-mile run on a Sunday in the off-season, into the mountains in the early hours of the morning, climbing the snaking roads, hearing the secret lives of animals on sloping fields, their bodies lost in mist . . . He had felt all that, out there, the haggard endurance of a ragged skeleton, the burning sensation of pain slowly uncoiling in his thighs, the controlled torture. Running became a drug, an inflicted resolve over the meaninglessness of that which was left behind in sleeping houses along the seafront in Dun Laoghaire and Bray. At the pinnacle of a climb, there was always that moment to stop and look, to take the eyes off the road and look down at the thin ribboned mist of smoke, the electric wires threading the sky. That was when his alienation held its still, immutable beauty. The land had a haunting aura. Visions of other lands were there. He could imagine the misted dawn of Africa unfurling in the sullen majesty of unseen mountains. He shared secret dreams with others. He remembered from his magazines an African saying on some yellow mountain, 'Before you can run with the pack, you must first run alone.'

Emmett felt the coldness. He was conscious of his own country, the smallness of the island shrouded in dampness, the dankness of fungus, the earth with its famine dead and blackened potatoes. The unforgiving infertility of that field out there, stone and mud. If there was kinship with Africa it was there in this famine death, in the underbelly of these unknown fields with forgotten cottages, the hidden past. Famine and blight lurked under the skin of earth. Emmett could almost smell the sodden flesh in those fields out there. He was amidst the dead, the tongueless, earless, eyeless corpses, inchoate memories like mist, whispering, unknown histories disembodied. It was the loneliness of those runs which resurrected the dead in the half-light of his dreams and journeys.

Slowly Emmett looked at Brennan with concealed hatred. His dreams were frozen. They were stuck in the middle of a torrential rain. Sleet fell in muted splats on the windows. The car was whistling in the wind. His teeth gritted. The menthol ointment was cooling on his legs. He kneaded the injury with the palm of his hand.

Mr Brennan pretended he was asleep.

Brother Madden materialized from the rain, tapping the window.

Mr Brennan yawned and rolled down the window. 'Yeah?'

'It looks bad.' There was an odour of bacon issuing from Madden's mouth. He walked off in the mud, rapping on other cars.

'You see now, you jumped your horses. You'll probably not have to run at all. And what would be the point in letting on to anybody that you had a bad leg? If they knew that, I'd bet Madden would have one of his fellas get you out there. Isn't that right? You know bloody well it is.'

Madden waddled about the cars like a crow. Brennan looked at Emmett. It was a war of waiting, of endless monotony. Emmett squeezed a worm of cream onto his thighs and shivered.

Madden gave a sudden roar, 'We're on.'

'That's it then.' Mr Brennan wiped a pasty spit from his lips.

People crept from the cars like creatures from the ark. Rain beaded every surface. Everything smelt like salt. Sea gulls squawked and hovered overhead. Mr Brennan gave his patented nod. 'Come here and gimme a look at that leg.'

Emmett sat at the side of the car, letting Brennan take his leg. 'Ah . . . right there.'

Brennan let his fingers trace the muscle from the hip to the knee. 'Tell me where it hurts the most.'

'Right there, on the inside of the thigh.'

Brother Madden spat in the mud. 'Is he all right?' His face was rosy and smooth. He had a big duffel bag slung over his shoulder with the singlets for St Brendan's and the holy water he made his boys drink.

'Are you off to an exorcism, Brother?' Brennan laughed.

Brother Madden smiled.

'Just giving him a rub down. We had a hard go last Tuesday on the mountains. He's still stiff.'

Madden led his boys off towards the field.

'Are you goin' to give it a go?' Brennan queried.

Emmett nodded his head. 'It feels a little better,' he said hesitantly, standing and testing the pressure on his thigh.

'Come on. Do it for your Da.'

Emmett felt the insincerity. 'Don't . . .'

Brennan grimaced and nodded. 'Come on, look, you're grand. In half an hour it'll be over, and then you can take your week. Right now, they won't believe you. They'll think you're scared. You don't want a reputation like that, now, do you?'

Emmett acquiesced. 'Right . . .' He tried to smile. He started running slowly. The pain knifed him instantly, his leg wobbling. He stopped and looked about him. Everywhere there were runners emerging in packs into the greyness. A megaphone warbled in the distance. One of the co-ordinators was marking the course with a wheel. The farmer drove his tractor up the back road, carrying bales of hay into the field, roaring his head off. The men were stomping about, rubbing their hands together, spitting, laughing, and coughing. A couple of dog-betting men had arrived in a Granada. Mr Thompson had set up his caravan and was selling tea, sandwiches, and curry chips. The morning stood in its own brooding stupor, the sun lost to the day.

Emmett ran in a stiff trot into an adjacent field. As long as he ran from the knees down the pain was abated. His pores opened and began to sweat. There was an earnestness about the morning, the myopic air, the dourness of sobriety. He tested his leg in the soft muck. The pain was excruciating when he pulled it from the mud.

Emmett urinated against the wall, feeling the hot trickle dribbling on his fingers. He pulled his sweats up. His leg was locked with stiffness. He fought the pain and tried to run, the torn muscle trembling. 'Come on, come on . . .' he said over and over to himself. He fell forward into the mud as his leg gave a twinge of pain, his hip giving out.

'Ten minutes!' the speakers sounded.

Emmett couldn't take the pain. He walked to Brennan, his body drenched in mud, his head held downward.

Brennan wheeled Emmett off to the side, his eyes burning. 'You fuckin' bastard. You get out there, you hear me?' His voice quivered on a shout.

'No!' Emmett roared. 'I can't even feel my leg, I swear to you.'

Brennan cocked his fist and smashed it into Emmett's face. He lunged forward, grabbing Emmett by the throat. 'You're fuckin' going to do what I tell you, you hear me?' Brennan spat into Emmett's face. 'You bastard. Get out there, or make your own fuckin' way home. Do you think I've nothing better to do than to fuck around with the likes of you?' Brennan could sense Emmett's body folding in his grip. He let go of him; Emmett fell to the ground.

The nothingness of the day and the hour was consumed by the dreams of those thousands of miles. Emmett felt the daze of the greyness, the sting in his face. His tongue was stuck in his throat. He was shaking with shock. He could see himself out there, alone with the silent alienation of his dreams, those things born in the coldness of fields.

Madden and Taylor came running over. 'Jesus Christ! What in the name of God – ?' Madden used his massive bulk, pushing Brennan away from Emmett. 'Are you mad?'

Taylor helped Emmett to his feet. 'What happened?'

Emmett kept his head down. 'Nothin'.' He hobbled under Taylor's arm to Madden's minibus.

'Five minutes.' The loudspeaker voice was distorted in the wind.

Madden shook his head in disgust. 'Is it your leg?'

Emmett nodded his head.

'I made that bastard what he is!' Brennan roared in the background. 'Get your fuckin' hands off me, Taylor!'

Madden laid Emmett down in the back of his bus, draping him with a woollen blanket. 'You just rest there awhile. I'll speak to the right people.' Madden shut the back of the van and ran off toward the start.

A gun shot out in the distance. Emmett was alone in the small compartment of the bus. There were faint roars and whistles outside. He closed his eyes. There was safety in the darkness. He could imagine them out there in the field and the rain. The myriad faces of the betting men poured into his head. They were there saying things with their eyes, rubbing the knuckles of their hawthorn sticks in contemplation. They knew a good thing when they saw it. They were crude farmer types who had an understanding for meat. And they said it to your father's face and looked at your mother, fine breeder that she was, a bitch in heat to rear a pup like you. The hoary, knotted, liver-spotted hands of men who had spent a life running fingers over the muscles of dogs and horses, betting men who could scare the shite out of a bookie, and they knew a good bloody thing when they saw one . . . they knew all the tricks, there now, poteen rubbed into the legs heats the muscles, sets them on fire. Oh, it kills the pain of fatigue, it drugs nicely, a drop is all it takes, and not too bloody much, or you'll be on your arse, drunk as a whore.

'You know, he gets it from his mother's side of the family.'

'Is that a fact?'

'It is by Jasus! They were all workhorses.'

And in his quiet gaze, Emmett felt the intoxication of sleep falling upon him. He could feel the rhythm of his breath, the cessation of pain in his leg. He would be out there again next week or next month. And he would be alone, running amidst immortals, feeling the faces of the dead looking at him with famished eyes as the rain poured into the dead earth.